The Anointed One

The Untold Story of Seth Paine, Midwest Abolitionist

Nancy Schumm

Biographical information, characters, and events are based upon true facts. Dialogue is based upon newspaper accounts, biographical information, and fictional supposition.

The Anointed One

Copyright © 2022 Nancy Schumm

Ellicott City, Maryland

All rights reserved. No part of this book may be used or reproduced in any manner whatsoever without the written permission of the author except in the case of brief quotations in critical articles and reviews.

For inquiries contact Nancyschumm2@gmail.com

Ebook ISBN: 978-0-9668749-5-2 (Paperback edition)

Library of Congress Control Number: 2021925269

Cover art by Stacy Headley and Jonathan Thomas, Postnet, Lake Forest
Front cover photo from the Saint Lawrence University Law Library, Pryce Lewis Collection.
Letter from Seth Paine to Stephen A. Douglas, University of Chicago archives, Box 10, Folder 13, dated December 14, 1857
Back cover photo, Chicago History Museum Public Domain photographs.
Author photo by Chehalis Deane Hegner
All other photo credits are cited alongside the photos.

Dedication

For my Debbie who talked the talk and walked the walk every day of your life. You still inspire me.

Acknowledgements

I would like to extend a special thanks to the following people for their help: Amanda Burgess, editor extraordinaire, who chewed the manuscript up and spit it back out; Patty Charhut for her undying patience, editing, and cheerleading; Debbie Adelizzi for making sure I stayed organized, and for calibrating my spiritual compass.

I would also like to thank Ray Syverson and Julie Vollbrecht from the Ela Historical Society and Museum, Ty Roher from the Waukegan Historical Society, Diana Dretske, curator and historian for the Bess Bower Dunn Museum of Lake County, Illinois, Al Westerman for his information on land purchases in 1840, Wally Winter and Bill Werheim (my biggest cheerleader), Chehalis Hegner and Arthur Gansen for patiently listening to me tell Seth's story. Elizabeth and Brooke Schumm for reviewing my first draft, Larry McClellan for never judging, for James Dorsey (deceased) whose work I expanded upon, Adam Selzer, the historian who helped me find Seth's remains, and editor Patty Dowd Schmitz. A book cannot happen without the support of good friends and family and I am grateful to have both.

I am humbled to tell this story of an everyday person who struggled every day to do good.

Nancy Schumm, June 2022

Epitaph

"It is not the critic who counts; not the man who points out how the strong man stumbles, or where the doer of deeds could have done them better. The credit belongs to the man who is actually in the arena, whose face is marred by dust and sweat and blood; who strives valiantly; who errs, who comes short again and again, because there is no effort without error and shortcoming; but who does actually strive to do the deeds; who knows great enthusiasms, the great devotions; who spends himself in a worthy cause; who at the best knows in the end the triumph of high achievement, and who at the worst, if he fails, at least fails while daring greatly, so that his place shall never be with those cold and timid souls who neither know victory nor defeat."

-Theodore Roosevelt

Table of Contents

Prologue	11
Introduction: Rebirth	13

Part 1 — 21

Chapter 1: The Beginning	23
Chapter 2: Heading West	41
Chapter 3: A Fire in His Belly	51
Chapter 4: Utopian Socialism at Cedar Lake	65
Chapter 5: Abolition	83
Chapter 6: The "Wild West" of Politics	97
Chapter 7: First Disenchantment	119
Chapter 8: Banker, Agitator	137
Chapter 9: The Banking Fiasco	147

Part 2 — 163

Chapter 10: Bridewell	165
Chapter 11: Accountability	177
Chapter 12: Rebuilding the Dream	185
Chapter 13: A Higher Calling	201
Chapter 14: Jail to the Battlefields	213
Chapter 15: Back to A New Reality	229
Chapter 16: Chicago's West Side	237
Chapter 17: Consumed	247
Epilogue: The Seeds Sown	254
Author's note	260
Timeline of Seth Paine's Life	263
Bibliography	269
Index	285

Prologue

We cannot all be privy to our impact on the world or the mighty trees that come from seeds we have sown in our lifetime. Sometimes our actions are like small saplings planted haphazardly. As they grow, they provide shade for a variety of lives without giving credit to those who dropped the seeds and started the journey. For Seth Paine, frustration with life or society as a whole did not hinder his quest to find meaning and purpose in his life. Seth could never fully imagine nor see the fruits of his labor in his lifetime, yet he sowed a vast, lasting, and progressive legacy. His journey was not easy and was frequently fraught with frustration, grief, and disappointment amidst his successes. These valleys in his life may have contributed to his early demise, but history reveals that Seth's seedlings left a larger imprint than he could have ever known.

Introduction

Rebirth; 1853

Chicago experienced its typical, random day of summer-like weather in February 1853. For the inmates of the Cook County Prison that beautiful day was barely noticed, and Seth Paine, in particular, was unaware of the sun's warmth. His body only registered the creeping chill of the prison floor where he lay. He would feel that chill long after his release, down to the marrow of his bones. He was heading down a moral path of slowly starving himself in response to the prison's swill disguised as food. His voice was growing hoarse from yelling about the prison conditions, and more importantly, about the appalling treatment of the humans within these walls. While he lay there, he felt helpless to assist the prisoners around him who were emitting sounds of suffering. It was reflected in their muted conversations, their whispering laments, and their soft, sad wailing. He had heard the officers beating prisoners whom they claimed were disobedient and his heart ached for them. The stench of male testosterone, fear, and human waste wafted into his nostrils, propelling his disgust to fear, and that fear to simmer over into boiling anger.

Despite their wanton punishment of certain prisoners, Seth knew that those same officers would not dare raise a strap to him. He could exercise options whenever he wished, but the cold isolation was awakening Seth to a realization that living up to his family's expectations was more daunting than he had previously imagined. During these long, cold days and nights on the prison floor, he silently wrestled with God about his purpose. On one hand, he knew his dedication to helping humanity was unwavering, but he worried to himself, "How can I best serve my fellow man now that I am going to lose my bank?" From what he read in the local papers, the public had ill views of the incarcerated, and a negative feeling about him already, despite all he had accomplished. Furious for letting his standing in society decline to this, he lamented to the concrete walls.

"Really?! When have I really suffered compared to others?" He recognized the irony of his situation as he muttered, "It does not seem right for me to be set free on bail when there are humans around me suffering so much." Stretching his back in a futile attempt to find comfort on the cold cement floor, he wondered, yet not for the first time, "Who. Am. I?" Not long ago, he would have described himself as a writer, banker, and humanitarian. Today, he faced three cement walls with a padlocked door. Yesterday, he envisioned a world where forgiveness, righteousness, spiritualism, and friendship ruled, where he was moving toward a mission bigger than he could have imagined. Today, he was just lost.

When his friend Daniel Davidson arrived to try to convince him to post bail at once, and relieve himself of this discomfort, Seth refused. "I am not ready," he said, "I am still trying to figure out how I even got here!" His voice carried a little too far, and Davidson gently suggested he speak more softly.

The warden of the prison, Cyrus Bradley, heard him and chuckled, though he was at his wits end with Seth.[1] Bradley, who had known Seth for almost 19 years, having met him shortly after he arrived in Chicago, told Seth upon arriving at the prison that he was embarrassed to call Seth a friend, and, frankly, Seth felt the same way about him. "What kind of man could treat humans this way and consider it justice?" Seth growled loudly to the walls in frustration.

"Keep quiet!" someone yelled back.

Seth ran his fingers through his bushy, reddish hair and scrappy beard, both grown in tribute to one of his ancestors and other family members who had been declared insane. They had espoused the belief, and Seth did now too, that when backed into a corner, one let basic grooming habits die. Wiping his hands on the long flowing white gown draped over his dwindling figure, he recalled in frustration how his voice had been silenced from public diatribes about his unjustified

---

[1] *Chicago Daily Tribune.* July 7, 1872. Page 5.

incarceration while hypocrites of banking and social responsibility roamed free. The irony was not lost on him that he had been jailed for bank fraud rather than for his work on the Underground Railroad. The thought drew a slight chuckle, but his voice, tinged with anger, clanged against the walls, "When I am really breaking the law, they look the other way, but when I am helping people legally, they arrest me!"

"QUIET!" another prisoner yelled.

Seth knew that several judicial trials awaited him, and as he considered them, dread started to seep in and stoke his anger. He anticipated how the press would further tarnish his reputation by mocking his values. He shared his thoughts with Davidson the next time he visited. "How did I—a green-mountain boy from Vermont, working my way up from penniless to great wealth, committing my life to helping humanity—end up in jail and lose my livelihood!?"

Davidson worried with him about his future, "We have to consider that this confinement may impede any future plans." The press, once Seth's ally, had turned against him now. And so he delayed posting bail while he fasted and lamented until he had surrendered his ruminations to a deeper mental space.

Seth would discover that this time in prison would lead him down a path of enlightenment, through fasting, prayer, and ceaseless reflection.

For the previous two years, he had been swept up in the Spiritualist movement. In that realm, séances had played a role in his daily decision-making and lifestyle choices. Emerging from his jail time, he would look to the outcomes of séances no longer. On one of his weekly visits, Davidson pointed out that Seth's faith in God still served as the foundation for his life choices. Seth appreciated Davidson's insight and he began to see how the spiritualists had not helped his inner peace. He had been led to foolish actions by the Spiritualists and this knowledge fed his anger and shame. As he wrestled with his present situation, he considered how his faith had gotten him through so many things before and imagined how his faith might help him here.

Seth could not see that, at the still young age of thirty-seven, his future was being shaped psychologically, affecting how he viewed those he worked alongside beyond these walls. The compassion he desired and was denied in jail and by the media would compel him to have more compassion for others experiencing incarceration and to take note of those who lacked compassion for their fellow humans. His prison experience would sharpen his acumen to identify his network of true friends. He believed he could forgive the friends not in a position to defend him publicly, but angrily realized many others had always been, and were still, his enemies. He knew that he needed to forgive them, but he was not quite ready to do that. Many of his enemies only wanted his land and wealth—wealth in which he ironically had little interest. Most notably, Seth would awaken to the idea that prison walls could manifest themselves in many situations even if they were not formed of brick and mortar.

After several weeks in prison he began to see how his anger had betrayed him, had blinded him to the warning signs that had ultimately led to his arrest, and how his partner Ira Eddy had also been affected. He remembered a discussion around the family table many years back; his grandfather had argued the fallacy of anger and the Book of James in the Bible. This memory caused him to pause, humbled in the recollection of his father quoting James 1:19-20, "Let every man be quick to hear, slow to speak, slow to anger, for the anger of man does not work the righteousness of God." With this sacred memory, Seth fell to his knees once more, this time in shame, and he continued in earnest prayer.

In those interminable days in the cell, Seth could see his recent past and all the incidents and people leading up to his incarceration. His perception of his own self righteousness came into sharp relief. He knew that to truly understand how he had landed here, he needed to go back to the beginning of his life. He needed to find his humble roots and, like an old vine, cut back to the root stocks.

After five cold, humbling, and enlightening weeks in jail, Seth finally permitted his friends to post his bail. He now felt prepared to face the world again. Later, he would dedicate his prison time in memory of his ancestor's martyrdom as well as his own pursuit of deeper knowledge of his life's purpose. When he left, a flurry of reporters were waiting at the entrance to scribble their bad press and mock his now disheveled appearance. But he knew in his heart that he was not the same man who had entered. Seth's choice to let his hair and beard grow in times of strife would come to symbolize how he could be both stopped in his tracks and reborn. Small acts of rebellion like those he practiced during his five-week prison stay gave him comfort whenever he felt imprisoned by life.

Incarceration can inspire that in a man.

Part 1

Charles Paine, sketch from Zadock Thompson, *1842,
Thompson's Vermont, Part III, Gazetteer of Vermont*

Chapter 1

The Beginning; 1816-1833

Central Vermont in 1816 was a mostly wooded landscape, nestled between two mountain ranges—the White Mountains of New Hampshire and the Green Mountains of Vermont—with farms dotted along the landscape and flowing rivers that provided the residents fresh drinking water and power to run mills. Small villages were forming and adjusting to post-Revolutionary War life, and fighting off bouts of disease that plagued early settlements. Seth Paine was born into this terrain.

As a young man Seth Paine's parents told him that his birth in April 1816 in Tunbridge, Vermont, was the joyful outcome of their attempt to keep warm during a summerless year in New England followed by a winter known as "1816 and froze to death."[2] Seth was the second living child of Elijah and Fanny Paine. The first child to have survived birth was their daughter, Ruth, born three years prior. The Paines' joy was doubled with Seth's arrival because he would carry on the family name.

---

[2] Though unknown at the time, the harsh winter of 1816 was traced to Mount Tambora, Indonesia. One of the largest volcanic eruptions in history in April 1815, claimed the lives of nearly 10,000 islanders and destroyed the homes of 35,000 additional families. Globally, a large ash cloud blocked the sun raising the earth's temperature by 5.4 degrees and causing frost every month of the year 1816 in New England, obliterating crops. It is estimated that 80,000 people perished due to the resulting famine and many others left Vermont.

As a seventh-generation male in the American Paines, Seth's parents took great care to choose a name that would reflect his responsibility to secure and carry the Paine legacy.[3] The name Seth in the Bible means "the Anointed One."[4] His father, a lawyer, and his imaginative mother reminded him of this responsibility often throughout his childhood as they told and retold stories of the legendary actions of other important Paine ancestors.

Young Seth listened and took his parents' prognostications to heart, believing that God had indeed assigned him a special mission. His family's confidence in him generated a brave self-assurance and a relentless drive to aggressively seek out his purpose, but as he got older, palpable angst over his predestined mission would torment him when he experienced setbacks. In his final days, he was still not convinced that he had lived up to his name, though many would argue that he did.

Seth did not fully embrace all of the conventions of the time. He did not understand why he was given more favor and praise than his sisters. Seth spent a great deal of time with his older sister Ruth and his sister Jane, one year younger, and he felt that they were just as competent of

---

[3] The American Paines were not related to Thomas Paine, who was born in England, participated in the American Revolution, and was critical of Christianity. There was no family connection in Seth's direct line of ancestry.

[4] From Genesis. The name Seth is a Hebrew baby name meaning: Anointed; compensation. Seth was the third son of Adam and Eve. Eve considered him to be a replacement for her dead son, Abel.

mind and spirit to do all the things that he was capable of doing. His parents' expectations for their girls did not go much beyond marriage, and that confused him. When he asked his parents and grandparents about this inequity, he was dismissed. Despite this, he would forever encourage and appreciate the feminine perspective on complicated issues he faced in life.

For the most part Seth was given the ability to question and challenge the family tenets, but as a young boy, he found value in observing how things were expected to be, then quietly determining his own path. This was due, in part, to the fact that he often felt unsatisfied with the answers he received to his questions. He believed that his parents led mysterious and confusing lives. Behind the scenes, he and his sisters held many conversations about the way things seemed in the adult world and the disparity between how adults acted and what adults said. Together the children dreamed of growing up, achieving greatness, and doing things better. Most importantly they discussed all the ways they would help the world.

Like other first generation families in post-Revolutionary America, Seth was expected to follow certain basic rules of civility determined by elders in his family. Seth knew that in other families breaking these basic rules could elicit fierce and sometimes painful discipline. His family did not follow the prevailing doctrine of "spare the rod and spoil the child." Instead, his parents believed that a stern look directed at him and gentle guidance would be enough to teach him civil responsibility, and this instilled in Seth a disdain for violence of any kind. Other expectations for Paine children included: listening closely and respectfully to others; only speaking when you know your topic and can do so eloquently; keeping your ideals at the forefront of your words and actions; and embracing responsibility wholeheartedly, especially with regard to family and community. Godly actions were the overarching compass for everything. Everything else in life would follow first family and then community.

Around the family dinner table Seth learned how each generation of Paines contained a soldier, a rebel, and someone who had explored, challenged, and wrestled with the religious conventions of the times. Around the table active and prolific Scripture-based discussions emerged. These conversations allowed the entire family to participate freely, question safely, and process Biblical chapters and verses. Empowered by this discourse, Seth's family felt well-equipped to encourage Biblical discussion with strangers whenever conversations cropped up. Seth embraced this ideology and saw it as the catalyst for all he did. Approaching his life as a series of adventures and schemes, Seth imagined every significant life experience to be his defining and Godly contribution to his legacy and the world. Each experience convinced him that he had the potential to cement his place in his family's history, if not in the greater history of America. Seth's consternation over any failure along his life path would propel him to seriously reflect and sometimes dramatically change his trajectory.

With his sister's urging, Seth decided that focusing on helping humans in need would become the most desirable pathway to occupy his community responsibility. Seth concluded that helping humanity would allow him to fulfill the obligations of family by teaching any family he might have about the importance of compassion, generosity, and God. He could imagine a life where he would establish a community worthy of his name, and it would be a place for humans in need to find relief. Surely, he thought, this lofty goal would make his descendants proud to tell the story of his legacy just as his parents told the story of their family.

Like so many others in New England and Vermont, most of the Paines were Congregationalists. The Congregationalists were by nature progressive, generally ahead of social trends in their compassion for suffering and elevation of social responsibility, but occasionally bull-headed in how, when, and where they practiced compassion. Each generation of Paines was "buoyed by the conviction that they were chosen by God to play a central role in the unfolding of human history" along with their fellow Congregationalists.[5] The Church followed a democratic model where all members had equal voting rights, which both guided and frustrated Seth throughout his life. The Congregationalists' belief system would butt against his own beliefs more times than he could predict. Seth wholeheartedly embraced social responsibility in all its forms with no limitations for his compassion, and he expected the same from others. When Seth saw a lack of compassion in anyone, especially those who aligned with the Congregational Church, he ached with disappointment.

The Paines had not always been Congregationalists. Family religious philosophy and origins could be traced back to the 14th century in Yorkshire, England. For six generations, those Paines had followed the standards of the Church of England until the "great migration" of 1626, when the Congregational Church was established in New England as a rebellion against the Church of England. In the culture of the early Congregational Church, church and state were clearly delineated, but both the government and the ministry worked together to ensure godly standards prevailed in the community as a whole. Even within the Congregationalists' democratic system of equal voting and decision-making, not all members had the same rights. The Church claimed that, "ordinary citizens had unprecedented power to make

---

[5] History of the Congregational Church. *Understanding Puritan New England.*

decisions about land and property and to hold their leaders in check."[6] In action, leaders still swayed voting decisions; women also had a voice, but no voting rights. The inconsistency of who received rights among the members was an important challenge for Seth's family. When church members challenged Seth's grandfather's leadership and ultimately removed him, the family relegated church to their home and the family dinner table, instead of the local meeting house.

Like his father, Seth's grandfather was also a lawyer. He had nine children who lived to adulthood with his wife, Lydia. When the epidemics of 1811 and 1812 took the lives of many children in Northfield, Seth's grandfather and his son Elijah (Seth's father) left Northfield to head south to Tunbridge to protect Seth's sister Ruth, who was just a baby at the time.[7] The men practiced law there together until the elder retired.

Seth's paternal grandfather and namesake helped establish Tunbridge in Orange County, Vermont after the Revolutionary War. He donated land in Tunbridge for the first schoolhouse in town and for the Hutchinson Cemetery where several Paines and other local families would find their final resting place. Twenty miles north of Tunbridge, his brother, Elisha, established Westminster and Northfield in

---

[6] History of the Congregational Church. *The Puritan Heritage.*
[7] Thompson, Z. *Thompson's Vermont. Part III Gazetteer of Vermont.* 1842. Page 129.

Washington County. Though 20 miles separated Seth's grandfather from his brother, the families were still closely connected and spent a great deal of time together. Seth wanted to follow the family tradition of building communities, but he saw that some used that position to inflate their egos, while others recognized the power, but maintained their humility. He carefully observed all of this and noted how he could do it better. He also observed a similar disparity within his family around religious belief and religious actions.

The Paine family homestead in Tunbridge was nestled in incomparable beauty, with a vibrant countryside rolling along the idyllic freshwater White River, surrounded by bucolic pastures and the Green Mountain range. Seth's parents enjoyed the peaceful nature of Tunbridge, a community that remains small even today. In this setting, Seth grew up roaming over mountain dales and fishing in the White River at the knees of his grandfather. His grandfather's patience nurtured Seth's boundless curiosity. From his namesake, Seth learned about the potency of independence, the reward of admiring and respecting all women, and that the success of owning land would be key to a good life. Though he was only a young boy at the time, Seth's character was defined through these lessons and his innate empathy for the elderly, the infirm, and children crystallized in these moments.

Seth's grandfather died in 1820, and his wife, Lydia, continued to live with the family until 1824 when, under failing mental health, she was placed in an asylum for the insane. Elijah's legal practice kept the family thriving until 1826 when he died unexpectedly at the age of 44. His father's death proved to be a pivotal challenge for Seth. Suddenly, his life's trajectory changed dramatically when he was thrust into the role of man of the household. Elijah's passing was very different from that of his grandfather. At Elijah's unexpected passing, the family home was thrown into disorder. There had been no preparation for such an occurrence, and at the tender age of ten, his mother expected Seth to step into adult responsibility immediately. The onerous pressure to make decisions about his father's internment combined with how to care for his grandmother, mother, and two sisters forced Seth to mature into a young man overnight.

After his father's death, Seth also witnessed firsthand the decline of his beloved grandmother as her dementia quickly accelerated. The experience instilled in Seth a compassion for loving someone with dementia, a malady that appeared in each generation of Paines. Lydia passed away in the asylum two years after Elijah's death, which as a 12-year-old, Seth had to manage.[8] He was tasked with clearing her belongings and planning her funeral, which he was able to accomplish neatly. At a young age, he already felt and thought like a grown man.

---

[8] Vermont vital records, 1720-1908.

Thankfully his schooling and frequent interaction with mature adults like his grandfather had prepared him to make adult decisions. He would work on problem-solving for the family on his way to school, or while he studied scripture. In these early years, his imagination did not extend beyond the small world of his immediate family and Tunbridge. He imagined that something was beyond his home, but he was so deeply engaged with family responsibilities that he assumed Tunbridge was where his future would unfold.

In his fleeting moments of free time Seth wondered if he would emerge a controversial hero in the family like his Uncle Elisha Paine, a formerly practicing lawyer who others described as "a man of unusual breadth and force of character."[9] Elisha played a large role in the spiritual revival of the region. The family had arrived in New England during the "First Awakening" in the early 1700's (1710-1730) to escape religious oppression, and nearly a century later, the Congregationalists were challenged for the same practice they had moved to escape. In Westminster and Northfield, Vermont, Elisha had taken part in the "Second Great Awakening" around 1825, when a schism occurred in the Congregational Church, forcing New England Christians into factions.[10]

---

[9] *Gazetteer of Orange County.* Vermont. 1899. Page 660.
[10] The Second Great Awakening in New England was led by Lyman Beecher, a New England preacher and evangelist who later moved to Ohio.

In the early days, the Congregational Church was so strong and membership so numerous in Vermont that other denominations paid a tax to them to practice different beliefs.[11] Elisha, in the footsteps of the early English Paines, advocated against the doctrines of the New England Congregationalists and its religious spirit. His protests, complete with white robes and long flowing hair, were so vehement that he was ultimately arrested for his public displays and imprisoned for several weeks on three different occasions during the "Awakening." His time in prison only forged his convictions, and eventually he left the legal field to become a minister. These dramatic protests colored many of the Paine family's religious discussions around the dinner table when Seth was a young man. The elements of this Second Great Awakening included the inclusion of both women and African Americans in the church.[12] Uncle Elisha taught Seth not to be afraid of calling out hypocrisy when he witnessed it and to be inclusive of marginalized citizenry.

Seth grew rapidly into a young man physically and mentally after his grandmother's death. He had thick reddish hair and a tall, lanky frame. His physical countenance commanded some attention, but the maturity and fullness of his spirit would expand even more once he was set free

---

[11] According to Euclid Farnham, President of the Tunbridge Historical Society. January 29, 2017 interview.
[12] U.S. History, Pre-Columbian to the New Millenium. _Religious Transformation and the Second Great Awakening_.

of his early household responsibility. Around the age of 14, Seth, his two sisters, and his mother were taken in by Seth's paternal cousin, Charles Paine, son of the infamous Elisha. The family moved up to Northfield and lived in one of Charles's homes, which he shared and rented to family and friends with specialized terms according to their need and means.[13] Charles greatly influenced young Seth through the kindness he demonstrated to his family, and their physical resemblance was uncanny. Charles was a force to be reckoned with in his own right and unstoppable in his tenacity and ambitions. As he spent more time with Charles, Seth concluded that the strong personalities of this half of the Paine clan may have influenced his grandfather's decision to move his father to Tunbridge so many years prior, rather than the threat of disease being their only motive. Seth's father had been gentler and quieter in spirit, while Charles's strong vocal opinions and decision-making were impressive and exciting to Seth.

Charles was active in local politics, eventually becoming the 15th Governor of Vermont (1841-1843). He established several businesses in Northfield in the early 1800s, including a town railroad center which fascinated Seth. The town center connected to the main railroad through Vermont, which Charles was largely responsible for establishing using

---

[13] U. S. Federal Census, Charles Paine, Chester, Windsor, Vermont 1820, Northfield, Orange, Vermont 1830. Charles's family grew from 5 in the 1820 Vermont census to 16 in the 1830 Vermont census. These early census records did not break out individual family members, only ages and gender.

his political connections. Charles's decision to build the railroad where he thought it should go rather than where commercial considerations might have made more sense, was a choice that still baffles historians in the 21st century.[14] Seth adopted Charles's approach to decision making when he faced personal challenges and business interests in his life. He was so influenced by Charles that he later named his firstborn son after him.

In the 1830s, Seth's mother, Fanny, was struggling with the financial challenges of running their household with only his father's estate to support them. In the probate record, shoes and all similar expenses for the children were documented painstakingly so the costs could be reimbursed to the executors.[15] Seth's mother recognized that the estate would not support them forever, despite additional help from her extended family. Wanting to spare Seth from the burden of working for the family's survival, she found companionship with the recently widowed Abel Keyes. Though Keyes was 20 years her senior, he was a robust, healthy man and a neighbor and friend of Charles Paine. Keyes had moved to Northfield around 1790 and purchased several of Charles' properties, which he improved and expanded. Locally, Keyes was known as Captain Abel Keyes because he was captain of the military

---

[14] According to Euclid Farnham, President of the Tunbridge Historical Society. January 29, 2017 interview.
[15] Vermont Probate Records. Elijah Paine. November 1828.

company, justice of the peace, selectman, and representative.[16] In 1833, on Seth's 17th birthday, Abel Keyes and Fanny Paine married.

Seth was supportive of his mother's marriage not only because he no longer had to fill the role of man of the house, but also because at 17 he knew it was time to make important decisions about his own future. His mother's marriage prompted Seth to consider an escape from Vermont. He was drawn to explore the world beyond Vermont and he presumed he could do a better job of making a name for himself away from his boisterous family. At the time, local newspapers in New England regularly enticed readers with stories of the economic prospects in the west and Seth consumed the information greedily. Land to the west was touted as cheap and bountiful, opportunities for work were many, and the long trek to get there was rife with risk, just the sort of challenge to inspire Seth. In the spirit of his ancestors, Seth began planning for a life in a new land.

******

In early 1834 Seth was further encouraged to put his plan into action when he was introduced to Chester Smith, an Illinois merchant who came through Northfield from Plainfield, Illinois, 40 miles southwest of the frontier town of Chicago. Formerly from Vermont himself, Smith

---

[16] *Vermont Historical Magazine.* Page 628.

had returned from Illinois and garnered wide publicity in the small town with his tales of the new frontier. From Smith, Seth and his family learned firsthand about several Paines who had lived in Plainfield as recently as 1832.

With open ears and wide eyes, the eager family took in Smith's Wild West tales. He told the story of how Fort Paine was built and named after Captain Christopher Paine in 1831, who had helped establish the Naper settlement and how a preacher named Uriah Paine was the victim of an attack during the Black Hawk War. This news struck Seth as the most significant of all, and he listened with rapt attention as Smith told the story. Settlers had abandoned Fort Paine and fled to Chicago after a massacre at nearby Indian Creek.[17] Preacher Paine stayed behind, purportedly to make peace with the natives. But, he was later found murdered and beheaded. Some presumed the Indians had beheaded him rather than just scalped him because of his long reddish hair and beard. Survivors said the Indians felt they "had killed one of the gods of the whites."[18] Looking in the mirror at his own reflection, Seth felt Smith's

---

[17] The settlement of the Illinois countryside included several forts to protect early settlers. One settlement was called Holderman's Grove near Indian Creek, where a particularly brutal massacre took place causing all surviving settlers to head to safety at Fort Dearborn in Chicago. Preacher Paine feared that Chicago had suffered the same fate and stayed in the region, where he was subsequently believed to be murdered by the Sauk tribe. (Blanchard spelled the name Paine in the original publication, later translations spelled the name Payne).
[18] Blanchard, R. *History of Dupage County*. O. L. Baskin and Company Historical Publishers. Lakeside Building, Chicago, Illinois. 1882. Page 39.

story was a sign for him to make a move.[19] High risk and potential heroism were just the sort of timely adventures Seth was craving.

Seth was also excited about other prospects in Illinois: the need for missionaries; cheap land ownership; and booming business were all lures he could not resist. Nothing was keeping him in Vermont now that his family was under the care of Abel Keyes. When Chester Smith prepared to head back to Illinois, he invited the young man to join him, and Seth eagerly agreed with the brazenness that eventually defined him. He took all the concerns and opinions of his family as encouragement. Even comments intended to discourage him were twisted in his mind to favor his departure. With his soon-to-be legendary charm, he convinced his worried family that this move west was best for all of them.

---

[19] Andreas, Alfred Theodore, *History of Cook County, Illinois, From the Earliest Period to the Present Time,* Chicago, 1884, In three Volumes. Page 315.

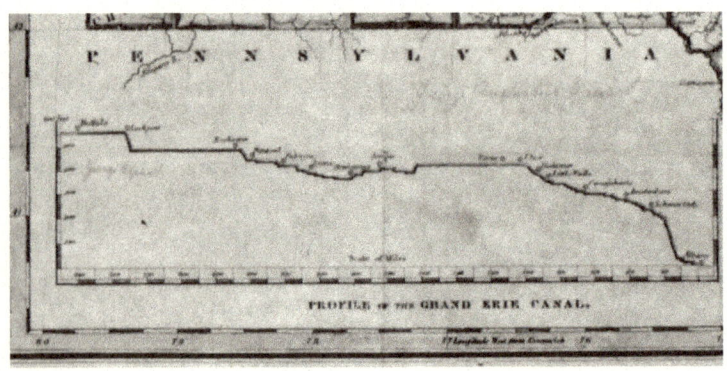

Profile of the Grand Erie Canal, Williams, William, and S Stiles. 1826. *The Traveller's pocket map of New York: from the best authorities*. Utica N.Y. The Traveller's pocket map of New York : from the best authorities | Library of Congress.

Chapter 2

Heading West; 1834

Seth had not traveled much beyond Tunbridge and Northfield or even over the next mountain in Vermont. He had very few personal possessions, so he packed a small rucksack, dressed in his daily attire and stepped out the door with Chester Smith in the spring of 1834. In his rush to escape Vermont, Seth's resiliency and youthful naïvete erased any fears that may have crossed his mind. He committed himself fully to the adventure into the unknown. In his mind he imagined with eager anticipation that traveling across the country would be like the migration his ancestors made across the ocean in 1626. Seth assumed that with pioneer blood in his lineage, any obstacles in his path would be overcome. His family christened his westward journey with a pocket full of money, his very own Bible, encouragement to stay indomitable in spirit, and an emotional shower of love and prayers.

If he found the new territory amenable, Seth decided, he would send for the rest of the family. Seth's enthusiasm sparked the imagination of his two sisters, his mother, and even his stepfather. They vowed to wait for word from him and consider a future move at that point. Most of the information about the west was from travelers returning to Vermont, like Chester Smith, or stories told by early missionaries, frontiersmen, and newspaper accounts of the wilderness of the Northwest Territory. While Northfield was evolving on political matters, New Englanders were still basking in the cultural restoration from the Revolutionary War and enjoying a generation of early patriotic citizenry, making them happy to stay put in Vermont even with uncertain harvests and short growing seasons. Seth had read about other states and knew he would pass through several new landscapes via multiple modes of transportation, and this knowledge fed his enthusiasm.

His first challenge was to get to and through the Erie Canal. In those days, the passageway was referred to as the Grand Erie Canal, and its opening in 1825 made travel feasible from New York to the West.[20] From Eastern Vermont, Seth and Chester Smith took a stage coach to Lake Champlain and from there a canal boat to Schenectady, New York. Two daily canal boats left Schenectady, connecting through Utica, and then traveled straight west to Buffalo along the Erie Canal. The New York portion of the trip cost around $7 per person and lasted a minimum of 72 hours. An abundance of cargo along the route meant a slower journey as freight was loaded and unloaded. Travelers could negotiate their fare if they were willing to move freight at each port.

Chester and Seth departed together on the boat, which proved to be a

---

[20] Williams, W. and Stiles, S., The Traveller's pocket map of New York : from the best authorities | Library of Congress. Canal Guide, for the Tourist and Traveler. LOC #G3800 1826.W5

relatively easy passage by water, and offered a fascinating journey through the land of trees that was New York. Seth found the entire process fascinating, and he didn't mind the work or the pace. He met other travelers and spent hours viewing the surrounding landscape, so different, he noticed, than the hilly regions of Vermont. Traveling only at the pace of the horse and mule teams pulling the canal boats, Seth watched his food supply dwindle, expecting it would have lasted for the entire journey. He had no choice but to spend money on food at trading posts along the route, depleting his meager savings quickly.

When Seth and Chester arrived in Buffalo, they discovered they would need to wait another four days until a boat would arrive to take them to Detroit, Michigan. By the time they reached Detroit, they decided to part ways. Smith had more money than Seth so he headed to Chicago overland on a speedier and more expensive stagecoach, while Seth traveled through the Great Lakes by steamship. Seth held no grudge for Smith's choice. In his mind, adventure did not need money. He only wondered if he would be able to procure free food along the way.

The spring of 1834 was marked by many dramatic stories about traveling through the straits of Mackinac.[21] Stories of the *Post Boy*, for

---

[21] An oath from the schooner was dated May 23, 1834 with Master R. Smith, and is held at the Burton Historical Collection at the Detroit Public Library.

example, exaggerated a capsize in the fall of 1833 along Lake Michigan. *Post Boy* had actually recovered from the event and went on to serve until 1841 when it exploded from gunpowder stored in its cargo hold.[22]

Seth used his last dollar to board the steam schooner *Commerce* for the long trip up through Lake Huron, the straits of Mackinac, then down Lake Michigan to Chicago. He needn't have worried about money for food because he had no appetite during the journey, which took 12 harrowing days. The stormy spring did not create smooth sailing for a mountain boy. In between the rocking waves, the *Commerce* made frequent stops for passengers to embark and disembark at various portages. These stops also gave them the chance to avoid traveling during storms, but did not guarantee that the decks were calm. Seth observed with wonder the Great Lakes, and the change from the eastern mountains and forests. He looked forward to stepping ashore and viewing the open prairie and flat land he had heard about from Smith. This anticipation kept his spirits up through the roiling waves, sleepless nights, and endless nausea.

When the *Commerce* finally arrived on the Lake Michigan shoreline, Seth's first glimpse of Chicago proved to be a disappointment. In 1834,

---

[22] Post Boy, 1832 Schooner. Alpena County George N. Fletcher Public Library. Great Lakes Maritime Collection.

most of Illinois was a vast and unexplored land, a parcel of the Northwest Territory conscripted into the United States from Napoleon's Louisiana Purchase in 1803. Vermonters had heard that the last treaty of Chicago was signed only a year earlier in 1833 at Prairie du Chien, Wisconsin. Most boats entered Illinois by landing on Chicago's underdeveloped shore. Though Seth was excited to arrive, the muddy landscape was bleak and depressing even as his relief to exit the schooner was growing. But disembarking would have to wait. First the boat needed to forge through the choppy water of Lake Michigan to the shore.

While the schooner navigated the chop, Seth learned from other passengers that Chicago was often described as a mudhole, situated on the banks of Lake Michigan and transected by a murky river sharing the city's name. First, a marshy swamp greeted the water's edge. After the ports and docks of New York, Ohio, and Michigan, this was a dramatic change. Those earlier ports seemed civilized and beautiful compared to what he could see over the side of the schooner, a vast sea of choppy water fringed by miles of marshy, tangled brush. Several decades would pass before boats would enter any harbor at the mouth of the Chicago River. J. B. Mansfield described the shoreline in 1899, "No docks, no lights, no tugs, and the passengers and light goods were put ashore by means of the vessel's yawls (small boats), as weather would permit."[23] Even after his first impressions, Seth would come to realize that Chicago's location, at the southwest corner of Lake Michigan, was the last waterway leading West. He could see that its location positioned the growing city as an important portal to the rest of the Northwest Territory.

Seth shivered alongside the others as he awaited his turn to hop into the small receiving boat. The boats could only take them so far, so the passengers then needed to wade the rest of the way to the shoreline. Seth considered for a moment if he wanted to get his boots wet or not. He chose not to, and holding his boots and knapsack, he stepped into the water. Quickly he felt a creeping numbness in his legs—his first experience of spring in Chicago. "Oh, folly!" he thought, "this water is COLD!" Seth groaned audibly as he struggled through the slapping, cold waves, and muddy substrate. As he clambered up the slope onto dry land, he cursed Chicago's spring and realized it was his 18th birthday.

On that day in 1834 Seth could see that Chicago was less of a "wild" frontier town as described by Chester Smith than he thought it would be. After donning his dry socks and boots, he joined a group of people

---

[23] Mansfield, J. B. ed. *History of the Great Lakes Volume I*. Chicago. J. H. Beers and Col. 1899. Chapter 35.

heading to the center of town and felt a sense of hope and optimism pulsing through the crowd. He overheard people discussing how Chicago was growing rapidly as a trading center and evolving into a thriving city. He could not help but feel a burst of anticipation and energy. The crowd's enthusiasm however, could not squelch the stench wafting in the air. Native tribes, as early as 1684 had named the area Chicagua because of the wild onions and skunk cabbage that grew profusely in the area around the shorelines and their signature smell.[24,25] Visitors eventually became immune to the stench as much as they did the mud sucking at their soles. To a wide-eyed Seth, the smell, the mud, and the gloomy spring weather were a challenge more attractive than the high waters of the Great Lakes. He brought his own hope with him into this adventure.

Though Seth arrived in Chicago penniless, what he did possess was youth, vitality, and a will to accomplish something important He set about looking for work and applying his soon-to-be renowned skill of attracting and securing friends.[26] He soon met Peter Cohen, a French

---

[24] Fraqualine's map of 1684
[25] Hyde, James Nevins. *Fergus Historical Stories Early Medical Chicago*. Fergus Printing Company, Chicago. 1879. page 4.
[26] Andreas, Alfred Theodore, *History of Cook County, Illinois, From the Earliest Period to the Present Time,* Chicago, 1884, In three Volumes. Page 315. "Tall and straight. He had a frank open countenance, and a pleasing and prepossessing address. His conversational powers were excellent and as a public speaker he was far above mediocrity. He was good humored, and made friends rapidly."

merchant in dry goods and a survivor of Napoleon's defeat at Waterloo. Cohen's shop was on Water Street in Chicago, situated among many other merchants. The meeting was providential for Seth, as Cohen could sympathize with the journey Seth had just completed and his need to find work. He took pity upon the bedraggled young man and, in a bit of a charitable act, offered him work in his shop to earn wages and his board. Seth recognized the gift of this opportunity.

As he laid his head down on his first night in Chicago, he humbly prayed that this might be the first of many opportunities. Drifting off to sleep, he told himself, " I can be anybody I want in this strange place." He had prepared no vision for what kind of business he would favor, where he would go from here, or how he would get there, but he knew with certainty that his adventure was beginning here in Chicago. He determined he would be gracious and learn as much as he could about this place while he worked out the other details. The next day he sent word to his family of his safe arrival.

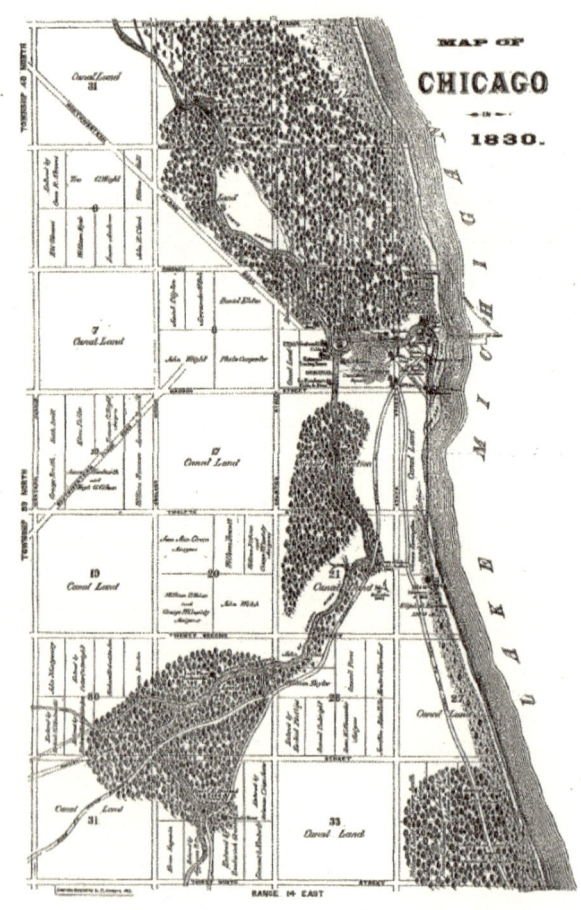

Map of Chicago 1830, Alfred Theodore Andreas, *History of Cook County, Illinois, From the Earliest Period to the Present Time, In Three Volumes,* Chicago, 1884.

Chapter 3

A Fire in His Belly; 1835

When Seth began working for Peter Cohen, neither had high expectations, but they quickly found that their personalities complimented each other well enough to form a successful business relationship. Seth was shocked to find that merchandise was coming in daily from the East. There were general stores in Chicago as he had found in other towns on the way West, and there were small shops like Cohen's where Seth helped to sell everything from tape and needles, to Eastern thread and Ohio butter.[27] Both men quickly realized that Seth was an exceptional salesman; not only because of his fearless, charming, and inquisitive personality, but also because he had an innate interest in people and the products they were selling. When they were not selling wares, they had discussions about their mutual dreams of a better life. Cohen had survived war, famine, family tragedy, and a trip across the ocean. Despite setting up a modest business in a new frontier, he was struggling with English. Seth had the mastery of English needed for sales, while Cohen understood market demands and suppliers. Together they were able to make money in ways that Cohen had not anticipated when he first offered Seth a job.

---

[27] *Chicago Daily Tribune.* July 7, 1872. Biography.

After a couple weeks of business, Cohen determined that Seth would be a good investment, and ordered Seth a tailored suit. He also taught him how to trim his beard and hair to respectable lengths to give him a more sophisticated appearance. With his new style, Seth began to expand his horizons and his role in Chicago with newfound confidence.

From Cohen's shopfront, Seth met adventurers from around the world, some passing through town on their way to new frontiers, and some planning to stay in the growing city. Seth was honing and practicing the art of sales, testing conversational styles and learning to listen actively to the experiences of others. As he mastered this art, Seth also learned about finances and came to appreciate the privileges that business and land ownership afforded men, in particular, through the melting pot of humanity that passed through Cohen's door. The more Seth talked to people, the more he wanted to be actively engaged in the community as a whole. He met many of Chicago's leading pioneers such as Mark Beaubien, Philo Carpenter, John Kinzie, and others forging their way in fledgling Chicago.

In 1834 Chicago was a town with wood-structures, gas lanterns, and confined spaces, at high risk for frequent and potentially devastating fires. The Great Chicago Fire of 1871 was many years away, but trained responders were critically needed to extinguish fires daily. When fires cropped up, local residents called upon the "bucket brigade" to help extinguish blazes. Volunteers would bring their own buckets to fill with water to fight the fires.

Seth joined the team of volunteer firemen at Station #1 in the heart of Chicago's downtown in 1835. This volunteer fire department materialized as a direct result of an ordinance that required a "store owner or dwelling occupant to provide one leather fire water bucket for each fireplace or stove in the building, to be hung in a conspicuous place."[28] The team was called the *Fire Guards Bucket Company*, organized through the Pioneer Hook and Ladder Company #1 and was located on Dearborn between Washington and Randolph Streets, not far from where Seth worked and lived. Fire department history remembers "Station #1 worked for the public good for many years."[29] Seth heard about their need for volunteers through Mark Beaubien and through this experience he eventually met many other men who would become local heroes.[30]

The men that Seth met while at the fire department were planning to buy land in the countryside surrounding Chicago, as soon as it was available for sale, while maintaining strong ties to the city. This seemed

---

[28] RJ Quinn Training Academy and Chicago Fire Department. *History of the Chicago Fire Department*. revised June 10, 2004. Page 1.
[29] Andreas, Alfred Theodore, *History of Cook County, Illinois, From the Earliest Period to the Present Time,* Chicago, 1884, In three Volumes. Page 228.
[30] Mark Beaubien was one of the first founders in Chicago and a member of the first fire brigade in Chicago with Seth.

like a good plan to Seth. He would cross paths with these men in times of fortune and failure in the future. Seth formed many formative relationships during this time including with Hiram Clarke,[31] Lewis Beecher,[32] Asher Rossiter,[33] Isaac Cook,[34] Cyrus Bradley,[35] and Ira Kimberly.[36] Some were older than he was and some were similar in age to Seth. From these friendships, Seth learned the value of networking and how small encounters could impact future events. Seth listened to the evolving ideas of these men as they worked alongside each other fighting fires and saving or losing structures. Each fire offered new challenges, more thrilling than Seth could have imagined, but he tackled each one with vigor and youthful innocence. He also began to dream of his own future in a way he had never had the freedom to entertain in Vermont.

---

[31] Hiram Clarke was a fellow firefighter and later part of the Congregational Church of Lake County, Illinois.
[32] Lewis Beecher became an early resident of Lake County. The Beecher name was associated with preachers, abolitionists, and New England influencers.
[33] Asher Rossiter was an influential abolitionist in Lake Forest, Illinois.
[34] Isaac Cook was a land agent who worked on the canals in Chicago (Chicago City Directories 1843).
[35] Andreas, Alfred Theodore, *History of Cook County, Illinois, From the Earliest Period to the Present Time,* Chicago, 1884, In three Volumes. Page 228.
[36] Andreas, Alfred Theodore, *History of Cook County, Illinois, From the Earliest Period to the Present Time,* Chicago, 1884, In three Volumes. Page 287. Dr. Kimberly was the clerk of the town meeting to decide whether or not Chicago would be incorporated and he was elected Trustee of the city on August 10, 1833. Kimberly joined Peter Pruyne to open one of the city's Pharmaceutical Stores located on South Water street, between Dearborn and Clark.

The members of the fire brigade were eager to be a part of Chicago's history and help shape Illinois politics. Most of them had roots in New England or New York, and like Seth, were lured to Chicago by the promise of cheap land, financial opportunity, and the assurance of adventure. They brought with them the "Yankee" value system which included many strong opinions about slavery. These values were familiar to Seth, coming from an antislavery state of Vermont and his Uncle Elisha's controversial battle with the Vermont's Congregational Church vision of equality.[37] Here, in Chicago, he met for the first time both enslaved and free blacks. He saw the suffering of the enslaved, and his stomach clenched when he considered the idea of owning another human. He found the idea inconceivable. Within the group of firemen, frequent discussions, and debates emerged about whether allowing or abolishing slavery was appropriate.[38] Slavery had been discussed in Seth's formative years, but the Paines had never considered the issue significant to them, since they had never owned slaves and did not know any enslavers themselves.[39]

---

[37] Arnosky Sherburne, M. *Abolition and the Underground Railroad in Vermont.* The History Press, Charleston, South Carolina. 2013. Page 20.
[38] New Englanders took a progressive stance against slavery, as the region had abandoned the pracice as early as 1808, when the federal government had mandated that slaves could no longer be imported to the United States.
[39] The language used to describe slavery, enslaved people, and freedom seekers has been updated to respect the families and descendents who were harmed by this practice following the guidance of the National Parks Service and the National Underground Railroad Network to Freedom Program.

The topic of slavery was especially relevant and openly discussed at the time as Illinois worked to revise its early established "Black codes" in 1835.[40] While Seth listened to the debates among his friends, he thought deeply about the issue himself. He observed how some considered slavery wrong because the practice allowed enslavers to be lazy. Others, he noted, believed owning slaves directly conflicted with the Christian value that all men should be given the opportunity to read the Bible, but laws prohibited all enslaved people from being taught to read. Still others were barely conscious of the issues presented by slavery because slavery did not impact their lives directly. As the frequency of these discussions increased, Seth's feelings on the topic solidified and ignited a spark within him, touching his humanity. Privately, he felt that all men were created equal and he had never considered that skin color could impact someone's ability to hold a job. But to hear other men talk, this was not a commonly held belief by decision makers, even in this new city. The more he heard the arguments about slavery, the more impassioned he became about the injustice of the practice. He pondered these feelings, but he kept them tucked away while working and fighting fires. He wanted to become better educated on the issue before he began to open his mouth and

---

[40] There were several iterations to the Black Codes of Illinois which were first developed in 1820 and revised several times until emancipation in 1863. Whenever they came up for revision, there were significant debates throughout the state.

speak. But secretly he considered slavery 'man-stealing.'[41]

******

In the summer of 1834, Cohen first showed Seth the prairie, a vast area that expanded beyond the city across present-day Wacker Drive. Seth was amazed. Chester Smith had previously described the prairie as an unexplored wilderness, but the expanses of open sky where pale skin turned red in the bright sunlight and the ground looked like a sea of waving grasses was beyond description for Seth. In the early summer light the grassy sea sparkled with dew, tall grasses, flowers, and golden duff. Seth admired Cohen's knowledge of these vast wild spaces and learned that the English word for "prairies" came from the French word for "fields." Seth could not hide his curiosity at what lay beyond and within that waving grass sea.

Their mutual admiration of the terrain drove them both to engage in many evenings of earnest discussion about the future of the city and what lay beyond it. Together Seth and Cohen robustly debated the new ideas they had heard during the day; progressive social movements in the world; humanity as a whole; and religion. Cohen was the first Jewish man that Seth had ever met and even in their differing religious views they found common ground in the Bible's Old Testament.

---

[41] *Chicago Daily Tribune.* July 7, 1872. Page 5.

City work was exciting, but when the weather allowed, Seth's innate curiosity and a need for fresh air drew him out to the countryside to explore. Once he left the muddy shores of Lake Michigan, he discovered the mysteries of the tallgrass prairie and was inspired to expand his dream out of the city and into the country as rapidly as he could manage. Less adventurous men had described travel through the countryside of the tallgrass prairie as disorienting and frightening, but Seth relished the peace and wildness of the terrain. In this natural landscape, he could envision Indians roaming, buffalo grazing, and wildflowers flourishing. He happened upon old cabins, farms, and villages, some long since abandoned, some currently inhabited. He would often bring wares with him to open conversations, friendships, and sales with these early homesteaders. As he explored, Seth began to imagine the opportunity to begin new communities with new value systems in the prairie, and committed to make that vision a reality.

When he would come back to Chicago, Seth and Cohen would discuss how buying land would allow them to establish new towns with their own guiding principles. They knew that the land was currently being homesteaded. It was not yet for sale, so all of these newcomers were dreaming just like Seth and Cohen.

Seth was expanding his understanding of what it meant to be a community. In particular, Cohen introduced Seth to the principles of

Charles Fourier, a French philosopher and Utopian Socialist. Fourier had taken advantage of Manifest Destiny in the early 1800s—which was the idea that development and expansion were inevitable because of the nature of man—to develop communities with a new social order shedding reliance on money and economics. Fourier criticized many existing societal practices and believed that the inequality of the poor was a root cause of all disorder. At the time, several successful test communities in America followed the Fourier model, including Utopia, Ohio, West Roxbury, Massachusetts, and Red Bank, New Jersey.

When Seth first heard about Fourier, he was impressed, particularly that Fourier's principles included equal rights for women and for blacks. Fourier also proposed the idea of establishing a central 'home' or 'grand hotel' in these communities where residents gathered for social discourse and communal exchange. From Cohen, Seth learned that residents in these Fourier towns had abandoned general trades for work favoring their individual strengths and skills. Seth began to dream about founding his own Utopian community, believing that buying land, his personality, and innate frugality were all he needed to create Utopia. The relationship between Cohen and Seth deepened and they formed a strong partnership based on this common vision while they continued to successfully sell Cohen's wares and save their money. Seth's confidence in his future was growing.

When word spread that the land offices were finally launching the sale of 40-acre plots in the area surrounding Chicago in early 1836, Seth seized the opportunity to spend his extra time finding a future homestead for himself and his family back East. His journeys into the prairie on horseback during that summer in Chicago were the highlight of his weeks. He worried a little that there would be no land left because he knew that the first round of settlement had already taken place with homesteaders, but he also had faith that there was a God-appointed place for him in the prairie. Ira Kimberly, having already staked a claim along an old Indian trail northwest of Chicago commonly known as the "Maunk-Suk" or the "Big-foot" revealed in confidence to Seth that more good land existed there.[42]

In the late spring of 1836, Seth first laid eyes on a region christened Cedar Lake. Acres of fertile prairie encircled an overgrown freshwater lake, rimmed with red cedar trees and dotted with old growth savannas intermixed across the landscape. Streams ran intermittently through the region and wild game roamed the countryside. Seth accessed the area via the old Indian trail Kimberly had told him about. When he saw the boggy, cedar-rimmed lake he knew he could convince others to support his community here. The afternoon he encountered the lake he set up a

---

[42] Sharf, A. F. *Indian Trails and Villages in Lake County, Illinois*. (ca, 1908). Page 1-2. The Big-foot trail led from Half Day (today's Vernon Hills) to McHenry County and eventually the state of Wisconsin.

camp and began to envision an entire settlement there. In his mind he saw farms, a sawmill, homes, and businesses. As the birds flew overhead and fish jumped in the water, he got carried away in his imaginings and became almost giddy with excitement.

Seth wasn't the first to believe farming would be ideal in the fertile prairies. Explorer, Louis Joliet, had commented on the Illinois prairies in his journals as early as 1673 when he said, "No better soil can be found…a settler would not there spend ten years in cutting down and burning the trees; on the very day of his arrival, he could put his plough (sic) into the ground."[43] Seth envisioned what the lake's shores would eventually look like as part of his first Fourier community.

After a couple days of dreaming, Seth rode back to the city to make concrete plans. He determined that he would bring his family from Vermont to be the first settlers around Cedar Lake. He began to plan the structures he would build, how he would arrange for the delivery of supplies, and who else could live in the countryside with him just like Fourier's vision.[44] He sent word to his family. "Come to Illinois!" he urged. "It is great farmland; we can secure many acres; and I can help you get settled. Together we can make things better."

---

[43] Madsen, J. *Where the Sky Began; Land of the Tallgrass Prairie*. Iowa State University Press. 1982.
[44] Haines, Elijah M. *Past and Present of Lake County, Illinois*. Chicago: Le Baron & Co. 1877. Page 270.

Before any purchase of land could be made, or even any move, Seth continued to save his money and plan for other residents. He frequently visited the site of his future village and he marked his intent by creating furrows and building a rough structure along the lake. His family was resistant, and initially, only his sister Jane made the journey in 1836. Jane and Seth lived in Chicago together until both married local Chicagoans. Seth began to look into how to purchase and secure the land around Cedar Lake, and through the Recorder of Deeds, he met his future wife, Frances. Jane met her husband, Caleb Fittz, an upholsterer visiting Chicago from Milwaukee around the same time. Ultimately, it was Jane who encouraged the rest of the family to move west and eventually they acquiesced.

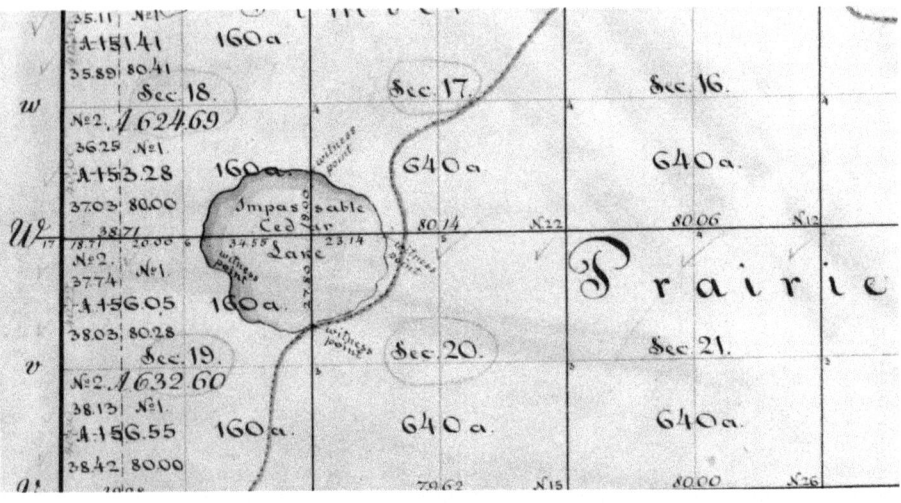

1836 Ela Township Plat Map Cedar Lake prior to being named Lake Zurich. The map was registered in the land office in St. Louis on June 24, 1840, public land records. The western edge of Ela Township was surveyed in the 3rd quarter of 1837 by James Galloway, surveyor.

Chapter 4

Utopian Socialism at Cedar Lake; 1836

Seth was anxious to get to work on his Utopian community. Like his ancestors before him, particularly his Uncle Charles, he knew that he needed people, resources, and labor to establish a town. With his belief that divine intervention would help him acquire the ideal property, he prepared to work. Recruiting people would only happen if he could convince like-minded friends, and family to move to the region. He would begin with a few cabins and then the real work would begin. Seth enlisted friends and sent frequent letters to his family, updating them on the progress. With Jane offering input, he began planning how he would lay out the first buildings. As he identified the supplies he needed, Seth envisioned how his Utopia would evolve from the land he had discovered at Cedar Lake and the labor and love of his residents.

Timber surrounded Cedar Lake on the northwest, while tallgrass prairie grew on the southeast side. First explorers of Cedar Lake considered it unnavigable in comparison to other lakes in the region, and it was documented that way on the original survey map.[45] Navigability was determined by the surrounding landscape. The terrain

---

[45] The western edge of Ela Township was surveyed in the 3rd quarter of 1837 by James Galloway, surveyor. The map was registered in the land office in St. Louis on June 24, 1840.

surrounding Seth's lake was flat, but prairie grasses grew as high as 12 feet and masked the waterway beyond which was a marshy, mucky stand of vegetation. These tallgrass vistas reached their peak in autumn and then remained upright until the harsh winter winds overtook the drying reeds, toppling them to reveal the terrain. Sometimes prairie fires—set accidentally or intentionally—controlled the excess duff, but mostly the grasslands were tall, dense forests of plantlife.

Primary surveyor of the region, James Galloway, found four witness points to mark the boundary of Cedar Lake on the official map, showing an old trail meandering around the north side of the swampy grasses adjacent to the water. This trail made accessibility better than first imagined. When Seth arrived in the late spring of 1836, after the winter winds had leveled the tallgrass, he saw the flattened landscape and the expanse of the lake hidden within. The brutal, unfettered wind made the environment exceedingly cold. However, the Vermont-bred Seth was undeterred by the weather.

After that first visit, he continued to come back to clear more land and every time he approached Cedar Lake, his heart began beating faster as if his destiny were guiding his every step. He was nervous, fearing that the plots would be scooped up by someone else before they were demarcated properly. Homesteaders were making their marks upon the land in the region.

The general process for homesteaders to lay claim to public land follows.[46]

1) First the Federal Government would announce that public land would be open for sale after it had been surveyed and approved by the President of the United States.
2) Pre-emption laws in 1835 encouraged claimants to settle early on public domain lands, as long as the land was free from Native American interests and was surveyed.
3) Claimants marked the boundaries of land they wanted to claim by erecting structures, felling trees or tilling or furrowing edges, basically taking possession prior to the official purchase; 1834-1837.
4) Federal land surveys for Lake County, Illinois began in September 1837 and ended in August 1840.
5) The Lake County land office, the Receiver's office, then opened for payment on pre-emption claims on September 30, 1840.[47]
6) Land patents, indicating formal ownership of the land,

---

[46] Thank you to Al Westerman, author of *Public Domain Land Sales in Lake County, Illinois*. Zion, Illinois. 2006.
[47] Per Al Westerman, this included most western townships of Antioch (West), Grant, Wauconda and Cuba. The earliest record for a pre-emption claim and purchase was on June 18, 1840 for land in Wauconda Township. Most pre-emption claims were from 1840-1842 but there were a few as late as 1847 in Lake County.

would be received from the government anywhere between 6 months to 2 years after payments were made.

The process could take several years. Land tracts tended to be selected first for three factors: access to fresh water, hardwood trees for building, and tillable land for farming. Prime plots were often located along old Indian and military trails and some had been claimed as early as 1834 by the first homesteaders.

Seth's Cedar Lake, hidden by tall grasses, had dismayed early speculators, and freezing temperatures had kept others at bay. Once he discovered the site, Seth made sure there were no marks from other homesteaders or Native American interests, and with the tenacity of a young man, he plotted to see the rest of his Utopian dream come to fruition. He observed that he was nearer to old Indian trails than he had originally thought which made bringing in equipment feasible. After clearing excess brush around the shoreline, Seth dammed a creek feeding into the lake ultimately revealing nearly 228 acres of open glacial water, full of edible fish. The surrounding wilderness was filled with wildlife. When the lake's shores were finally cleared Seth could barely contain his excitement.

Understanding of the land process in Illinois was initially completed at the Government Land Office in Chicago. It was common practice for homesteaders, after first cultivating the soils and building structures on their desired property, to save their money before the Land Office opened for payments. Seth, like many others, took advantage of the time gap between claiming Cedar Lake and purchasing it to get to know people familiar with the process for land acquisition. Even though he was a young man, Seth's confidence led him to introduce himself to Colonel Edmund D. Taylor. Other young men might have been intimidated by Taylor who served as a private during the Winnebago War before moving his family from Kentucky to Springfield, Illinois in 1814.[48] Taylor moved his way through military ranks and then into the Illinois State Senate from 1834-1835. In 1835, he was appointed by President Andrew Jackson as the *Register of Public Monies* in Chicago, which was quite an important role.[49] Taylor was working with James Whitlock who was the *Receiver of Public Money*.[50] Together Taylor and Whitlock would be responsible for coordinating the sales of nearly 400,000 acres of land in Illinois between 1835 and 1839. Seth's friendship with Taylor and Whitlock paved an inside track to making

---

[48] As a young man, Taylor joined the Historical Society of Illinois in Springfield where he worked with Governor Edward Coles and several other legislators. His work led him to run for the State Senate in 1830 for Sangamon County. In 1832, he ran again and defeated the young lawyer, Abraham Lincoln. During the Black Hawk War, Taylor earned the rank of Colonel.

[49] Edmund D. Taylor Biography. *The National Magazine,* volume 16. April-November, 1892. "The Originator of the Greenback Currency."

[50] Westerman, A. *Public Domain Land Sales in Lake County, Illinois.* Zion, Illinois 2006. Page 9.

sure his land transactions were legitimate.

The first land tracts were sold as 80 acre parcels and some were given away to prominent men who had served in the military. The region was arranged according to section, township, and range, generally with 32 sections in each county, each section measuring 160 acres. The first round of 80-acre tracts sold for $1.25 an acre. Early purchasers needed to submit their names to the *Register* (Taylor) and then take their receipt to the *Receiver* (Whitlock), who accepted and recorded the payment. Whatever land was left unsold from the first round of 80-acre purchases, the federal government then offered for private sale on a first-come-first-serve basis. Cedar Lake was in this second round of purchase opportunities.

The lag time between claims and purchases made a lot of people nervous because some land speculators had money available to pay for land even if they had not officially claimed any. While Seth continued to work in Chicago, he attempted to spend as much time as possible in Cedar Lake to make sure he had proof of his claims while he saved his money until the formal payment would be required at the *Register's* office.

In the meantime, Seth, along with other speculators, formed "claim associations." These associations were made up of people who supported one another to ensure that when payments were required, members would have the cash ready for the purchase. Fearing the possibility of "claim jumpers", Seth formed claim associations with family and friends in Vermont such as Daniel Baldwin, a Paine family friend whose name was on several early deeds with Seth.[51] With the support of these associates, Seth could continue his work in Chicago while others kept an eye on the land itself, assured that when the time came he would have the capital to purchase it.

Baldwin, along with many other New Englanders were drawn to land prospects in Illinois after the economic panics of '36, '37, and '39 in New England. Motivated families were migrating to Illinois to establish their own hamlets of religious freedom on this new, inexpensive, and fertile land. Many Congregational Church families from Vermont and other parts of New England found Lake County as attractive as Seth did, and some were familiar to the Paines.

******

In addition to being the *Register,* Taylor had a Chicago-based dry goods business called Taylor, Breese & Co. After Seth's mentor Peter Cohen moved out of Chicago in 1837 to pursue work in Michigan, Seth

---

[51] Daniel Baldwin is mentioned in the Vermont Historical Magazine, page 659. His name appears with Seth's on 7 land tract purchases found at the Bureau of Land Management, Government Land Office Records.

was invited to work with Taylor.[52,53] The move from Cohen's retail storefront to selling dry goods for Taylor, Breese & Co. was smooth as Seth never forgot a face and his natural charm inspired trust among his customers. This new work further improved Seth's financial situation and expanded his savings.

As Seth and Taylor worked together, Seth continued to dream beyond business about his future. After some time, Taylor suggested that Seth might enjoy the company of James Whitlock's sister, Frances. Seth, a young, ambitious, and business savvy man, made an attractive potential suitor for the sassy Frances Jones Whitlock. Both Whitlocks were the children of Major Ambrose Whitlock, a survivor of Anthony Wayne's Army of Indiana during the War of 1812. They had been born in Kentucky and moved with their father to Illinois after losing their mother when they were young. Frances was schooled in society through her father's social prominence. When they met, Frances was drawn to Seth's confidence, handsome disposition, and tall stature. He was not arrogant and she was entranced by his charm and humble nature. Her admiration grew when he listened to her advice and demonstrated that he believed her to be equal in intelligence and ability to himself. Seth saw in Frances a hearty pioneer spirit and warm-heartedness to compliment his lofty dreams. Frances shared his compassion and his

---

[52] *Chicago Daily Tribune.* June 10, 1872.
[53] Chicago City Directory. 1839.

Utopian vision which he had eagerly shared with her before he proposed. Seth realized he could learn a lot from Frances and Frances felt that Seth was a man who would let her personality and fortitude shine. Shortly after Seth met Frances, they were married on August 31, 1836.[54] Once married, they relocated from Chicago to Cedar Lake. Seth was ecstatic.

The young couple constructed their home by Cedar Lake and moved in before Christmas in 1836. That year on December 20th, the thermostat dropped unexpectedly from 40 degrees Fahrenheit in the morning—preceded by a large ominous cloud of wind, cold, and ice that shattered the temperature in the course of a few hours—down to zero degrees. Stories of the day recall that, "Men froze to their saddles; frogs froze, petrified with their mouths open."[55] That Christmas, Seth and Frances were comfortably oblivious in their new home.

Seth's family from Vermont finally arrived in Illinois in October 1837 along with his stepfather, Abel Keyes and his son, Joseph, who was heading for Wisconsin.[56] Seth's mother, Fanny, was feeling

---

[54] Illinois State marriage archives say the wedding was August 31, 1836. Andreas, Alfred Theodore, *History of Cook County, Illinois, From the Earliest Period to the Present Time,* Chicago, 1884, In three Volumes. This volume says the wedding was August 25, 1837.
[55] Bedell, J. *A Tour Through the Western States* - "The Sudden Freeze". Long Island City: Star Book and Job Printing Office. 1867. Pages 40-41.
[56] *History of Jefferson County, Wisconsin, Containing a History of Jefferson County.* Western Historical Company, Chicago. 1879. Page 347. Joseph was Abel's son from

particularly restless since Ruth married and moved to Connecticut with her husband's family in 1837. Abel and Fanny decided that moving with a caravan of wagons like Joseph's would be safer than traveling alone. Abel, a man known for his restless temperament, was not patient enough to stay in one place too long, so he was anxious to head to this new frontier.[57] Moving by wagon, the families took overland trails, making the journey less arduous. Abel and Fanny arrived in Cedar Lake where Seth had prepared a home for them. Seth knew that having Abel, an experienced pioneer, in Cedar Lake would assist the neighbors with any potential claim issues. Meanwhile, Joseph moved on to Wisconsin. With Illinois' close proximity to Wisconsin, the family felt that Abel could travel back and forth to visit his son and to help him set up the community of Lake Mills in Jefferson County.

When Abel and Fanny arrived, Seth and Frances were waiting for them. Fanny barely recognized her son who she had seen only three years prior. The man who stood before her looked so much like her first husband, Elijah, that at first glance, she thought she was hallucinating. Seth rushed forward to embrace his mother and swept her up in his arms in a giant bear hug, "Mother!" he exclaimed with tears in his eyes. "Thanks be to God for your safe arrival."

---

his first marriage, born in 1794, Page 540.
[57] *Vermont Historical Magazine*. Page 628.

"My boy," she whispered in his ear.

As they separated, Seth pointed to the pretty woman he had been standing next to and said, " Mother, I want you to meet my wife, Frances." Fanny, without hesitation, embraced Frances wholeheartedly and said, "Praise the Lord and welcome to the family." If Frances had any doubts about Seth's family and his dedication to women, they were erased when she saw the respect and admiration he held for his mother. Fanny quickly became the mother Frances never had as a child.

Seth's sister, Jane, came to Cedar Lake in January 1838. Jane was newly married and she and her husband were eager to help settle the town.[58] Jane knew that having her family nearby would help her when her husband was traveling. Jane's husband, Caleb Fittz, was an upholsterer who worked between Chicago and Milwaukee. In time, they would return to Chicago where Jane's husband would be elected Justice of the Peace in the 1850s. But, in these early days, the family needed each other to gather food, cook, prepare for foul weather, find supplies, and build a burgeoning community at Cedar Lake. With his family settled, Seth could commute to Chicago, only a half day's ride away. Though the roads were still rudimentary in 1838, their path would become smooth with frequent travelers and the delivery of goods from

---

[58] Milwaukee marriage license, January 11, 1838. The 1840 Federal Census lists the family with Abel Keyes.

Chicago northward to Wisconsin.

Between 1833 and 1840, the State of Illinois was working to develop a Township and County form of local government. Lake County, Illinois, where Seth's Cedar Lake was located, stretched west from Lake Michigan to the Fox River, south to the Cook County border, and north to the Wisconsin border.[59] As it was forming, Lake County boasted eight election precincts including the voting district Seth named Zurich. [60,61] There was already another Cedar Lake in the county, so Seth, as one of the largest claim holders in the area, was asked to come up with another name.[62] Some records claim that Seth remembered Fourier was a fan of Zurich, Switzerland which is why he chose the name. Others claim that the land nearby had features similar to Switzerland, and thus made Zurich a good namesake.[63] Ira Kimberly's land just west of Seth's Cedar Lake also boasted Swiss features, with its hardwood forests, natural ravines, and rolling countryside. Seth may have also heard of the beauty of Zurich from his mentor, Peter Cohen. Regardless of his

---

[59] Officially, it would be established by an act of the State legislature in 1839.
[60] Haines, Elijah M. Past and Present of Lake County, Illinois, Chicago: Le Baron, 1877, and cited in Dretske, Diana, *What's in a name? The Origin of Place Names in Lake County, Illinois,* Lake County Discovery Museum, January 1, 1998.
[61] It was officially registered as Lake Zurich by Paine in 1856, though many called it that in earlier years and the town was officially incorporated as Lake Zurich in 1896, well after Paine's passing.
[62] The existing Cedar Lake is located in central Lake County along today's Route 132 in Lake Villa, Illinois.
[63] Albert F. Scharf (cartographer 1900) mentions that Honey Lake (in adjacent Ela Township) looked like Switzerland to many early settlers.

source of inspiration, Seth found that being the first landowner in the area had its advantages, changing the community's name from Cedar Lake to the voting district of Zurich in 1843.

The community around Zurich began to evolve quickly. Following the Fourier design, Seth's first major structure after building homes was a large community center he named the Humanity Stable—later known as the Stable of Humanity—which would serve as Zurich's central hub. [64] On the ground floor of the Stable was a Union Store where residents could buy shares in the business and partner in decision-making. Local residents purchased or traded goods, receiving credit for current or future needs. The second floor functioned as a community center with a large meeting hall for groups to gather. Smaller rooms in the Stable offered space to people who needed temporary housing. Here in this center of his community, Seth began to see ways to help humanity. Rather than operating these rooms as a hotel, charging for their use, he only asked for free-will donations, from travelers who passed through town, people he met who needed assistance, and eventually freedom seekers from slave states. Seth was not the only family member to want to assist those who needed support. The 1840 Lake County census shows that his stepfather and mother had a free black man living with

---

[64] Partridge, Hon. Charles A. *Historical Encyclopedia of Illinois and History of Lake County*. Chicago Munsell Publishing Company. 1902. Page 679.

them on their farm.

Seth knew that constructing buildings required a connection to a mill for lumber. In pursuit of that goal, Seth introduced himself to Philetus W. (P.W.) Gates, who ran Gates Iron Works on Canal Street in Chicago. Gates hailed from New York and was a hard-working, industrious man in the process of building an innovative empire in Chicago.[65] When Gates wanted to test out his revolutionary steam-powered mill, Seth saw the mill's great potential and became the first in Lake County to establish a steam sawmill on Flint Creek, adjacent to the lake. The sawmill would provide the much needed wood to build homes, and provide jobs while testing out Gates' new model. The enterprise was deemed a success and Gates was grateful for the confidence Seth had in his idea, forming a lifelong friendship between the two men.

Seth did not forget his friendship with Peter Cohen and how transformative that early opportunity had been for him, so part of his mission also became to provide jobs, resources, and the same welcome to people coming to his burgeoning community. His heart was full as he watched his Utopian town come to life. Not only was his generosity extended to strangers passing through, but he also encouraged and mentored other young men and women, just as Cohen had done for him,

---

[65] P.W. Gates was born in Tioga, New York in 1817 and had his first Iron and Brass business in Chicago by 1840 on Canal Street, near where Seth worked.

helping them to dream. Seth spoke of his Utopian plans to anyone who would listen and his connection to families from New York and Vermont brought in other residents who appreciated his vision and bought property in partnership with him. His early investments in real estate accumulated over 2,200 acres in total spread out over Will, Cook, and Lake Counties. The majority of his land holdings surrounded the lake in Zurich. This early success led him to believe that he could accomplish anything and help anyone in need. Seth's enthusiasm and confidence gave him the ability to form steadfast relationships with people, a gift that would serve him well as challenges arose.

As his land holdings grew, Seth's interest in politics and world affairs was also expanding and he was getting bolder about expressing his views to any willing ear. Initially, he stuck to social movements and business, but as time went on, his willingness to discuss religion and politics became notorious. He was someone oblivious to the power that came with his privilege. For Seth, money was merely a tool that would allow him to help people, build a better community, and do good things.

The population in the wilderness around Chicago was growing. As more New Englander's arrived, they brought news of the abolitionist movement that had been gaining ground through the activities of William Lloyd Garrison.[66] Garrison's followers were bringing

---

[66] William Lloyd Garrison was a strong abolitionist and publisher of the *The Liberator,*

abolitionist values with them with the aim that Illinois would remain a 'slave-free' state. Seth welcomed them to the region and he would later wholeheartedly and enthusiastically become a supporter for the cause.

In these early years around Lake Zurich, things were cozy in Seth's home. His family surrounded him and around the evening dinner table, they debated controversial topics, discussed their biblical values, and laughed away any problems. At 22 years of age Seth had created his perfect home.

---

an anti-slavery newspaper on the east coast.

Riot in Alton, Illinois, October 1837.
Woodblock print from 19th century poster print, public domain. Missouri History Museum Photograph and Prints collections. Illinois. n29376.

Chapter 5

Abolition; 1837-1843

Like many young men who embrace ideas before having the life experience to back them up, Seth fell wholly into the abolition movement when he met Henry Blodgett. He had first heard about Blodgett and his family from Chester Smith. Seth met Blodgett when he was working on his Lake County land claims.[67] Blodgett recognized his surname and asked Seth about his connection to the fort. Blodgett was a man who had been in the midst of the Indian Wars and survived the massacres at Fort Paine. His parents, Israel P. and Avis Blodgett, were legendary pioneers. Blodgett was a young attorney in 1836 as well as a humanitarian and abolitionist. By the time they met, Seth had been learning quite a bit about the abolitionist movement and he had seen a copy of William Lloyd Garrison's newspaper *The Liberator*.[68] What continued to move Seth toward the abolitionist cause was the absurdity of the idea of treating any man differently simply because of the color of their skin. He had been raised to believe that he was morally obligated to love all of his fellow men equally.

Blodgett was an eloquent and dignified storyteller. Through his

---

[67] *The Biographical Directory of Federal Judges.* A public domain publication of the federal Judicial Center.
[68] *The Liberator,* a newspaper dedicated to discussing and promoting the abolitionist cause, was started in 1831 by William Lloyd Garrison in New England.

stories, Seth could not only see the atrocity of enslavement, but was also moved to join the cause for abolition. Blodgett told a particularly poignant story about his mother, Avis. Avis Blodgett lived in the countryside of DuPage County, Illinois around 1835. Blodgett recalls,

> "A man on horseback rode up to the door, leading two negroes, whose hands were tied and who were held by a rope passed from their hands to the pommel of the saddle. He asked mother if she would give them a drink of water. She took a tin pail and a cup and went to the spring….filled the pail….and began giving the negroes a drink. The fellow cursed her and asked her why in the devil she was giving water to them….said that he asked for water for himself, not them. She answered that the spring was there, he could help himself; that these men couldn't do that, and therefore, she was giving them the water and not him."[69]

Seth appreciated Avis's audacity and aspired to have that kind of foresight and courage.

Blodgett's parents were a part of the Underground Railroad, a pathway to freedom for the formerly enslaved, run by advocates of the abolitionist movement who wanted to take action. The Underground Railroad's name of origin is not officially verified, but is likely derived

---

[69] Blodgett, Henry W. *Autobiography of Henry W. Blodgett*. Waukegan. 1906. Page 16.

from a news reporter who described the disappearance of an enslaved person as if he had traveled on, "a secret route, not overland like a railroad, but like an underground railroad."[70]

The Underground Railroad network was a closely guarded clandestine organization with members sworn to secrecy.[71] Members served as station masters, conductors or operatives and they provided temporary sanctuary, transportation, and other support to freedom seekers, helping them find their way to freedom in the northern states or Canada.[72] In 1834, Illinois State law forbade private citizens from providing assistance to freedom seekers. To be a part of the Underground Railroad, you needed connections to other station masters.[73] Blodgett was Seth's first connection to the Underground Railroad in Illinois, but Elijah Lovejoy was Seth's inspiration to join the antislavery movement and the Underground Railroad network.

---

[70] Foner, E. *Gateway to Freedom.* W.W. Norton and Company, New York. 2015. Page 6.

[71] Courtland, T. M. Jr. *Southern Illinoisian.* Carbondale, Illinois. June 18, 1972. Page 8. It is estimated that nearly 100,000 enslaved people escaped using the Underground Railroad from the 1830's through the Civil War. Nearly 6,000 are estimated to have come through Illinois.

[72] Station masters provided shelter or hiding places, conductors helped to provide safe passage, and operatives helped to make arrangements if a freedom seeker was caught. This language was adopted following the guidance of the National Parks Service and the National Underground Railroad Network to Freedom Program.

[73] After the Civil War, the network took years to unravel. Much of the Underground Railroad's secrecy was lost to history. Those who assisted the formerly enslaved and those who escaped to freedom's stories largely went unwritten.

The story of Elijah Lovejoy in Alton, Illinois, grabbed the attention of many people in late 1837 when the news of his murder by an angry mob circulated around the state.[74] The Lovejoy's were known as a family of zealous and controversial abolitionists, actively advocating for Garrison's antislavery movement. Elijah's brother, Owen Lovejoy, was an unreserved orator and an active station master on the Underground Railroad in Princeton, Illinois. Another cousin, William Lovejoy, ran a stage line from Chicago to Waukegan in 1836 and was also rumored to have harbored freedom seekers in his coaches.

The antislavery movement was gaining traction in the region, but was still seen by many as a cause that bordered on being un-American as it was seeking to change an institution that had been supported by the founding fathers. Therefore, those who were involved were quiet about their support for fear of being considered radical. The Lovejoys placed themselves visibly on the front lines of a national debate asserting that the premise of slavery itself was against the will of God.

Elijah Lovejoy started an antislavery newspaper in St. Louis, Missouri in 1835, in the spirit of Garrison's *Liberator*. Missouri was established as a slave state after the Missouri Compormise of 1820, with many early residents originating from Mississippi and bringing the

---

[74] The Midwest Lovejoys were descendants of Abiel Lovejoy (1731-1811). The Lovejoy ancestry is traced back to the 17th century Massachusetts Bay Colony.

practice along with them.[75] Lovejoy's paper, the *St. Louis Observer*, published articles supporting the abolitionist movement, which was very unpopular with enslavers. In 1836, the lynching of Francis J. McIntosh in Missouri inspired Lovejoy to pen a headline for an article in the *St. Louis Observer* on May 5 suggesting that public support of the tragedy had effectively "ended the rule of Law and Constitution in St. Louis."[76] In response, in July of 1836, an angry mob destroyed his printing press, forcing him out of St. Louis. Undeterred from sharing his message, Lovejoy moved across the Mississippi River to Alton, Illinois where he continued his work. In Alton he joined the newly formed Anti-Slavery Society becoming more and more vocal against slavery. Along with his supporters, which included Henry Ward Beecher and Henry Blodgett, Lovejoy attempted to guard the new press against the threat of seething mobs.[77] On November 7, 1837, a large mob stormed his new offices in Alton. In the ensuing melee, they murdered Elijah

---

[75] Missouri Compromise | HistoryNet, The Missouri Compromise drew the north/south line of slavery and was along the southern border of Illinois.
[76] Neuman, Caryn E., The First Amendment Encyclopedia presented by the John Seigenthaler Chair of Excellence in First Amendment Studies, Elijah Lovejoy | The First Amendment Encyclopedia *The Alton Observer* article in the *Missouri History Collections, May 5, 1836.*
[77] Henry Ward Beecher, brother of Harriet Beecher Stowe, was a Minister from Connecticut who mastered a stutter before evolving into a social reformer, abolitionist, and women's suffrage advocate. He was described by his biographer Debby Applegate as, "an odd combination of western informality, eastern education, and unabashed showmanship." Beecher's 'gospel of love,' set the groundwork for theological and social reform.

Lovejoy while he protected the building. They set fire to the space and destroyed the press. Instead of squelching support for the antislavery movement, Elijah Lovejoy quickly became a martyr.

Each time Seth crossed paths with Blodgett, his passion for speaking out about the injustice of slavery grew stronger. Seth was intrigued by the connections that the Blodgett family had with men like Elijah Lovejoy, Henry Ward Beecher, and other well-known progressives. Following Blodgett's retelling of Elijah Lovejoy's martyrdom story, Seth became an eager follower of the movement. While traveling, selling goods, and setting up his community around Zurich, Seth began to seek out and attend antislavery meetings in the Chicago area. At one of these meetings he met Theron Norton, who would offer Seth his next business opportunity and further his connections to the cause.

******

In 1839 Seth left Taylor, Breese & Co. and formed a partnership with Norton which they eventually named Paine and Norton.[78] The pair set up shop at 117 Lake Street in Chicago and sold dry goods such as flour, sugar, and oats, and they exported products like pork, beef, and lard.[79] Together Paine and Norton built a strong and lucrative enterprise, selling nearly $30,000 in merchandise in their first year.[80] They also

---

[78] Norton was the 'Co' in Taylor, Breese & Co.
[79] Fergus' Chicago Directory. 1839. *Norton, Theron.* Alphabetical Listing of Workers.
[80] Goodspeed,W.A., Healy, D.D. *History of Cook County, Illinois.* Goodspeed Historical Association. 1909. Pages 91-92.

invested briefly in the Chicago Marine and Fire Insurance Company, which operated like a modern bank–loaning and receiving money.[81]

The Norton family had East Coast connections and were a part of the abolitionist movement from their Congregational Church roots. Norton's family lived a few miles north of where Seth had settled in Lake County and had invited other like-minded New Englanders to join them there.

At the time, churches were forming all over the region. On February 20, 1838, 16 residents met in Alfred Payne's log cabin near Fort Hill in Mechanics Grove (today's Mundelein) bringing 'the old Puritan spirit' together to form the Ivanhoe Congregational Church.[82] The members who signed into service brought their records of good standing from their prior churches in New York as well as their antislavery values.[83] At this time the church was part of the larger national order of the Presbytery and followed the constitution of the Presbyterian Church of the United States.[84] This congregation became the foundation for

---

[81] This engagement did not last long, but it linked Seth to E. I. Tinkham and J. Y. Scammon. This was also his first exposure to the world of banking.
[82] *Ivanhoe Congregational Church Records*. Self published by the church, June 15, 1973. Copy from the Cook Memorial Library, Libertyville, Illinois. Cover page.
[83] Four members of the Clark family, three from the Harden family, two from the Hoffman family, four from the Payne family, one from the Schanck family, one Norton, and one Gridley comprised the initial group.
[84] *Ivanhoe Congregational Church Records*. Self published by the church, June 15, 1973. Copy from the Cook Memorial Library, Libertyville, Illinois. Members held services for the next 18 years in various homes and schoolhouses until 1856 when they erected a formal structure.

several others to form in the county.

Seth considered himself a devout Christian. However, his upbringing with the Bible as a dinner companion and his family's early challenges with the Congregational Church made him resistant to attend formal church services. But, his partnership with Norton offered him a connection to the local members of the Congregational Church. Even as he worked closely with them, Seth's ability to mingle with groups but not join them as a member was a practiced trait that served him well but eventually left him on the outside as movements gained traction. At this time, any eager volunteer was embraced and welcomed into the fold of the abolition movement.

At the national level, the abolition movement remained controversial. Although Lovejoy had encouraged many private supporters like Seth, others found the cause absurd and would ridicule those who felt they needed to act against slavery.[85] Seth was unfazed by the often negative response to his increasingly frequent discussions about the cause. By 1843, he had officially secured and paid for his land and his first son Charles had been born. Having a son made Seth protective and more confident in sharing his views on slavery to create the world he wanted for his son and family. He appreciated his family's values on the matter and was determined to see his son grow up in a

---

[85] City Publishing Company. *Portrait and Biographical Album of Lake County, Illinois*. Chicago: Lake City Publishing Company. 1891. Page 270.

world where his fellow man was not oppressed.

In the beginning of 1843, the Congregationalists in Lake County began to host a variety of events intended to recruit support for the antislavery movement. These events would bring national speakers and emancipated slaves together to encourage voting for antislavery delegates for public offices. Seth initially balked at encouraging support for elected officials. Seth spoke out about civil government and instead encouraged the Fourier tenets he embraced, claiming that "civil government should be abolished on the theory that all restraint by law was in violation of natural law."[86] He found others interested in joining and living without civil government which was an unusual arrangement for the region. Fair trade through his community store and purchases made with merchandise credits based on personal trade, had proven to Seth that his store had no need for civil regulation.

In 1841, Seth's connections helped him secure a post office in Zurich with his stepfather appointed as the first Postmaster. The President of the United States, at that time John Tyler, approved post offices based upon population, political connections, and access to travel routes.[87] Having a post office in town significantly affected trade routes,

---

[86] Halsey, J. J. *A History of Lake County, Illinois*. Chicago, Illinois. Roy S. Bates. 1912. Page 428.
[87] Albert Scharf in 1908, credited the Honey Lake Area as resembling "little Switzerland" with its elevation shifts. Honey Lake, an impoundment along Flint Creek, was about 0.25 miles due west of Lake Zurich.

development, roadway establishment, and community growth. The residents Seth attracted embraced his philosophies, but other surrounding communities were beginning to form with standard economies. Seth wasn't the only one to see the value of the land in Lake County; by 1840, 2,905 residents lived in the county, expanding considerably from the first non-native resident Daniel Wright who had arrived in 1833.[88]

In July 1842, Seth sold his portion of the business to Norton, to spend more time in the countryside maturing his community and deepening his connection to the abolition movement.[89] He began to invest in the infrastructure of his community while maintaining close ties to the city of Chicago. Under the cloak of secrecy, he was invited to work with other station masters to support the Underground Railroad.[90] Through his connections, Seth made it known that his "Humanity Stable" would provide a safe haven for freedom-seekers.[91] Legends of the Underground Railroad from that time, depict wagons hiding escaped

---

[88] Lake County, Illinois History, blogspot. Friday September 18, 2009. Daniel Wright, claimed that the native Potawatomi helped him build a cabin in June 1833.
[89] Andreas, Alfred Theodore, *History of Cook County, Illinois, From the Earliest Period to the Present Time,* Chicago, 1884, In three Volumes. Page 408. Note the source is misspelled in this volume, Chicago city directories of 1839 confirm the name is Norton not Norson.
[90] Siebert, W. *The Underground Railroad from Slavery to Freedom.* The MacMillan Company, London. 1898. Page 404.
[91] Lake Zurich, IL. Encyclopedia of Chicago. *Lake Zurich history*. Chicago History Society.

slaves under straw or animal hides until they could be safely transported to Chicago's lakeshore, where they could find a boat bound for Canada.[92]

Illinois State Black Laws would punish those who assisted freedom seekers as well as the freedom seekers themselves. Any violation carried with it a risk of $500 in fines and five years in jail. Still, Seth was not deterred from the cause. When he was appointed Zurich Postmaster by then President Tyler in 1843, he felt the clout of that appointment. Seth's personal and professional success fed his growing feeling of invincibility. He recognized that advocating for the abolition movement would require the attention of more passionate leaders. As soon as he was invited to, Seth stepped into a leadership role, willing to embrace any risk that might follow.

His family fully supported his endeavors. Seth's wife, Frances, embraced his ideals wholeheartedly. Around their Sunday dinner table, the Paine's openly discussed the injustice of slavery and how they could assist the cause, just as they had discussed controversial topics when Seth was growing up. His sister Ruth and her husband moved from Connecticut to Illinois around 1843, his sister Jane moved back to the

---

[92] Blanchard, Rufus. *Discovery and Conquests of the North-West, With the History of Chicago*. Volume 1, O.L. Baskin and Company Historical Publishers Lakeside Building. 1882. Volume 2 1900. Page 286.

city with her husband and new baby. Seth came to appreciate his time with his sisters and their spouses, as well as his mother, stepfather, and his wife's family members, who often joined them. At this table they would argue the merits of these humanitarian efforts, discuss the news of the day, and read the Bible.

One evening after another spirited discussion, Seth walked from his front porch to the lake named after his town. He stood on the edge of the quiet banks and reflected on the blessings that he had received here. As the golden sun was setting, he felt the conviction that this was where he was meant to be. Life was good around his lake. He had a growing family, a beautiful community, and a cause worthy of his name. He felt at peace and ready to take on the world.

Owen Lovejoy Home in Princeton, Illinois as it looks restored in 2015. Photo from the author's collection.

Chapter 6

The "Wild West" of Politics; 1843-1846

Public speaking came easy to Seth. Stepping up to the podium to introduce the first speakers at an abolition event in Lake County in 1843, he felt both nervous and elated. This was his golden opportunity to inspire more of Lake County's residents to embrace the abolitionist movement. Seth's eagerness inspired in his audience both admiration for his energy and eye-rolling at his naïvete. He began his speech with a quote from William Lloyd Garrison's weekly *Liberator* newspaper which he had recently subscribed to. As he read it, he imagined Garrison personally calling his audience to arms with his words: "I am in earnest — I will not equivocate — I will not excuse — I will not retreat a single inch — AND I WILL BE HEARD."[93]

For emphasis, he paused between the words to let them sink into the minds of his audience and he felt Garrison's passion pour forth from his mouth. As the breathless crowd hung on his every word and those to follow, Seth saw how powerful Garrison's words were, and the important role they played in influencing the public's opinions on controversial issues. This event would be the first of many others in the region for Seth speaking publicly about the abolition of slavery.

---

[93] William Lloyd Garrison and The Liberator. *U. S. History Online Textbook.* 2017.

As Seth traveled to participate in abolition events, he sought out and met inspiring speakers and like-minded individuals who he would later invite to events in Lake County. His mission was to advocate for peaceful action to end slavery. Unlike the followers of John Brown who called for aggressive measures, Seth believed in the words of the Psalms; "With patience a ruler may be persuaded, and a soft tongue will break a bone" (Proverbs 25:15).[94]

In tandem with the cause to support the enslaved, the growing Washington Temperance movement also attracted Seth's attention, as the two causes were closely intertwined by their participants and by conservatism.[95] The Washingtonian Temperance Movement was calling for the Federal government to abolish liquor completely in the United States. Their approach was different from many anti-liquor movements, encouraging harmonious, persuasive public presentations rather than shouting at people or humiliating them. The Movement not only allowed, but also encouraged women's involvement, which was progressive for the time.

Through his participation in the local chapters of both movements, Seth had a front-row seat to progressive political activity. Garrisonian

---

[94] John Brown was fast becoming another vocal abolitionist, but unlike Garrissonians, he advocated for forceful action against slavery.
[95] Dumbarton House. Washington D.C. January 2020 Newsletter. "In the year 1800, the average American over the age of fifteen consumed thirty-two gallons of hard cider and beer, seven gallons of distilled spirits, and one gallon of wine."

followers, including Owen Lovejoy recommended that concerned citizens lead the effort to form *Anti-Slavery Societies* throughout Illinois and build the abolitionist movement.⁹⁶ Followers like Seth, began to organize meetings and conventions to bring the cause's message to more people. Though William Lloyd Garrison himself had been nearly killed by a crowd in Boston in 1835, he had not been deterred from his passion for the movement. Seth admired these progressive leaders and he courageously and wholeheartedly adopted their words and actions in his own political leadership.

John Tyler was in the middle of his term as President of the United States in 1843. Tyler ascended to the role after the unexpected death of William Henry Harrison. It was a pivotal year to expand the abolition movement. While President Tyler was a firm believer in state rights to establish laws about slavery, the Oregon Trail had just opened which meant that slavery could potentially extend beyond the existing borders of the country. The abolistionists feared this would bring more human suffering and expand slavery's reach. At the same time, Texas was in conflict with Mexico, which meant that slavery could possibly extend further south into Mexico. Although Tyler ran with Harrison on the Whig Party ticket, he was later called *His Accidency* by the Whigs who abandoned him when he pushed for policies that would allow the states

---

⁹⁶ Owen Lovejoy was the brother of the martyred Elijah Lovejoy and became a dedicated organizer after his brother's death.

to make their own decisions on pressing issues. Tyler's position of less federal involvement and more state control delayed many progressive movements including the abolition and temperance movements that Seth was a part of. Despite the national political climate, the abolition movement gained ground in Lake County with Seth at the helm.

In September of 1843, Seth's stepfather Abel Keyes passed away while visiting his son in Jefferson County Wisconsin.[97] Shortly thereafter, Seth's mother moved in with his growing family. His mother's presence gave Seth more time to devote to his causes and prepare for presentations and events.

The abolitionist movement's most ardent supporters in the early days were the Congregationalists in Illinois. As new churches were being formed, they had the option of being either Congregational or Presbyterian, or to maintain their affiliation with both denominations.[98] In 1844, when the revised Illinois state law forbade anyone from assisting the formerly enslaved, the Congregationalists split from the Presbytery. Within the Presbytery, heated discussions took place over whether the church would follow the laws of the land or the laws of God. Presbyterians felt that if they were outspoken about the abolition

---

[97] *The History of Jefferson County, Wisconsin*. Chicago Western Historical Company. 1879. Pages 540, 546.
[98] Millburn Congregational Church Records. Historical Millburn Community Association Inc. 1912.

cause, that was sufficient. By contrast, the Congregational Church felt they needed to do more than speak about the issue. Seth sided with the Congregationalists—agreeing that abolishing slavery would require not only words but action. Though he took a leadership role in church activities, he still avoided membership in the church itself.

In 1845, local Congregational churches in Lake County organized a widely attended conference series about the abolition of both liquor and slavery. The Chicago regional press paid close attention to the agitated crowds and published the names of everyone involved. Seth was at the forefront, and listed as the President of the local Temperance Society.[99] Joining him were neighbors, Congregational ministers, and other prominent members from around Lake County.[100] Following these encounters, Seth began to interact with the press regularly and enjoyed sharing the messages of the Anti-Slavery Society and Temperance movement with a wider audience.

Seth attended a local speaking engagement which featured Ichabod

---

[99] Halsey, J.J. *A History of Lake County, Illinois.* Chicago, Illinois: Roy S. Bates, 1912. Page 92 lists an article from *The Porcupine.* Waukegan, Illinois. June 11, 1845. Reports a call to organize a "County Washington Temperance Society." Signers were Josiah Wright, D. O. Dickinson, E. W. Hoyt, M.P. Hoyt, W.F. Shepard, Theron Parsons, Thomas Haggerty, Samuel M. Dowst, Nathaniel P. Dowst, William B. Dodge, William Ladd, Hiram Clark, **Seth Paine**, and C. C. Caldwell.

[100] Later, On October 9, *The Porcupine,* in Waukegan reported that **Seth Paine** was listed as president of the temperance promoters with VP; M. P. Hoyt, Theron Parsons, Ransom Steele, W.F. Shepard, and Milton Bacon. R.D. Maynard was secretary. Meeting held at the Methodist Church in Libertyville.

Codding and Sojourner Truth in the Spring of 1845.[101,102] At the same meeting, *Liberty Minstrel* author George Washington Clark gave an impassioned presentation accompanied by a choir from the Quinn Chapel in Chicago.[103,104] Clark began his presentations by saying, "Let associations of singers, having the love of liberty in their hearts, be immediately formed in every community."[105] His music elevated the event and proved to be inspirational, drawing more crowds and complementing the heavy political speeches at events.

Codding had a long history of speaking out against slavery in New England.[106] In 1840, Codding was one of several who discouraged including women in the Anti-Slavery Society in Massachusetts. However, five years later, he began to shift his position towards the involvement of women in the movement. He and other abolitionists could not deny the powerful message women like Sojourner Truth

---

[101] Abraham Lincoln Presidential Library archives. *Codding, Ichabod.* Biographical Sketches, Box 3, Memorandum envelope. Page 7.

[102] *Ivanhoe Congregational Church Records.* Self published by the church, June 15, 1973. Copy from the Cook Memorial Library, Libertyville, Illinois. Page 5.

[103] *Ivanhoe Congregational Church Records.* Self published by the church, June 15, 1973. Copy from the Cook Memorial Library, Libertyville, Illinois. Page 5.

[104] The Quinn Chapel in Chicago was part of the African Methodist Church beginning with a seven member prayer band and an active group of abolitionists who also were part of the Underground Railroad.

[105] Clark, G. W. *The Liberty Minstrel.* Leavitt & Alden, Boston: Saxton & Miles, N.Y., Myron Finch, N.Y., Jackson & Chaplin, N.Y. 1844.

[106] Codding was an Illinois abolitionist who also became an editor of the Wisconsin newspaper *The Christian Freeman* under the leadership of Sherman M. Booth.

preached during their speaking tours.

Sojourner Truth was born Isabella Baumfree in Dutch speaking Ulster County, New York in 1797. Her parents had been brought to New York with the slave trade in the late 1790s. As a young girl, she was sold four times to different enslavers, and despite being promised her freedom she was not emancipated by her enslaver in 1826. Consequently, she emancipated herself. She was assisted by New York residents who were members of the Dutch reformed church. Guided by God, she changed her name to Sojourner Truth and committed to Methodism and the abolition movement. During her lifetime she spoke passionately about women's rights, prison reform, and human suffering. [107,108] Social reformers like William Lloyd Garrison, Susan B. Anthony, and Wendell Phillips provided her platforms to speak nationally on these topics.

Seth and Codding bonded over their mutual passion and established a quick and dedicated friendship. Seth was mesmerized by Truth and her message of hope through storytelling. Prior to her death in 1883 she gave an example of one of her speeches in an interview with the *Inter Ocean* in Chicago. Speaking English with her Dutch accent she said,

---

[107] National Women's History Museum. *Sojourner Truth*. 2019.
[108] African American Odyssey. *Sojourner Truth*. 1864. Sojourner Truth's first language was Dutch, but she learned English too. She believed that she was called by God to travel around the nation--sojourn--and preach the truth of his word.

"Chillen, I talks to God, and God talks to me. I goes out and talks to God in de fields and de woods. Dis morning I was walking out, and I got over de fence. I saw de wheat a-holding up its head, looking very big. I goes up and takes hold of it. You believe it, dere was no wheat dar. I says, 'God, What is de matter wid dis wheat?' Su' He says to me, 'Sojourner, dere is a little weasel in it.' Now I hears talking about de constitution and de rights of man. I comes up and I takes hold of dis Constitution. It looks mighty big, and I feels for my rights; but dar ain't any dar. Den I says, 'God, what ails dis constitution?' And He says, 'Sojourner, dere is a little weasel in it!'"[109,110]

The effect her stories had on audiences was incomparable.[111]

By spring of 1845, many new and inspired supporters were joining gatherings in Libertyville, Half Day, and Waukegan as a result of the Anti-Slavery Society events.[112] Some came to hear what all the fuss was about; others were moved to get involved. The burgeoning attendance of these events began to require more space. Tobias Wynkoop, a Libertyville man of dubious character, offered the members of Ivanhoe

---

[109] Chamberlin, E. *Chicago and its Suburbs*. Newspapers in Chicago, described the *Inter Ocean* as a paper owned by J.Y. Scammon in 1872, which evolved from a prior paper called the *Republican Journal*, T. A. Hungerford & Co. 1874. Page 268.
[110] The weasel was felt to be responsible for destruction of wheat in the early West.
[111] *Inter Ocean*. Chicago, Illinois. Saturday, December 1, 1883. Page 9.
[112] The town of Half Day is today's Village of Lincolnshire.

Congregational Church free wood to build a new facility to accommodate the growing crowds. Church members would be required "to get it across the river....In spite of the obstacle in the way, the offer was accepted, and Hiram Clark went with four yokes of oxen... and hauled the timbers to the river, and with much difficulty, it was taken across."[113,114] The new structure solved the meeting space problem in the central part of the county. Seth had offered his stable for use, but the Congregationalists felt that it was too far to travel to Lake Zurich. The church also hesitated to garner a dependent relationship with Seth because of his reluctance to join them formally.

In June of 1845, Seth participated in a religions convention at Half Day, about 8 miles from Lake Zurich, for "prayer and consultation, and to adopt a course to suppress slavery, intemperance and Sabbath desecration."[115] A number of prominent men joined the convention including; Joseph H. Payne, John Strang, D.O. Dickinson, William B. Dodge, Theron Parsons, Robert Pollock, Seth Paine, John Easton, F.H. Porter, Father William B. Dodge (and 20 other members of the clergy and residency of Lake County.[116] As an attendee rather than a leader,

---

[113] Hiram Clark was a firefighter with Seth in 1835 and also a Congregational church in Ivanhoe who helped build the first church in Lake County
[114] *Ivanhoe Congregational Church Records*. Self published by the church, June 15, 1973. Copy from the Cook Memorial Library, Libertyville, Illinois. Page 4.
[115] History of Lake County, Illinois. *Porcupine*. April 28, 1846. Page 131.
[116] Dunn Museum: Lake County Forest Preserves. Lake County History. <u>Reverend Dodge and the Anti-Slavery Movement</u>. June 18, 2019. William B Dodge (1783-1869)

Seth began to sense a differing opinion amongst the attendees. He listened closely to men who were new to him. What he was hearing began to make him uneasy about where the movement was headed.

Heading into 1846, that unease grew when a group of Chicago businessmen of considerable wealth organized a meeting in Antioch, Illinois, to form the *Lake County Anti-Slavery Society*. The new society planned for its own year of additional inspirational conventions, partnering with other advocates from around the state. Seth, who had been networking all around the northeastern counties of Illinois, worked with his own coalition to form the *Lake County Liberty Association* in March of 1846. Both groups wanted to abolish slavery, but each had different opinions about the role of politics and physical and vocal action on the topic. The *Anti-Slavery Society* felt strongly that the cause should stay out of politics, but the *Liberty Association* believed that without political clout to back the movement it would lose traction and ultimately fail.[117] Some members belonged to both groups, and the division between them inhibited progress in the county and deeply frustrated Seth.

While the factions struggled, political decision makers in Illinois

---

came to Lake County in 1844 from Massachusetts. He was an abolitionist, preacher, and stationmaster on the Underground Railroad, affectionately called Father Dodge.
[117] This challenge was felt as early as 1839 by the followers of William Lloyd Garrison.

were debating a revision of the Illinois Black Codes.[118] The Black Codes of Illinois, were established in 1819 and ratified in 1820, shortly after statehood. These early laws mandated that, despite being free, blacks could not vote, testify, or bring suit against whites, gather in groups of three or more without risk of being jailed or beaten, could not serve in the militia, and were unable to own or bear arms. Blacks living in Illinois were required to obtain and carry a Certificate of Freedom with them at all times, otherwise, they were presumed to be slaves. The Illinois Constitution also allowed for indentured servitude at the time, in the Southern Illinois salt mines. The mines provided significant income for the state and an important presence in what was considered vulnerable frontier territory.[119] The Black Codes went through several revisions, most of which tightened gaps in the early regulations to better protect enslavers including amendments increasing the fines associated with fraternizing, harboring, or assisting freedom seekers. Zebina Eastman, a strong advocate for the cause and newspaperman, would argue that Illinois had become, "the blood-hound of the whole slave region…which only the future could curse with slavery…and a model for the National Fugitive–Slave Law of 1850."[120] In 1846 these codes were undergoing yet another revision and in March the Liberty

---

[118] WTTW. *DuSable to Obama, Early Chicago, Slavery in Illinois*. From an interview with Glennette Tilley Turner.
[119] Eastman, Z. *The Black Code of Illinois*. Chicago Historical Society. 1883. Page 29.
[120] Eastman, Z. *The Black Code of Illinois*. Chicago Historical Society. 1883. Page 45.

Association met to discuss them. At the first Lake County Liberty Convention, Seth Paine was elected as the Association's president.[121] In this role, Seth openly denounced the Illinois Black Laws.[122]

In the weeks following the convention, the Liberty Association established committees to select candidates that were aligned with the movement to be nominated for political office in the 1846 election. Through these committees, they selected Henry W. Blodgett as State Representative, Robert Pollock as County Commissioner, and Theron Parsons as Sheriff, among others.[123] These offices played a critical role in voting on issues os slavery and assisting supporters of the cause. Seth's outright denouncement of the codes was considered a rebellious act. Seth, however, was amused and encouraged, thinking, "Finally, I am having an impact!" Many Congregationalists, as well as his friend, Henry W. Blodgett, supported him even as a more serious rift was growing within the movement.

Seth was able to ignore tension in the movement. Finally at the helm of a humanitarian cause, he reveled in the heady feeling of power. He was advocating for change, and change was happening. Along the way, Seth was making friends, meeting influential people, bonding with

---

[121] Halsey, J. J. *A History of Lake County, Illinois*. Chicago, Illinois. Roy S. Bates, 1912. February 3, 1846. Page 93.
[122] Also called the Black Codes of Illinois.
[123] *The Porcupine*. Waukegan, Illinois. May 18, 1846.

like-minded folks and making space for women within social movements. Simultaneous to his causes, his wife gave birth to two more sons, Seth Jr., and William, and he was feeling his family's warmth and support. He was an adult doing adult things. He would begin and end each day filled with the wonder of doing God's work.

During his time in the spotlight, some of the friendships he formed became more important as time passed. He befriended Owen Lovejoy and he tightened his friendship with Ichabod Codding and James H. Collins, another popular speaker and advocate at antislavery events.[124, 125] At a Kane County Anti-Slavery convention in 1846, Seth met and befriended Allan Pinkerton, who was hosting similar gatherings to those Seth was hosting in Lake County.[126] They bonded over their common goal of helping their fellow men while keeping an arm's-length distance between the church and the cause. Pinkerton and Seth also shared a disdain for conventional politics. The pair had a mutual

---

[124] Kelsey, C.L. *Bureau County Republican.* June 16, 1864. OWEN LOVEJOY'S TRANSFORMATION FROM THE LIBERTY PARTY TO THE FREE SOIL PARTY, By the Rev. William F. Moore, Illinois State Historical Society Symposium, December 1, 2001. Owen Lovejoy's second transformation came in 1840 at the State Anti-Slavery Society meeting in Princeton when the Society refused to endorse political candidates. Lovejoy organized that Party in Bureau County with "twelve disciples" none of whom deserted him for the next twenty-four years.
[125] Cook, F.F. Bygone *Days in Chicago.* A. C. McClurg & Co. 1910. Page 64. Collins was another member of the Underground Railroad with Charles Volney-Dyer and others in Chicago.
[126] *Chicago Daily Tribune.* June 10, 1872.

acquaintance—Charles Volney-Dyer.

Charles Volney-Dyer was part of the region's groups who were merging local societies and expanding them in the city of Chicago. In 1846 with Zebina Eastman, Owen Lovejoy, and Luther Rossiter (of Lake Forest), Volney-Dyer held a *Liberty Party* convention in Chicago. [127,128] These frequent conventions built credibility for the movement, garnered support, and drew new members wanting Illinois to remain a free state even as political pressure grew. Volney-Dyer was an important link between Pinkerton and Seth as a fellow station master on the Underground Railroad, Seth had engaged with him in Chicago during several transfers of freedom seekers.

In 1846 Allan Pinkerton's prominence was growing in the Chicago region. Pinkerton, the son of a police sergeant, arrived in America in 1842 from Scotland. He worked as a skilled barrel maker in Kane County, Illinois, when his career took a serendipitous turn. While he was out searching for wood, he discovered a group of counterfeiters hiding in the forest. Rather than confront them, he followed them and gathered information on their activities which he later turned over to the Kane County Sheriff.[129] The sheriff admired Pinkerton's work, and

---

[127] Zebina Eastman was the publisher of the Abolitionist newspaper the *Western Citizen*, along with many other anti-slavery writings.
[128] Halsey, J. J. *A History of Lake County, Illinois*. Chicago, Illinois. Roy S. Bates, 1912. Page 94.
[129] Bourke, C.F. *The Strand Magazine*. Volume 30. 1905. Pages 494-495.

hired him as a Kane County detective in 1845. It was this work that linked Pinkerton to the abolition movement and Volney-Dyer. Pinkerton was known as a man of deep integrity and considered one of the best judges of a man's character.[130]

At the national level, tensions were mounting on all sides around the issue of slavery. In May 1846, in response to the proposed Wilmot Proviso—which designated any parcels of land acquired from Mexico as free from slavery—a large contingent in Lake County challenged the proviso and the local newspapers put out a call to arms in the war against Mexico.[131,132] The reaction inspired more dedication by abolitionists as they feared they were losing ground.

Seth was enjoying an active relationship with the local press. After a particularly heated debate at a Temperance meeting in June of 1846, Seth wrote a letter to the editor of the *Lake County Herald*. In the letter he criticized the local County board for not acting upon an opportunity

---

[130] Mills, L.L. *In Memory of Allen Pinkerton, At his Late Residence.* Chicago. July 3, 1884.

[131] History. The Wilmot Proviso. 2019, June 7. The Wilmot Proviso was designed to eliminate slavery within the land acquired as a result of the Mexican War (1846-48). Soon after the war began, President James K. Polk sought the appropriation of $2 million as part of a bill to negotiate the terms of a treaty. Fearing the addition of a pro-slave territory, Pennsylvania Congressman David Wilmot proposed this amendment to the bill. Although the measure was blocked in the southern-dominated Senate, it inflamed the growing controversy over slavery, and helped bring about the formation of the Republican Party in 1854.

[132] Halsey, J. J. *A History of Lake County, Illinois.* Chicago, Illinois: Roy S. Bates, 1912. Page 94.

to vote against liquor establishments and he chastised a member of the board for passing falsehoods in the press. "Is it a source of regret to me to have to call in question the acts of a public officer for delinquencies of any kind, but painful as the duty is, I cannot, I dare not omit it."[133] An anonymous reader wrote a letter in response criticizing Seth for his attack on the commissioner, to which Seth replied, "Someone who lacks the moral courage to sign his real name to the productions, has passed judgment upon my reply...Let me say to them that I have rights to call public attention to, gross and palpable violations of principle and duty by public functionaries, whether they be the county Commissioners of Lake County or a professed minister of the Gospel of Chicago...Is it wrong? Is it destroying public character to speak of his official act in its plain unvarnished truth?"[134]

Seth's compatriots did not seem to mind his use of the press. In June of 1846, a Whig convention at the Fort Hill schoolhouse attempted to find leaders to represent the county in the state legislature.[135] The Whigs wanted the federal government involved in the abolition of slavery. At that local convention, the Whigs' nominated D.O. Dickinson for the state legislature. These acts were important in growing local support for the cause, but the State's Democrats still dominated the August election

---

[133] *Lake County Herald.* May 1846.
[134] *Lake County Herald.* June 1846.
[135] Near today's Mundelein.

that year.[136] The abolitionists responded to election results by stepping up the pace of advocacy and hosting additional events nearly every week throughout the year.

Between all the meetings, Seth continued to build his Utopian community around Lake Zurich. The revenues generated by his Union Store played a successful and integral role in the town's growth. He was again assigned as postmaster and increased his involvement with the local Washington Temperance Society founded by the Methodist church. He hosted as many meetings as possible at the Lake Zurich community hall. Though many groups he belonged to overlapped in their ideology, his nonconformity to the social confines of both the church and politics, coupled with his wide range of acquaintances, made him begin to seem radical to some of the groups' members.

Seth's reliability as a station master on the Underground Railroad furthered his friendship with his fellow conductors. Harvey B. Hurd, a lawyer in Chicago, related a story about an event in the summer of 1846 involving Charles Volney-Dyer, James Collins, Allan Pinkerton, Daniel Davidson and Seth Paine.[137] Volney-Dyer's offices, located at 71 South Clark Street, were considered an important hub of Chicago's

---

[136] The Democratic party in Illinois in 1846 favored states rights.
[137] Blanchard, R. *Discovery and Conquests of the North-West, With the History of Chicago*. Volume 1. O.L. Baskin and Company Historical Publishers Lakeside Building. 1882. Volume 2, 1900.

Underground Railroad. Hurd recalled, "One night a number of runaway slaves were brought into the offices and slept on the floor...early in the morning they were taken to another place and their clothes were exchanged for others...and their slave names were exchanged for new ones...thus newly born into liberty, some of the most distinguished names in American history." He continued, "Not too long after, the Marshall knocked on the door and demanded to be shown the slaves, but they were long gone."[138] They had already been shuttled to the docks at the end of Clark Street and onto boats waiting to take them through the Great Lakes to freedom. It is estimated that nearly 200 freedom seekers found their way north in this manner through Chicago and the Great Lakes.

At the federal level there was one solution proposed to resolve the problem of slavery that caught Seth's attention. It involved establishing colonies for formerly enslaved people in other lands, even back in Africa. In November of 1846, Seth wrote a lettter to the editor in the *Western Citizen* pertaining to the debate of what a post-slavery America would look like. "I am unwilling to acknowledge that the Christian Religion is insufficient to break down the cruel, oppressive, and wicked prejudice against the colored man. If one in them....treated the colored

---

[138] Blanchard, R. *Discovery and Conquests of the North-West, With the History of Chicago*. O.L. Baskin and Company Historical Publishers Lakeside Building. Volume 1,1882. Volume 2 1900. Page 306.

man as though he was a man, the object sought by colonization would be accomplished upon righteous principles and his rights regarded as sacred as those of any other man. *Five hundred dollars for refusing to starve a man to death! Oh, Christian where is thy blush?*"[139] His friends and allies applauded his strong words, but opposition against him was simmering.

By the end of 1846, Seth Paine was 30 years old, owned 2,200 acres of land, and had a small fortune. He had some political clout, was well known throughout Chicago, had a wife and three small boys, and a blossoming Utopian community he called home. He owned several businesses, a Union Store, hosted a school, and managed a refuge for humanity from the corner stable. Seth felt that the world was his oyster, and his passion for causes opposed to and acting on societal injustice was growing exponentially. He had little concern for how others viewed him. Seth believed his mission was greater than most men's, and he felt deeply about many topics. Where he had been silent earlier in his life, now he began to speak openly about his convictions. He felt that slavery in any form was wrong and that God was working through him to see it cast off the planet. His Utopian framework supported his belief that everyone had a duty to support each other, feed each other, and

---

[139] *Western Citizen.* Volume V, Number 17. November 17, 1846.

treat each other fairly and without prejudice.

Around the family dinner table, Seth was the patriarch, leading discussions with his wife, mother, and children about current social issues. The Bible was a primary influence in discussion, followed closely by Fourier's tenets, and Seth's glass-half-full view of the world. Seth was committed to shaping his children's minds the way his own mind had been influenced as a youth. Indeed, his children had first-hand knowledge of the importance of assisting their fellow men and played active roles in the clandestine activities of their father. In return, Seth protected them from public scrutiny, even as he increasingly found himself a person of note in local news reports and neighborhood gossip.

A modern photo of a large rock, locally called Kuhn's rock in the woods in Lake County. It was known to be a hiding/meeting spot for travelers on the Underground Railroad. Photo from the author's collection.

Chapter 7

First Disenchantment; 1847-1850

Seth entered 1847 with the optimism that it would be a pivotal year for the abolitionist movement. He was not wrong. However, it did not unfold as he expected. A new wave of migration to the western United States was underway in 1847. President Polk's successful negotiation with Britain in June of 1846 had secured the Oregon Territory south of the 49th parallel which encouraged this migration.[140] The war with Mexico over the territory of Texas was over, but Texas' status as a free or slave state was heavily debated after the Wilmot Proviso had failed in 1846. Nothing was settled at the start of 1847. Newspapers were becoming a major source of national news even in smaller communities around the country—telling tales of westward "Yankee" travelers.[141] Many of these travelers came through Illinois, adding not only more residents in Illinois, but also bringing new supporters of abolition.

This was the era of Manifest Destiny, but underneath the movement of people, beliefs, and ideas, tension simmered as people debated whether these new territories would lead to more slave states or inspire

---

[140] The area included modern day Oregon, Idaho, and Washington states.
[141] Yankee was a term used to refer to New Englanders, dating back to the 1700's and the revolutionary war when British soldiers would mock the amateur nature of the New England colonists by calling them 'yanks' or yankee doodles.

an end to slavery. The Missouri Compromise of 1820 was outdated and despite effectively drawing a dividing line between North and South slave territories when it was created, it had not been updated to include the addition of new territories. The controversy was at the forefront of daily discussion, creating a ripple of unrest throughout the country.

Seth could see and feel change coming, motivating him to work harder to be a part of the change. He was hopeful the country would choose to end slavery particularly after the successes in 1846. In early February 1847 Seth attended the Elgin Anti-Slavery Convention. The convention's principal speaker was Owen Lovejoy, the late Elijah Lovejoy's brother and a founder of the Chicago Liberty Party. Attendees noted, "If the people of Elgin can withstand what he has said, and still cling to their parties, I cannot think what they are made of. I do not see how they can help being real strong Liberty party folks."[142] Lovejoy led the way for the Liberty Party to commit to upholding Christian ideals in its manifesto. Aligning itself with the Congregational Church, meant that the Church weighed in on all local party candidates and leaders. Seth, like his Uncle Elisha before him, believed religion could co-exist with politics without rejecting individuals with different beliefs. Even with his own strong biblical convictions, Seth felt that

---

[142] Sugar Grove Historical Society. Sugar Grove's Historic Role in the Kane County Anti-Slavery Association and Underground Railroad. Quoted by Caroline Gifford in a letter to her father.

recruiting others to the antislavery movement should be focused on the cause rather than creating restrictions on who could participate.

Seth remembered how desperately the cause had needed support just recently. In frustration Seth appealed to the press and publicly criticized the Liberty Party for this decision. When the Liberty Party brandished their decision publicly they stated, "We reject as untrue and evil [the dogma of the so-called Garrison], or non-resistant abolitionists…We recognize the principles of Christianity as the only sure foundation on which we may hope for permanent reform in this or any other cause."[143] This statement made clear that the Liberty Party would publicly denounce anyone who would not first embrace their Christian ideals including Seth and his good friend Allan Pinkerton. This position violated not only Seth's personal principles but also the resolutions that the Lake County Liberty Party had adopted 10 months prior: "That the objects of this association are to do all it can consistently with Law, Humanity and Religion to effect the entire condition of slavery in the United States…its object it will endeavor to accomplish this…to obtain subscribers for the campaign (to elected office in 1847)…who will move immediately to free our country and state from this foul reproach."[144] Seth was conflicted. As his anger at the Liberty Party's new direction

---

[143] Sugar Grove Historical Society. Sugar Grove's Historic Role in the Kane County Anti-Slavery Association and Underground Railroad.
[144] *The Porcupine.* Waukegan, Illinois. April 7, 1846.

festered and grew, he officially withdrew himself from the party by publishing a post in the *Western Citizen* with the help of his old friend, Zebina Eastman.

Seth was not alone in his frustration. One sympathizer wrote to William Lloyd Garrison on March 16, 1847, saying:

> "Dear Sir – Enclosed, I send you the communication of Mr. Seth Paine, defining his position in relation to the Liberty Party, which I cut from today's 'Western Citizen.' Mr. Paine has been a prominent member of the Liberty Party for something more than two years, and during that time, has probably made more sacrifice of time and money for the upholding of the party, than any other member of it in the State. I was present at the Elgin Convention, and though a member of the Liberty Party, justice required me to corroborate the statement which he makes, relative to the convention. Much as I have hoped from that organization, and strong as is my faith that a higher and nobler spirit will yet rule in its councils, still, there is no concealing the fact that there was a gross and successful attempt to suppress and stifle discussion on the legitimate application of our abstract principles. Of this attempt, the mass of the convention were not

guilty and for that reason, I still adhere to the party; But, did I believe that the leaders at that convention were for the future to guide and rule the organization in the State, as they did there, I should change my position. Although, heretofore, Mr. Paine has been regarded, by many, if not all, as one of the strongest and purest men in our ranks, there are now wanting those who now hound him with the cry of 'crazy!' 'fanatic!' and even 'knave!' But, for all that, Mr. Paine is not alone; there are many here, and I rank myself among the number, who occupy the position of Beriah Green, and with him we say, 'If such is to be the policy of the Liberty Party, (regarding the discussion and legitimate application of our principles to ALL men,) we renounce it.' I send you this, because I believe you stand in about the same position to the Liberty Party, that does to the other great parties of the country. Yours for the slave."[145]

The author of the heartfelt letter to support Seth's decision is unknown, but his reference to Beriah Green was unmistakable. Reverend Beriah Green was an advocate not only for abolition, but also for formerly enslaved Americans to have equal access to education and all benefits

---

[145] *The Liberator*. Boston, Massachusetts. April 9, 1847. Page 1.

of citizenship. A minister and theologian, Green was the president of the Oneida Institute in New York, a Garrisonian college. He agreed to be the president of the Institute only if he was given free rein to accept anyone he determined creditable regardless of their race. Many other religious institutions opposed him and his ideals and in 1845 his school was forced to close. Reverend Green cut ties with the traditional abolition parties after this.[146]

On March 24, 1847, Seth again expressed his frustration to the press. He called out the Liberty Party for voting against the Wilmot Proviso.[147] He was particularly affronted that they had slighted his good friend Pinkerton, who had been nominated as a delegate for the Constitutional Convention but later rejected because of his professed atheism. In April Seth wrote, "the Liberty Party has proven that they are as much disposed to reject and suppress the truth as any other party."[148] Local and national media were starting to pick up and recirculate his opinions. Seth repeated his stance in a letter published in the *Lake County Visitor*, Henry Blodgett's weekly newspaper later in April. As Seth's views became more widely disseminated he appreciated the importance of the press. Referencing the Bible he stated, "do not merely listen to the

---

[146] National Abolition Hall of Fame and Museum. Beriah Green. Reverend Green is credited with educating over 100 Black students at the Oneida Institute including Alexander Crummel, an important 19th century intellectual.
[147] *Rockford Forum*. March 24, 1847. Page 3.
[148] *Janesville Daily Gazette*. April 10, 1847. Page 8.

Word, and so drive yourselves. Do what it says! Anyone who listens to the Word but does not do what it says is like someone who looks at his face in the mirror and after looking at himself, goes away and immediately forgets what he looks like." (James 1: 22-25). His statements were also gaining recognition by men in leadership positions within the party.

With controversy simmering, Owen Lovejoy's friend and lawyer James Collins complained that other significant political causes required as much attention and advocacy as the antislavery movement. Collins held some influence with Lovejoy because he had defended him successfully in court when he was charged with harboring two escaped slaves. Collins, a neighbor of Seth's in LaSalle County, argued that the Liberty Party would do better to support a broader platform of reform to include free trade as well as equal rights for all men. His plea to Lovejoy's Liberty Party suggested that "some of his Chicago friends who supported free trade felt they didn't receive fair treatment at the Elgin Convention."[149] The Liberty Party ignored those pleas and pursued further solidifying the connection between religion and the antislavery movement.

Seth wrote a letter to Garrison's *The Liberator* in July claiming the

---

[149] Illinois State Historical Library. *Letter from James Collins to Owen Lovejoy*. March 17, 1847.

Liberty Party would be a "death to progression." In addition, he spoke to reporters at the *Chicago Journal* about other flaws of the Liberty Party and accused them of "aiding and comforting the enemy."[150] He also commented on the overarching enslavement of all humanity, saying, "the primary object of civil government is to secure justice, our ultra-Abolitionist sentiments cause us to believe in the declaration that *all men* are created equal without the accidency of birth or color."[151] Society was not ready to accept the implications of his thoughts and he felt the push back; people chided him for his convictions. But he was undeterred. His anger grew even more toxic with anyone opposing his views.

In confidence to his friend Allan Pinkerton he righteously proclaimed, "the star of political abolitionism as a single party idea is on the wane, and there is a good time coming boys!"[152] Seth could see how damaging the growing division could be for the cause, but he could only do so much to stop it.

Seth took matters into his own hands by focusing on building support for his convictions around Lake Zurich. In 1849 he and ten other men established a local League of Universal Brotherhood, a

---

[150] *Chicago Journal*. March 24, 1847.
[151] Halsey, J. J. *A History of Lake County, Illinois*. Chicago, Illinois: Roy S. Bates, 1912. Page 96.
[152] Quote from the *Chicago Journal*. March 24, 1847.

private group committed to following the tenets of Elihu Burritt of Connecticut.[153,154] Burritt, after being inspired poverty he witnessed in Ireland, had recently organized the Brotherhood with the mission to, "Oppose Slavery, Work for temperance, and achieve World Peace."[155] The broad mission aligned closely with Seth's own and he was able to find others who shared this passion in Chicago and around Lake Zurich. Like the Underground Railroad, the League functioned as a clandestine humanitarian club taking on social causes and assisting others with kindness, generosity, and secrecy. The league members all had affiliations with the railroad and lumber industries, either directly with iron works or with millworks. Like Seth, they were mostly men in their 20s and 30s who had found success early in their lives and wanted to help humanity. Thanks to Seth, the League owned a number of properties near Lake Zurich and the neighboring community of Long Grove, which included trails and a few large stretches of vacant land.[156] Seth donated a series of parcels totaling 250 acres to the group.[157] Some of the parcels were covered in timber and others were open prairie.

---

[153] The men included; David Harrower, John William, Andrew McKnight, John Porvell, George Young, Robert Willson, Alexander Cumming, Mr. Drysdale, William Angy, James Walker, and Seth Paine.

[154] Burritt also organized an international congress of the Friends of Peace in Brussels in September 1848. Eventually, he was appointed by President Abraham Lincoln as United States consul in Birmingham England.

[155] Central Connecticut State University. *Elihu Burrit 1820-1879*. Description of Elihu Burritt and his League after the Peace Congress of 1849 in Paris.

[156] Meaning there were no dwellings as of the 1861 plat map of the County.

[157] Land records. Lake County, Illinois. Deed #375. March 13, 1849.

They all had access to three major roadways linking Chicago, Elgin, and Waukegan to each other and to Wisconsin.[158,159] These pathways were important to assist freedom-seekers along the trail to freedom through woodlands and open space on private property.

Despite all of the progress happening locally around social issues, Seth still seethed about what had happened in the Liberty Party. He kept up with the news of the people who he had previously worked with through travelers passing through town and national newspaper stories. As they continued to climb in their positions Seth spoke openly about his anger again in the media. "The entire human race was in a condition of moral slavery, more terrible than slavery in other forms. He considered the institution of marriage under the existing system as one equally oppressive with African slavery."[160] This eye-popping comment, documented by the press and snickered about by his neighbors and detractors, did not however reflect his own marriage. Instead Seth felt marriage was an opportunity to form an equal partnership, contrary to how society viewed it at the time. Seth not only

---

[158] Waukegan was originally named Little Fort until 1849 when residents changed it to 'Waukegan' the Potawatomi name for fort.

[159] The roadways included here are today's Rand Road, Old McHenry Road (the Old McHenry-Chicago Trail which heads west from route 83), and the Elgin-Waukegan Road (which bisected the County from the southwestern edge heading north). The original road ran from today's Rte 14 over to Algonquin (Freeport Road) from Lake Zurich to Elgin.

[160] Halsey, J. J. *A History of Lake County, Illinois*. Chicago, Illinois: Roy S. Bates, 1912. Page 273.

spoke about this but he lived his life this way.

Seth expanded his community center adjacent to the Union Store, and officially christened it the *Stable of Humanity* in 1850.[161] He took this opportunity to share with those passing through the Fourier idea that people in communities should assemble together often for 'social intercourse and free discussion of subjects relating to their welfare.' As word spread through the region about this large and free open meeting place, a congregation of Methodist worshippers began to host a variety of events and held regular calls to worship in the Stable.[162] The Stable would prove to be an excellent way for Seth to spread his message of hope and humanity for all and it proved to also be a good way to irritate his detractors. Whenever he heard that his establishment was garnering attention from his critics, a smile would play across his face and he would think to himself, "I will show them what a real Christian looks like."

In 1850 the Stable was one of the county's largest buildings. Measuring 50 feet wide by 150 feet long and three stories tall, it had a meeting space in its basement large enough for public gatherings. Along with meeting space, the building also featured "a large store, a school

---

[161] Halsey, J.J. *A History of Lake County, Illinois*. Chicago, Illinois: Roy S. Bates, 1912. Page 273.
[162] Halsey, J. J. *A History of Lake County, Illinois*. Chicago, Illinois: Roy S. Bates, 1912. Page 428. Reiterated by *Portrait and Biographical Album of Lake County, Illinois*. Chicago: Lake City Publishing Company. 1891. Page 698.

room—the use of which was donated to the public free of charge—and several suites of rooms for families who were allowed to move in and stay free of rent as long as they liked and move out to make room for others."[163] The building also contained a private academy complete with a schoolmaster named Mr. Gordon Dresser.[164] Seth agreed to furnish this school free of rent in his Stable and it is said that he "kept his word."[165] The teachers were paid by Seth, and educated many of the area's children. The academy was impressive compared to the small one-room school houses in the region. At one point, nearly 100 people lived in the guest rooms at the Stable.[166] By concentrating on the development of his own community, Seth was able to create the Utopian vision that he felt the world needed.

******

On September 18, 1850, the federal government passed the Fugitive Slave Act—as a compromise between the southern slave-holding states

---

[163] Halsey, J. J. *A History of Lake County, Illinois*. Chicago, Illinois: Roy S. Bates, 1912. Page 428.
[164] Ann Sargent also taught at this school, she was an aunt of Edwin Winter, Mr. Gordon Dresser stayed with the Academy at the Stable of Humanity for nearly 2 decades.
[165] Brockway, L. *History of Lake Zurich*. An address by Lewis O. Brockway to the Lake Zurich Community Women's Club, September 25, 1930. From the Ela Township Historical Society records.
[166] Halsey, J. J. *A History of Lake County, Illinois*. Chicago, Illinois: Roy S. Bates, 1912. Page 131.

and the northern Free Soil Party.[167] The act made it a federal offense to assist freedom seekers and offenders were subject to jail time and a $1,000 fine. It was also known as the "Bloodhound Law" because bounty hunters, federal officers, slave patrols, and even dogs were encouraged to track down the formerly enslaved to return them to enslavers for a reward. Rather than discourage them, the law actually served to unite the Whigs, independent abolitionists, Liberty Party members, and Congregationalists throughout the Chicago region. Local news articles responded to the act with a renewed dedication to the cause's critical mission. Local abolitionists from other counties demanded support in Lake County in October 1850, calling for an immediate repeal of the act and asking all men to vote for antislavery candidates in the 1850 election. Seth attended regular events supporting the repeal of the act and the political climate shifted exponentially in the movement's favor. The Fugitive Slave Act inspired additional supporters as many "Northerners were deeply offended by the law and came to view slavery as a threat to their own rights."[168] Seth also felt the act was a personal affront and he refused to pay property taxes for

---

[167] The Free Soil Party opposed slavery's expansion into any new territories or states. The Free Soil Party's slogan was "free soil, free speech, free labor, and free men." They generally believed that the government could not end slavery where it already existed but that it could restrict slavery in new areas.

[168] *Smithsonian Civil War, Inside the National Collection.* Forward by John Meacham. Page 49.

several months in protest.[169]

Many Chicagoans largely ignored the new law. Passionate abolitionists worked together to thwart bounty hunters while they continued to assist freedom seekers. With Seth's regular travel between Chicago and Lake County, he was an active conductor assisting many formerly enslaved people during these years.[170] Seth often hosted them at the Stable, an illegal act, but no one reported his movements or reported his involvement to federal authorities. The Underground Railroad was busier than ever and Seth once again found himself in the thick of many progressives. "The slave hunters were not less active; the whole state of Illinois was corralled for fugitives, the hunters being bold and defiant, offering liberal rewards for assistance, while the Underground Railroad men were subtle and determined; the former under the regime of law, the latter under the palladium of justice."[171] Between Chicago and the surrounding region, a large volunteer network formed. Over 200 formerly enslaved people are estimated to have passed through Chicago and its suburbs before the Civil War.[172]

---

[169] It did not take long for him to realize the government could seize his property for not paying taxes and he eventually paid them in order to keep his land holdings secure.
[170] Siebert, W.H. *The Underground Railroad from Slavery to Freedom.* The MacMillan Company London, New York 1898. Page 404.
[171] Blanchard, R. *Discovery and Conquest of the Northwest with the History of Chicago.* Volume 2, Pages 305-306.
[172] Cook, F.F. *Bygone Days in Chicago.* A. C. McClurg & Co. Chicago 1910. Page 68.

Seth completed two census reports in 1850. On November 27th 1850, his survey in Ela Township, Lake County, listed him as a farmer. On December 18th 1850, he listed himself as a merchant in the town of Salisbury in LaSalle County.[173] In LaSalle County, Seth invested in and managed a bank with his friends Edward Taylor and Churchill Coffing. [174] Seth held interest in the bank for over a decade. Living in LaSalle County also put Seth in the center of the western branch of Underground Railroad activity in Illinois, and he found comfort and inspiration from relationships with his fellow conductors and station masters.

A young law clerk, Calvin DeWolf—a lawyer with offices adjacent to those of Volney-Dyer—described the relationship between conductors, "our offices might reasonably be named the Chicago Depot of the Underground Railroad. James Collins had his office nearly opposite, and next door were the most devoted and energetic friends of the colored man. LC Paine Freer, S. D. Childs, Daniel Davidson and his brother Orlando, and Seth Paine."[175,176]

---

[173] He is recorded as living in both towns with his wife, three children, a nephew, and his wife's brother.
[174] Baldwin, Elmer. *History of Lasalle County, Illinois.* Chicago, Rand McNally and Co. Printers. 1877. Page 364. Churchill Coffing was a lawyer, abolitionist and businessman who hailed from Salisbury, Connecticut.
[175] Calvin DeWolf and Charles Volney-Dyer were well-known, and esteemed agents on the Underground Railroad.
[176] Blanchard, R. *Discovery and Conquest in the North-west with the History of*

Around this time, an emerging religious movement called Spiritualism piqued Seth's interest. While he admired and encouraged the Methodists and begrudgingly supported the Congregationalists, the Spiritualist movement inspired Seth in a new way. It also fed his lingering anger towards those who disapproved of his abandonment of the Liberty Party years earlier. His work with the Underground Railroad, business success, press engagements, and land ownership filled his head with the sense that he was invincible. He would soon discover that he was not.

Chicago. Told in a letter by Harvey B. Hurd, Page 306.

William Lloyd Garrison's *Liberator,* article, 1847.
Public domain records.

Chapter 8

Banker, Agitator; 1849-1852

Spiritualism came to Chicago in 1849.[177] Though it had a foundation in Christianity, Spiritualism centered around the idea that earthly humans could communicate with the departed in the spirit world through séance, rapping, and other vibrational methods. The practice became popular in the 1840s among the middle and upper classes and also included healing, visions, levitation, and speaking in tongues. The modern movement of Spiritualism arrived in the United States when the Fox sisters, of Hydesville, New York brought it back from the United Kingdom in 1848.[178] When 'rapping medium' Mrs. Julia Lusk came to Chicago in 1849, Seth was intrigued.

Interest in communing with the dead was not a new concept in the 1840s. Ghostly communication was recorded in ancient times and even the Bible documented the dead returning to earth to speak to the living. One of Spiritualism's earliest adoptees in Chicago was Ira B. Eddy.[179] Seth met Eddy through the Temperance movement and his brother, Dr.

---

[177] Andreas, Alfred Theodore, *History of Cook County, Illinois, From the Earliest Period to the Present Time,* Chicago, 1884, In three Volumes. Pages 353-354.
[178] Leah, Margaretta, and Catherine Fox were three sisters from New York who were credited as part of the origin of the Spiritualism movement.
[179] Hardinge, E. *Modern American Spiritualism, A Twenty Year Record.* New York, by the author. 1880. Page 378.

Thomas M. Eddy, a Methodist minister and fellow Garrisonian supporter in Chicago. Eddy was born into Methodism and first adopted Spiritualism in 1849 after meeting Julia Lusk. Lusk allowed Eddy to communicate with a recently departed friend, sealing his belief in the practice. He felt that the Methodists lacked certain believable doctrines about the Devil and Hell.[180] In the fall of 1850, Seth was introduced to Eddy when he sought a business space on Clark Street in Chicago for a new enterprise under the title of Seth Paine and Co. The location was near the offices of Volney-Dyer and other Underground Railroad station masters and was also a space for Seth to stay when he was in the city.

In the same building, Eddy had a large space on the third floor that he had named *Harmony Hall*. After he joined the society of Chicago Spiritualists, he invited them to hold meetings in the room, and quickly became the first president of the Chicago Spiritualist Society. Around 1852, another Spiritualist medium, Mrs. Herrick came to Chicago to work with Lusk. Herrick was a brilliant lecturer and frequently used demonstrations and séances to promote the practice. The more Seth encountered the Spiritualists the more he embraced their doctrine. He was especially impressed that women held prominent leadership roles within Spiritualism.

---

[180] Andreas, Alfred Theodore, *History of Cook County, Illinois, From the Earliest Period to the Present Time,* Chicago, 1884, In three Volumes. Pages 353-354.

As the Spiritualists continued to capture the attention of the public, the media was raising questions about their growing influence over many affluent Chicagoans. The strong Christian community of Chicago did not appreciate the Spiritualists taking funds from their churches and influencing parishioners in practices they considered questionable. An article published in the *Evening Post* described what the reporter witnessed when he attended a meeting hosted by Mrs. Herrick in 1852 involving proceedings which included séances and manifestations. The reporter declared, "I am not prepared to pronounce all the phenomena genuine, yet I believed some of them to be so."[181,182] Even with the press coverage, the Spiritualist movement continued to gain traction. Seth began to imagine the opportunities for Spiritualism and banking to merge together and mutually benefit humanity.

In the early 1850s, all of the private banks in Chicago could trace their roots to George Smith. Smith was a land investor and real estate financier originally from Scotland. After a brief start in Chicago in the early 1830s, Smith moved his investments to Wisconsin, where he held significant property. He returned to Chicago with additional capital around 1839 which allowed him to back a business model to issue creditable certificates in exchange for money. This model gave Smith

---

[181] Andreas, Alfred Theodore, *History of Cook County, Illinois, From the Earliest Period to the Present Time,* Chicago, 1884, In three Volumes. Pages 353-354.
[182] *Common Sense*, quoting an article of the *Evening Post* from the 1850's. Volume 1-2, 1874.

and his banks significant clout and influence in Chicago's economy. Smith's banking influence also assured that interest, fees, and loan qualification criteria were centralized. He was the most successful banker in Chicago, with a long track record with the Wisconsin Marine and Fire Insurance Company as well as with George Smith and Company in Chicago.[183] *The Chicago Democrat,* a newspaper owned by John "Long John" Wentworth, supported Smith's banks by speaking favorably about them whenever possible.

Illinois banking regulations changed in 1851 allowing banks to register through the Secretary of State, allowing them to issue bank notes for the first time. Earlier banks had been started by individuals who backed investments with gold and silver, and the Illinois Constitution issued bank notes based on that value. However, in times of financial panic like in 1837, when people rushed to banks to request their funds be returned to them immediately, the banks failed. The change in regulations allowed the banking industry to quadruple and competition increased among bank owners as new banks were backed by railroads, real estate, and other industries.[184]

Seth's early forays into banking extended from the Chicago Marine and Fire Insurance Company to investing in the LaSalle County bank in

---

[183] Encyclopedia of Chicago. *Banking, Commercial*.
[184] Many people did not trust railroads or their shareholders because funding for rail lines was challenging to secure. As such new rail lines often faltered or failed quickly.

the 1840s with Edward Taylor and Churchill Coffing. The LaSalle bank helped fund plank road projects in Chicago's western suburbs. With the success of the LaSalle bank, his projects around Lake Zurich, and his deepening friendships with powerful men in Chicago, Seth felt it was a good time to start a progressive bank in Chicago. To test this, Seth began to strategize ways that communicating with the dead might help earthly investors. He discussed his vision with Eddy who eagerly encouraged him and Seth boldly sought additional investors for his banking idea—which he was sure would be revolutionary.

Seth's team made plans to officially open a new bank in 1852 as a unique financial institution under the principles of *pure* Christianity and Charles Fourier.[185] Complementing the bank's activities, Seth also planned to publish his message of faith and Utopian socialism in a new newspaper he called the *Christian Banker.* The motto of his newspaper would be, "The Love of Money is the Root of All Evil." Seth saw his paper leading the movement for justice, righteousness, and Christian values. He funded the paper himself to avoid any risk of contaminating his message with advertising or pandering to other ideals. With the principles he touted, he was confident that other newspapers would pick up on his messages, pointing out deficiencies among leaders not yet committed to the antislavery movement and any other issues he felt

---

[185] In this case only loaning money to or taking money from Christians who were approved by Seth and his team.

were important. Seth was confident that with this motto, all the Christians in the city would be thrilled to invest money in his bank. Seth Paine and Co decided to open one bank in Chicago and another in Waukegan.

Seth began to embrace the concepts of Spiritualism with gusto. He spoke in earnest to audiences at Eddy's Harmony Hall. Attendees described him as "an excellent speaker although a bit radical."[186] Appreciating his contributions to their goals, Mrs. Herrick jumped in to support Seth assuring him that his banks would cater solely to the righteous and be fully supported by the visions of the Spiritualist mediums. Seth began to see the future unfold: with money, his bank, and his own newspaper pointing out blatant hypocrisy, outlining Christian values, and supporting the humanitarian efforts he cared so deeply about.

By the time Seth's banking project was underway in 1852, both his idealism and his anger were driving his actions. On the one hand, he wanted to be a financial resource to people with similar value systems, who did decent work, and needed help in the spirit of true charity. On the other hand, he wanted to prove that his approach to addressing social issues was truer to Christianity than the Church's approach. What

---

[186] *Semi-centennial History of the University of Illinois.* Volume 1, University of Illinois. 1918. 3rd Industrial Convention. November 24, 1852.

he did not take into account was the public's growing fear of the Spiritualist movement and the power of those who opposed him.

Seth was convinced that his bank would be an important support system for all people, or at least "good" people. Seth had never needed banks to fund his activities, but he knew that the continued settlement of Chicago would require investors and banking to keep going. Seth felt that many of the banks were not helping the people who needed help the most and was appalled to see them making money on the backs of hard-working citizens by charging interest instead of providing interest to their shareholders. Since these banks were supported by the same men who held conflicting beliefs about slavery and religion, this dual injustice fueled his anger.

Seth had determined that his new bank would be different. Their rules were:

- We loan to no one to pay debts.
- We loan to no one to aid in murder of anything which has life.
- We loan nothing on real estate - believing that real estate cannot be bought and sold and that possession with use is the only title.
- We loan nothing to aid in making or selling intoxicating

liquors or tobacco in any of its forms.[187]

Eddy, who would eventually become President of Seth's Chicago Bank, elaborated on the bank's mission to the media, "its mission is a great one. No less than to assist directly in lifting up and bringing forth to the light the now dormant energies of the mechanics and common people. The people who have been crushed by the aristocracy of money power."[188] This mission garnered a great deal of the press's attention. Initial responses to the bank's opening were very guarded and focused on Seth's principles, "to his vision, the affairs of this world were badly out of joint. They were sadly in need of reorganization, and it required Seth Paine to adjust things properly. So he left 'Lake Zurich' and his farm, and returned to Chicago to teach his old friends and the world at large how banking could be carried on in accordance with what he deemed a higher law than the banking law of Illinois - the Law of Humanity."[189] Pride ruled Seth's mind and he was convinced that his new bank would be his greatest contribution to humanity yet.

At the age of 37, Seth believed he had enough experience to accomplish whatever he set his mind to since he had never failed at

---

[187] *Daily Register Gazette. Chicago's Early Banks.* Rockford, Illinois. Friday, December 7, 1928. Page 17.
[188] Goodspeed, W.A., Healy, D.D. *History of Cook County, Illinois.* Goodspeed Historical Association, 1909. Page 152.
[189] Andreas, Alfred Theodore, *History of Cook County, Illinois, From the Earliest Period to the Present Time,* Chicago, 1884, In three Volumes. Page 540.

anything before. In the evenings he defied the law to help humanity through the Underground Railroad and participated in Spiritualist rituals with dancing and séances.[190] In the daylight he was a wealthy, outspoken businessman. Prior to the bank's opening, the public often called upon him to comment on civic matters. Though he was somewhat controversial for some he was embraced by the progressives and his ideas were published in newspapers across the country. Seth felt sure he was heading in the right direction.

---

[190] *Chicago Daily Tribune.* July 7, 1872. "The Underground Railroad enterprise had never seen a more effective agent than he in those days."

Copy of Bank of Chicago two dollar bill. Public domain records.
(From the author's collection.)

Chapter 9

The Banking Fiasco; 1852

The population of Chicago had reached nearly 50,000 in 1852, double what it had been in 1849, and it would double again by 1857. New residents were excited to see what Chicago could offer them, and Seth was eager to unveil his new bank model to the influx of new citizens. Despite the booming population embracing progressive ideas, Chicago was founded on traditional religious principles and many powerful people wanted it to stay that way. They were keeping a close eye on Seth as he announced the goals of his bank. They thought he only wanted to increase his wealth and power and put them out of business. His critics did not understand his altruistic intent and saw him as a threat they needed to destroy before he destroyed them. In his own obstinate style Seth ignored the cautions of his friends. His swelling pride drove him to forge ahead with his banks and his new newspaper.

Now that the market was ripe for new banks, many opportunities arose for creative and exploitive banking strategies. *The Chicago Democrat* took the opportunity to evaluate them all publicly and the public responded in kind.[191] Those who were not favored by its editor

---

[191] Goodspeed, W.A., Healy, D.D. *History of Cook County, Illinois.* Goodspeed Historical Association. 1909. Page 150.

Wentworth were critiqued mercilessly. Wentworth spared no detail when he attacked them, describing,"irregular or illegal banks had a better opportunity to make money than those which were organized under the State bank law and adhered strictly to its provisions. They could issue money, receive deposits and at the same time do a shaving, brokerage business and could take wild-cat financial matters to extremes. On the other hand the prudent regular banks were restricted in their operations and hence lost much of the business which went to the irregular banks. The regular banks accordingly demanded that such a change in the law should be made as would drive the irregular bankers out of business."[192] Normal citizens found it all both confusing and entertaining.

Seth's bank stood in the heart of the business district in Chicago along Clark Street. It was next to the recently formed Pinkerton's National Detective Agency, operating under the motto, *"Pinkerton Detectives Never Sleep."*[193] Seth's plan was taking some time to be implemented and being near his friends gave him more confidence as he waited. Many of them were concerned that this effort would jeopardize their work on the Underground Railroad. These long established, trusted networks shared a deep loyalty to each other and to

---

[192] Goodspeed, W.A., Healy, D.D. *History of Cook County, Illinois.* Goodspeed Historical Association. 1909. Page 151.
[193] Pinkerton had found a niche market for his services with the railroads who were arriving in Chicago and had plans to expand west.

their causes, but could be easily compromised with too much publicity. They were finding that station masters associated with the Spiritualists attracted more media attention, potentially risking exposure for their highly secretive activities.[194]

With great fanfare and coverage in the local newspapers, Seth and Eddy's bank opened in August of 1852. Christened the *Bank of Chicago,* the nickname "Spiritual Bank" became the public's favored moniker for the business.[195] The local Rockford paper reported that two women called the Fox Sisters led board members through séances at the opening and another well known spiritualist, Mrs. Herrick was hired as a teller. Reporters described that, "in the hall above his bank Paine and his friends gathered in séances to call on the souls of Alexander Hamilton for financial advice."[196] At Seth's bank, they made sure that women, spiritualists, and even the formerly enslaved were served equally. Seth explained, "our basis for making loans is the established character of the borrower. He must be a temperate, honest and religious man or woman."[197]

---

[194] Mason, E. G. of the Chicago Historical Society. *Early Chicago and Illinois.* Fergus Printing Company, Chicago. 1890. Page 110. Discusses Philo Carpenter, and the Underground Railroad at Randolph, Morgan, Washington and Carpenter Streets.
[195] Andreas, Alfred Theodore, *History of Cook County, Illinois, From the Earliest Period to the Present Time,* Chicago, 1884, In three Volumes. Page 315.
[196] *Daily Register Gazette.* Rockford, Illinois. December 7, 1928. Page 17.
[197] Andreas, Alfred Theodore, *History of Cook County, Illinois, From the Earliest Period to the Present Time,* Chicago, 1884, In three Volumes. Page 540.

Seth's banking plan followed the model of the Utopian bank Charles Fourier had envisioned. The bank issued credits in the form of one, two, and three dollar bills, a common practice at the time. Seth's *Bank of Chicago* bills featured elegant portraits of Henry Clay, George Washington, and Senator Stephen Douglas, all perceived to be men of fine character. The bank opened with $6,000 in equity and at the outset had many depositors. However, only a couple months after opening, in October 1852, the bank had attracted more attention for its radical ideals than its financial credibility.[198] Seth's second hire was his wife Frances who worked alongside Mrs. Herrick as a teller. Often, Frances had Seth's youngest daughter along with her. The local media ate up the quirkiness and turned the bank's way of conducting business into fodder for a number of articles—making fun of bankers consulting the dead on banking decisions, and handing their money over to women.

Meanwhile, Seth basked in the public attention that the bank was generating. He became involved in many state activities including the establishment of the University of Illinois. During this time, discussions were circulating about using federal funding to support higher education.[199] Dr. John A. Kennicott invited him to the Third Industrial

---

[198] Andreas, Alfred Theodore, *History of Cook County, Illinois, From the Earliest Period to the Present Time,* Chicago, 1884, In three Volumes. Page 541.
[199] By 1865, land grant universities were being established across the country, focused on agriculture and the advancement of industry.

Convention in Chicago to discuss establishing a land grant university on November 24, 1852.[200] Dr. Kennicott, convention moderator and a well-known horticulturist and agriculturist, described Seth as a man who possessed "all the fire of his singularly energetic, and progressive mind and rather visionary genius."[201,202] At the convention Seth spoke eloquently on the need for progress. He had strong feelings that progress in industry would assist farmers. Farming was 50% of the industry in the country and ongoing discussions revolved around how to better support farmers both locally and at the federal level. As a farmer himself, Seth was always looking for ways to improve efficiency. Based on his experience with Gates Metal Works and his early mill along Flint Creek in Lake Zurich, Seth felt that methods to reduce the reliance on the physical labor of men could be achieved through industry advances. [203] To the crowd gathered, Seth was critical of the old way of thinking, describing it as detrimental to the promise of the present and future times. In his usual manner, Seth was ahead of his time.

---

[200] The University of Illinois Urbana-Champaign was established as a public land-grant university in Illinois in 1867. It served as the flagship institution of the University of Illinois system.
[201] Dr. John A. Kennicott helped to encourage and supported the establishment of land grant colleges in the United States and Illinois in particular with his enthusiastic assistance and support. He lived in Glenview, Illinois..
[202] *Semi-Centennial History of the University of Illinois*. Volume 1, University of Illinois. 1918. Pages 44-45.
[203] National Research Council. *Colleges of Agriculture at the Land Grant Universities: A Profile*. Washington, DC: The National Academies Press. 1995.

On December 9th 1852, the Bank of Chicago opened its second branch in Waukegan under the leadership of John Holmes, Chauncey T. Gaston, and Cyrus M. Hawley. The bank operated under the umbrella of Seth Paine & Company. Seth sent a press release to the *Chicago Daily Tribune* to announce that his mother would be a teller and quoting the Bible he said, "give of her the Fruit of her Hands, and let her own Works Praise her in the Gates!" (Proverbs 31:31)[204]

A week later, on December 15th 1852, Seth announced the imminent publication of his first issue of *Christian Banker*. While the bank and the newspaper were unique in their objectives, public attention and competitive media outlets mocked Seth's attempt to manage the narrative around his ideals. Events that occurred at the site where the Spiritualist Society met and where his Chicago bank operated, were irreversibly intertwined, and under the public's microscope.[205]

The same day, *The Chicago Democrat* mockingly noted that they wished the paper success writing, "the stuff it is likely to be made of will be harmless; but as to the system of wild-cat banking it is established to support, we confidently look to the legislature to clap a summary extinguisher upon it, among its earliest acts. If it does not, the country will; by means of 'Christian banking', be very shortly placed in

---

[204] *Chicago Daily Tribune*. December 9, 1852. Page 2.
[205] *Illinois State Register*. Springfield, Illinois. December 15, 1852.

a condition to require the exercise of a vast deal more 'Christian' patience, under losses than we believe it to be possessed of." The *Democrat* wrote about all the Chicago citizenry cringing in anticipation of the impending *Christian Banker* periodical while a cyclone of trouble was growing around the antics of the Spiritualists and Seth Paine.[206]

In the midst of the eager anticipation for his paper to be published, 1852 saw political progress in Illinois, with voters selecting several Whigs for state office including Seth's friend Henry Blodgett who took a position in the House.[207] Seth put pen to paper and published his first issue of the *Christian Banker* on January 5th 1853. Along the masthead, Seth coined his bank the "Bank of Utopia".[208,209] In addition to this announcement, Seth called out the hypocrisy of the banking industry in his first issue.

Seth would soon feel the sting of Chicago's powerful and unforgiving press. The first editor to take notice and mock the paper was *The Chicago Democrat's* Wentworth, saying that the *Christian Banker* focused on "calling out sarcastic comments," Seth's intent was

---

[206] *Chicago Democrat* as quoted from the *Daily Illinois State Register*. Springfield, Illinois. December 15, 1852. Page 2.
[207] Halsey, J. J. *A History of Lake County, Illinois*. Chicago, Illinois: Roy S. Bates, 1912. Page 132.
[208] *Chicago Daily Tribune*. Wednesday, December 22, 1852. Seth's business names included: Paine, Brothers & Co. for the Waukegan branch of the Bank of Chicago, and Seth Paine & Co. for the Chicago branch.
[209] *Christian Banker*. January 5, 1853.

to support his bank, "eight issues printed, from the back room of his bank on Clark Street intended as an elaboration of the bank of Utopia…but as its influence became felt and its power augmented it would be called the bank of the people and as it advanced in cosmopolitan finance and depository accretion it would be called the Bank of God."[210,211]

Having seen advance copies of the paper, Seth's rival bankers plotted an end to the peculiar bank. They refused to honor the notes from the Bank of Chicago and ultimately pressured the courts to take action against him. In the midst of celebrating his first publication, Seth, along with several other local bankers, was indicted for illegal banking. The charges against him initially were for issuing three-dollar bills, signing promissory notes, offering bills of credit, and signing bills.[212]

The *Weekly Wisconsin,* drawn into the stories about the banks in Chicago, published an article on the banking wars in Illinois, saying, "according to the Chicago papers the regular banks of Illinois have succeeded in getting about a dozen of the irregulars indicted by the grand jury." The paper continued, "but the joke is that many of our regular bankers are irregular. Thus they carry water upon both

---

[210] *Chicago Democrat* as quoted from the *Daily Illinois State Register*, Springfield, Illinois. December 15, 1852. Page 2.
[211] Andreas, Alfred Theodore, *History of Cook County, Illinois, From the Earliest Period to the Present Time,* Chicago, 1884, In three Volumes. Page 238.
[212] *The Weekly Wisconsin.* Milwaukee, Wisconsin. January 5, 1853. Page 4.

shoulders."[213] Crafty, powerful Chicago bankers and an opportunistic press used Seth's passionate words against him. Seth soon realized how rapidly his public reputation had changed for the worse. As noted in the *History of Cook County*, "the circulation thus became a source of constant annoyance to him instead of proving, as he had hoped, a source of profit to himself and a blessing to Chicago."[214]

In desperation Seth reached out to his circle of friends and supporters who encouraged him to defend himself in his paper. "Seth Paine, and his connexion (sic) with the Illinois River Bank had shown that he had been twenty years in Illinois, knew everybody in the West, had passed through the trials of financial disease in '36, '37, '38, and came out unscathed—credit untainted—don't owe a man a dollar in the world."[215] Meanwhile, behind his back, hearings were held to determine whether or not the grand jury allegations against him warranted a trial.

Undaunted about what might be coming, Seth published the next issues and included praise of his friends who he called, "real reformers" followed by slanderous statements about who he thought of as his enemies, "contrast these names with your Judas's."[216] Not only did he include these sweeping statements and their purported violations, he

---

[213] *The Weekly Wisconsin*. Milwaukee Wisconsin. January 5, 1853. Page 4.
[214] Andreas, Alfred Theodore, *History of Cook County, Illinois, From the Earliest Period to the Present Time,* Chicago, 1884, In three Volumes. Page 543.
[215] *Christian Banker*. January 19, 1853. Page 1.
[216] *Christian Banker*. January 12, 1853. Page 1.

listed them by name. He included his long-standing critique of the Congregationalists, "I was declared to be a Christian but not worthy of membership with Congregational-ism. They admitted that I was ready for the portals of Heaven, but not for the Congregational-ism of the West Side."[217] Within his critique he did however praise them for their dedication to the antislavery cause.

In response, *The Chicago Democrat* wrote, "it certainly is a curiosity in its way. Such a strange mixture of assumed benevolence and malinity, sanctity and slander, we have seldom seen."[218] The following week of January 19th 1853, as the indictment's details came together, Seth wrote again about the people he felt were his enemies—specifically those from Lake County and the Chicago suburbs. Seth claimed that D. O. Dickinson was working hard to turn the public against his Bank of Chicago because Dickinson and his friends wanted to establish their own bank.[219] Dickinson had attacked Seth's earlier bank connections, and Seth published that Dickinson and his friends were "possessed of neither honesty nor respect for humanity."[220] The more he wrote, the more desperate he sounded and the more his anger came through in his tirades. Though several

---

[217] *Christian Banker.* January 12, 1853.
[218] Goodspeed, W.A., Healy, D.D. *History of Cook County, Illinois.* Goodspeed Historical Association, 1909. *Democratic Press.* January 14, 1853. Page 152.
[219] *Christian Banker.* January 12, 1853.
[220] *Christian Banker.* January 19, 1853.

circumstances brought the bank to the authorities' attention, Seth's publication of the *Christian Banker* newspaper elevated press complaints and drove his enemies into action, with the goal to shut down his bank as quickly as possible.

The bank, while under investigation, was still operating until in late January when a man named Ezra L. Sherman arrived at the bank and attempted to exchange bills which he claimed were from the Bank of Chicago. When a bank officer along with Mrs. Herrick, the teller, refused to redeem the bills, Sherman began to fuss loudly and a crowd began to gather. Mrs. Herrick became indignant and asked him to leave. Seth, hearing the fuss, promised the bills would be honored, but he asked Sherman to step outside. Sherman refused and later testified that Seth—who had never been prone to aggression—pushed him out of the door. The incident attracted the attention of the local constable.

Seth was unraveling and his behavior was becoming more erratic. He was brazen in his comments to the press and his actions, sparing no one in his criticism. "By his indiscriminate attacks on everybody and everything, outside of his own circle, he alienated the common sympathy which otherwise might have been bestowed upon him. He became Ishmael among Chicago bankers."[221,222] Soon after, every one of Seth's bank notes presented to other banks was very quickly returned to him unpaid. With every public critique there was a run on his bank, forcing Seth to pay out his investors. Some days he refused to issue credits and he found strange ways to delay honoring the requests.

The *Chicago Daily Tribune* described another incident on February 5th 1853, "fifteen minutes were passed by the crowd in gazing at Seth Paine, standing dressed in a kind of morning gown, without a neckerchief, a wide collar turned over, arms crossed, eyes shut, and in a kind of trance. He was said to be communing with the spirits, what spirits we did not learn. On waking up from this, a series of angular spasmodic gesticulations followed, apparently directed to W. W. Stewart, who held a bill of the 'Bank of Chicago', which Mr. Eddy and Mr. Paine had refused to redeem. These gesticulations partook in part of the character of the mesmeric manifestations…Mr. Stewart was frequently called 'a cowardly representative of this dastardly crowd,' but continued 'in quietness to possess his spirit', and calmly repeated his request that his bill might be redeemed, but to no purpose."[223]

---

[221] Ishmael was a son of Abraham who was both blessed and cursed because he was the son of Abraham's wife's servant. God decreed, 'His hand will be over (against) everyone, And everyone's hand will be against him.' Genesis 16:12.
[222] Andreas, Alfred Theodore, *History of Cook County, Illinois, From the Earliest Period to the Present Time,* Chicago, 1884, In three Volumes. Page 543.
[223] *Chicago Daily Tribune.* February 5, 1853.

Seth's odd behavior continued: "Soon after this Mr. Payne (sic) suddenly leaped on to the counter and harangued at some length, after his usual chaste style, as seen in his paper. Two ladies were present behind the counter, supposed to be Mrs. Payne (sic) and Mrs. Eddy, and at one point in the exercises, an infant was brought forward and held up to the crowd by one of the actors, who said: 'Behold the infant, except ye become as this little child, ye cannot enter into the—Bank.' Several in the crowd seemed to enjoy the personal tirades and attacks, and some who held bills of the bank would not present them, saying, 'They had no fear the Bank would break.'"[224] The police were eventually called. The *Chicago Daily Tribune* reported that, "the whole scene was a strange mingling of the ludicrous and melancholy. It remains to be seen whether the Bank will persist in refusing to redeem any of their bills. If so, the consequences are plain and inevitable."[225]

That dramatic report unleashed a firestorm of additional media reports and began to be picked up by news outlets around the country, including this one from the *Fredonia Censor*:

"On Friday the 4th someone carried a $5 bill to the bank for redemption with a cigar in his mouth. Paine told him no one who smoked, chewed, or drank liquor, could have their money

---

[224] *Chicago Daily Tribune*. February 5, 1853. *A Run on the Spirit Bank*.
[225] Fowler, Henry, The Bank of Chicago and Spiritualism, *Chicago Daily Tribune*. February 10, 1853.

redeemed. The rumor soon spread through the city that Paine & Brothers could not redeem their bills. Everybody who had any of their money in [the bank's] possession immediately hurried to the Bank, where a crowd of some hundreds were soon congregating, and much excitement prevailed. Seth, reduced to a skeleton for the want of food, his face covered with a beard uncut for months, his sunken eye gleaming with all the wildness of a maniac's, and spoke for several hours (as moved by the spirits) with outlandish gestures. Some money was redeemed by Eddy for those who neither smoked, chewed or drank. At dark the crowd dispersed. Next day, however, as soon as the bank was opened, the crowd gathered again, and in the afternoon, assumed quite a mob-like appearance. Paine took an iron poker and Eddy a hatchet and were proceeding to clear their office, but found themselves disarmed in less time than it takes me to write it. The cries of 'tar and feathers', 'smash in the windows', and 'drag 'em out', were now loud. The arrival of the City Marshal and several police officers, however, prevented violence. The officers of the law closed the Bank, placing papers, books, etc., in proper hands for adjustment. Paine and Eddy were examined before a jury."[226]

---

[226] *Hornellsville (New York) Tribune.* March 5, 1853. *The Spirits in Chicago—Spiritual Banking.*

Seth had been fortunate that his brother-in-law Caleb Fittz warned him that he would be arrested. Caleb had heard the rumors and told Seth what to expect and how to behave when he was arrested. He listened to Caleb's advice, but was so righteous and desperate when the magistrates appeared on February 6th, he could not believe it was really happening.

The *Chicago Daily Journal* summed up the excitement, "SETH PAINE was arrested on a charge of assault and battery upon E. L. SHERMAN, and in default of bail, on the indictment found against him for illegal banking. This we trust will put an end to a monomania which has embraced many worthy people in its grasp, and given the vicious and the depraved an undue influence over them."[227] Press coverage of Seth's arrest varied; claiming that he had printed illegal bank bills, to saying that he had been speaking the "pugnacious and defiant truth".[228] Either way, Seth and Eddy were arrested and sent to Chicago's newest jailhouse— Bridewell.

---

[227] *New York Daily Times*. February 18, 1853. *The End of a Delusion*. Copied from *the Chicago Daily Journal*.
[228] *Chicago Daily Tribune*. July 7, 1872, Page 5.

Part 2

Sketch of Bridewell, 1851, from Cook County Sheriff records.

Chapter 10

Bridewell; 1853

The newly constructed Chicago jail, Bridewell, was named after a British hospital turned workhouse in England and was located at Polk and Wells Street on the east side of the river. Seth was appalled by the abuse he witnessed describing the 'house of terror' where prisoners were beaten to break their spirits to the local news reporters at his weekly hearings. Seth started off difficult and continued his unruly behavior in jail—holding a mirror up to his former acquaintance Cyrus Bradley for serving as a foreman in this fortress of evil and inhumanity. He often compared the conditions at Bridewell to the atrocities of slavery. The stories ruffled the feathers of the police chief and the warden Bradley, who attempted to have Seth indicted again for inciting a riot at Bridewell.[229] At every opportunity, Seth reminded Bradley of their time volunteering on the fire bucket brigade together when they were both humble young men with a world of possibility and promise in front of them.

When a second indictment proved unsuccessful, Bradley worked to qualify Seth to be released on bail but Seth refused to leave, saying, "he

---

[229] *Rock River Democrat.* February 22, 1853. Page 2.

would not pay tribute to Caesar in any form or shape."[230] Meanwhile Seth channeled his anger through the press where he was reported to have not only described the living conditions vividly, but the quality of the food which he reportedly "flung back" at the warden. Seth was so disgusted by the food offered at Bridewell that he adopted a vegetarian diet for the remainder of his life.[231,232] Initially he wanted to stay to rail against both his enemies and the conditions in this *Augean Stable* of humanity, but ultimately he also needed the time to think.[233] In his cell, his words and his thoughts were the only thing he had to worry about absent the distractions of his business and family.

Being dropped from his world of comfort into the cells at Bridewell was a surreal awakening. In his nightmare come to life, he found himself mocked by the public, by his fellow prisoners, and by Bradley. His close friends encouraged him to ignore the press, but many strangers found the whole charade entertaining. Over time, he came to humbly reflect on his own actions with embarrassment.

Compared to the world he had known and even the melee at his weekly hearings, life in the jail continued to drop him to his knees. The

---

[230] *Chicago Daily Tribune.* July 7, 1872. Page 5.
[231] Life on the Veg: Early Vegetarianism in America | New-York Historical Society. Vegetarianism came out of British society in the mid-1800s and very few Americans embraced the trend.
[232] *Chicago Daily Tribune.* July 7, 1872.
[233] The Augean Stables were where Hercules had his fifth labor cleaning the horses and cattle of King Augeas.

first grease-congealed meals, the bone-numbing cold of the cells, the miserable sound of prisoners weeping, the rancid smell of human waste, and the deafening clank of iron doors proved to him that imprisonment was truly a crass punishment.[234] The acute sensory overload humbled him to realize its transformative and enlightening power. He felt deeply that his actions had been taken for the good of humanity, and yet here he was in jail. He tried to understand why the press had turned against him so quickly. "How could this circus exist in the world unchecked?" he wondered? He had been so sure of what God had wanted him to do. But, his current, brutal reality challenged this paradigm.

******

On February 12th 1853, the local newspapers prepared the world for the first trial related to the Bank of Chicago reporting, "Paine is in Jail, Herricks going on trial on Thursday."[235] The *Democratic Press* said, "the banks have been alarmed; the public has been excited; there appears to be an underlayer of spite or ill will towards banks and banking in this city."[236] In fact, more than just banking was on trial. The proceedings quickly came to include an assessment on the validity of

---

[234] *Chicago Daily Tribune*. July 7, 1872. Page 5. The newspaper described the prisons as possessing 'time honored abuse' which included 'the word of every sheriff's satrap as law'.
[235] *Daily Intelligencer*. February 12, 1853. Wheeling, West Virginia. Page 2.
[236] Goodspeed, W.A., Healy, D.D. *History of Cook County, Illinois*. Goodspeed Historical Association, 1909. Page 153.

alternative religious practices and the role of women in society.

On February 15th 1853, the courthouse opened to what was commonly called the 'Trial of the Spiritual Mediums'. The press coverage stretched as far as the east coast, where they concluded, "the bank appears to have been a spirit swindling shop in good earnest."The Spiritualist mediums were on trial for inciting a riot with Sherman, in what the press also summarily coined, 'The Spiritual Bank Affair'.[237] First to testify was Mr. Sherman who recalled that he went into Paine's bank the week prior with bills from the bank and asked to redeem them. In response, Paine and Eddy told him they would hold a séance to determine if the notes should be paid. When they returned to the waiting area, the men reportedly refused to redeem the notes. Shortly after, he testified that two men came behind him, dragged him to the back door, and threw him out under Paine's orders. Mr. Sherman also recalled that Mrs. Herrick was present throughout and Eddy eventually said he would pay on the notes, but this was never completed.[238] After Sherman's testimony, Herrick was asked about her spiritual communications and whether they affected her sanity. Other witnesses testified that Sherman had provoked and insulted people at the bank.

The press avidly followed the trial. They accused Seth of having a

---

[237] *Baltimore Sun*. Baltimore, Maryland. February 18, 1853. Page 1.
[238] Synopsis of a combination of newspaper reports on the trial.

'shinplaster bank'. The term shinplaster was often applied to banks and bankers who held unusual practices. Shinplasters created paper money worth less than a couple dollars that was considered valueless by other banks. Sherman's testimony confirmed suspicions that the Bank of Chicago did not value their own notes to patrons the spiritualists determined were not worthy. The workings of banks would be studied, critiqued and mused upon for a long time following the resolution of the trials.[239]

The crowds who attended the trial were less interested in the bank's operating model, and more interested in the stories about séances and Spiritualist practices. The press concluded they were very similar to Swedeborgians capturing the imagination of citizens all over the country.[240] As if to quell speculation on their reporting biases, many papers shared the same story over and over. The stories sold newspapers and the courtrooms were, "filled to overflowing at an early hour." The press drew conclusions stating, "of course the Spiritual Bank has burst as all other fanatical bubbles must."[241]

Despite this the papers noted, "a great deal of mischief and

---

[239] *Hornellsville (New York) Tribune.* March 5, 1853.
[240] *Western Citizen.* February 22, 1853. Swedeborgians were followers of Swedish Lutheran theologian, Emanuel Swedenborg, who accompanied his preaching with mystic illuminations.
[241] *Wheeling Daily Intelligencer and the Pittsburg Journal.* Thursday, February 17, 1853. First Edition, Page 2.

swindling has grown out of this Seth Paine scheme of banking, yet when a rapper or medium announces himself in any of our towns our people rush to witness his impositions and hold conversations with the shades of departed friends. There is always a fee for a conversation and the villainous tricksters generally make a good thing of it."[242] The Spiritualists attracted an extensive following of people both locally and nationally because of their quirky practices and eventually published a journal out of Chicago. However, even with all the media attention, they never claimed as strong a foothold in Chicago as they did in other cities like New York.[243]

Trying the case in the press, the *State Capitol* paper reported, "the Spiritual banker of Chicago, in consequence of his refusal to redeem the shinplasters put out by himself and Mr. Eddy pretended to be governed by a communication from Jefferson, Washington and Hamilton banking."[244] The debates about these practices raged on between the public and the press.

Between all of the press, the first case tried in court boiled down to determining whether or not the bank had 'incited a riot'. The prosecution focused on the management practices at the bank and

---

[242] *Daily Illinois State Register*. Springfield, Illinois. March 5, 1853. Page 2.
[243] Andreas, A.T. *Brief History of Spiritualism in Chicago, 1850's through 1870's, History of Chicago*. Chicago. 1884. Page 831.
[244] *Daily Illinois State Register*. Springfield, Illinois. March 5, 1853. Page 2.

accused the Spiritualist mediums as having influenced, "men of property, and who hitherto have had credit given them for at least ordinary intelligence, would submit to be led by silly women as to the disposal of their property and their reputations." But, the judge was determined to focus on the issue of whether or not the charge of breaking the peace was warranted. One disclosure that brought great excitement was the fact that "Paine had little or no capital in the bank; that all the stock amounted to some 4,000 or 5,000 dollars, deposited by Ira B. Eddy, and about $3,000 by other persons."[245] The judge ultimately declared that those involved in breaking the peace would be fined $500 each and Seth Paine was additionally charged with assault and battery upon Mr. Sherman.[246]

******

On March 5th 1853, Seth published the following public statement, "we shall re-appear shortly with our *Christian Banker*, when a tale will be unfolded that will make the ears of this city and worlds tingle; and shall prove in due time that not only is not the Bank of Chicago, or the spirituality of Seth Paine bent or broke – but will live and live forever." [247] As soon as he distributed this statement he regretted doing so.

---

[245] *Chicago Daily Tribune*. February 10, 1853. The Bank of Chicago and Spiritualism.
[246] *New York Daily Times*. February 18, 1853. The End of a Delusion.
[247] *Daily Illinois State Register*. March 5, 1853. Springfield, Illinois. Page 2.

The backlash only added to Seth's anguish while he ruminated inside Bridewell's walls. Continued coverage of the case made national news regularly. While the crowds of reporters grew, Seth considered his options. After five weeks, he felt ready to leave Bridewell. His friend and fellow abolitionist Daniel Davidson, posted his bail. A fellow station master on the Underground Railroad, Davidson had worked with Seth for many years in Chicago.[248] After posting bail, Seth's friends urged him to lay low in Lake Zurich and not engage with the newspapers until his next trial. When he was released, the newspapers reported that no one was happier to see Seth Paine out of prison than Warden Cyrus P. Bradley. One paper claimed, "that the (prison) officers rejoiced when Seth walked out the door."[249]

Resigned to face his uncertain future, Seth went home to Lake Zurich while he awaited the next trial. After his release, he abandoned his "oddities of dress" and temporarily stopped publishing the *Christian Banker*.[250] He continued to read the stories published about him and his perceived crimes. The media portrayed Seth's impending trial as a joke, speculating that he had resisted bail for so long based on the guidance from departed former presidents.

---

[248] Blanchard, R. *Discovery and Conquests of the North-west, With the History of Chicago.* Testimonial of Harvey Hurd, Volume 2, Page 306.
[249] *Chicago Daily Tribune.* July 7, 1872. Page 5.
[250] *Chicago Daily Tribune.* July 7, 1872. Page 5.

Of particular fascination continued to be the accounts of how the Spiritualists practiced their faith. The *Hornellsville, New York Tribune* reported, "at their medium meetings they frequently had spiritual demonstrations similar to Rochester knockings… At other times they had Spiritual Dances…Some of the women—a few of whom are known to be of an abandoned class—would whirl about, throwing their arms around them like a Quixotic windmill until completely exhausted, and then tumble…on the floor, putting Bloomerism to the blush by the immodest exposure of the nether limbs."[251]

The first trial attempted to prove that Spiritualism was not a true religion and positioned Seth and the spiritualists as lunatics.[252] The hearings were described as a general wash-day of the creeds.[253]

> "Every head-centre of diverse doctrine in the region was subpoenaed, and J. Y. Scammon, the Rev. R. W. Patterson, the Rev. Dr. Burroughs, a brace of Methodists Elders, a stray Shaker and Quaker, a traveling Mormon, and a score of others, were each brought separately to tell the jury 'what they knew about' Swedenborgianism, Presybterians, Baptism, Miracles, Effectual Calling, Election, Et in omne genus.[254] There was not enough

---

[251] *Hornellsville (New York) Tribune.* March 5, 1853.
[252] *Chicago Daily Tribune.* July 7, 1872. Page 5.
[253] *Fredonia* article February 1853. Referring to the fact that persons representing nearly every creed were brought into the trial to attempt to discredit Spiritualism.
[254] Jonathan Young Scammons was a renowned lawyer, abolitionist, newspaperman

evidence to convict the mediums of inciting a riot and for a time, Seth Paine picked his *Christian Banker* out of the wreck of his bank, and withdrew to the quiet shades of Lake Zurich."[255]

The first trial was over and the verdict, though in his favor, did not feel like a victory to Seth. Ira Eddy, purchased Seth's interests in the bank in April 1853 and the bank officially shuttered its doors on July 9th 1853, less than a year after opening.[256] Seth personally felt that he needed to redeem every note the bank issued and reconcile with everyone whom his bank had impacted.

As Seth returned to Lake Zurich on the local stagecoach, the bumps in the road lulled him into deep thought. Seth was disappointed in humanity. He had witnessed all the dreams of his youth shattered and he mourned his loss of innocence. His soul felt more adrift than ever and he wondered if he might actually be insane—though his friends and family tried to convince him otherwise. It was an issue he felt compelled to address eventually, but for now, he was headed home. He thought about King David and reread Psalm 16, "Preserve me, O God, for in thee I take refuge. I say to the Lord, Thou art my Lord; I have no God apart from thee." His family's warm refuge reminded him again of

---

and sometime banker. When John Wentworth accused him in *The Chicago Democrat* of being a wild-cat banker, Scammons sued him and won.
[255] *Chicago Daily Tribune*. July 7, 1872. Page 5.
[256] *Weekly Wisconsin*. April 20, 1853.

his humanity and grounded him. On his first night at home as he and Frances lay together, he took a deep breath and listened to the gentle rise and fall of her breath. He closed his eyes and let his anxiety fade into the darkness.

Letter to Stephen Douglas, 1856. University of Chicago, Guide to Stephen A. Douglas Papers 1764-1908, Box 10 Folder 13, Correspondence 1857, December 14. From Seth Paine

Chapter 11

Accountability; 1853-1854

After a few days recovering in Lake Zurich, Seth sold some of his property to pay his debts and prepare his finances for the upcoming trials. He decided to address the public's speculation about his soundness of mind by checking himself into an asylum for a couple of days. In the mid-19th century, sanity, or lack thereof, was an important indicator for society of a person's ability to manage wealth or property. Few people recovered from insanity and due to Seth's recent behavior, there was rampant speculation that he was insane. Given his family history, Seth certainly felt it could be possible, so he committed himself just to be sure. His lawyers discouraged him out of fear that his reputation would be ruined if he were officially declared insane, but in his usual stubborn way, Seth insisted.

The filth and conditions at public asylums across the United States was publicly exposed in 1847 and many were undergoing reforms by 1853. One of the key advocates on asylum conditions was Dorothea Lynde Dix (1802–87)—a teacher in Boston—who had observed the conditions firsthand and was working to change them. At the time, "insane Persons confined within this Commonwealth [of Massachusetts], in cages, closets, cellars, stalls, pens! Chained, naked, beaten with rods, and lashed into obedience! (Dix, 1843: 4) In reply to an often proposed question —Whether similar cases of suffering…can be found in other States beside Massachusetts? —truth and justice oblige me to answer that I believe they exist in all the States of the Union."[257] In response to her initial study, she was hired to prepare a report on the conditions in Illinois asylums in 1847. Her results were presented to the Illinois State Legislature and prompted plans to reform the existing institutions and build the first state hospital in Jacksonville around 1848.

Seth compared the conditions at the asylum to Bridewell. Similar to prison, the wailing of his fellow humans, the stench of waste, and a claustrophobic feeling filled his days. However, the asylum was warmer, the food slightly better, and the staff more compassionate than the prison guards had been.

Exempt from responsibility, Seth had more time to contemplate the condition of man, his family, and to prepare to face his future. "Perhaps we are all only one or two steps from insanity," he thought, as he offered advice to the other residents. He was also compelled to work out solutions to problems between other residents and with the staff. He remembered visiting his dear grandmother Lydia in the asylum as a boy.

---

[257] Howarth, R. J., Aleguas, S.A. *Through a glass darkly: patients of the Illinois State Hospital for the Insane at Jacksonville, USA (1854–80)*. University College London. Page 3.

Thinking back, he recalled how disconnected she seemed and yet was still her beautiful self. Despite his efforts to assist in improving the place, the institution insisted he leave a few days after his arrival. The press reported that the asylum "determined that Mr. Paine was not qualified naturally for his inhabitancy of the asylum for the short time that he was there; that he was merely hyper-reformatory and perhaps illogical in the nature of his schemes for the amelioration of the human race."[258] In other words, he was not insane. All he had been through in the past few months had just given him pause and mellowed his mind.

Seth implored his legal counsel, E.W. Tracy and George W. Meeker, to push for a speedy resolution to the trials he faced.[259] Meeker was an early Chicago resident and well-connected lawyer. He had a lifetime handicap as a result of childhood paralysis. His career had seen his storefront on Lake Street become the location of the first Federal Courts in Chicago. Later he was part of a partnership with J.Y. Scammons to develop an industrial school, and eventually he served a commission on the Circuit Courts in 1848.[260] Seth knew him from his work with the abolitionists. Meeker had tried the first fugitive slave case in Chicago

---

[258] Andreas, Alfred Theodore, *History of Cook County, Illinois, From the Earliest Period to the Present Time,* Chicago, 1884, In three Volumes. Page 320.
[259] E. W. Tracy was a law partner of George W. Meeker, long time attorney and abolitionist in Chicago.
[260] Andreas, Alfred Theodore, *History of Cook County, Illinois, From the Earliest Period to the Present Time,* Chicago, 1884, In three Volumes. Pages 156, 211, and 217.

on June 7th 1851. The case involved, "one Morris Johnson, alleged to be a runaway slave. Crawford E. Smith, of Lafayette County, Missouri by power of attorney to Samuel S. Martin, of Chicago, had him arrested as his slave. William, who had escaped from his premises July 4, 1850." The trial lasted three days and Meeker eventually acquitted the man because of a discrepancy in the description given of the formerly enslaved man and the man he saw in his courtroom. This acquittal was believed to be, "largely due to the unpopularity of the law, and the unwillingness of the Bench, Bar and people of Chicago to act as negro-hunters for Southern slave holders."[261] As a friend to the suffering, Meeker was a formidable defender of Seth's rights.

With his prison and asylum experiences behind him and his own anger cooled, Seth allowed his legal team to speak for him. He also resumed his former grooming practices learned long ago to distract him from the trial and subsequent press response. Beginning in early 1854, the trial set a momentous legal precedent for the entire Spiritualist movement, ultimately determining that Spiritualism "was established among the creeds, because it was not established to be anything else."[262]

When the time came for the banking charges to be tried, the debts had all been paid and the bank was closed. The judge dropped all

---

[261] Andreas, Alfred Theodore. *History of Cook County, Illinois. From the Earliest Period to the Present Time,* Chicago. 1884. In three Volumes. Page 454.
[262] *Chicago Daily Tribune.* July 7, 1872. Page 5.

banking charges against Seth on the condition he no longer engage in banking. After an anti-climactic end to the banking trial, with his paper discontinued, Seth withdrew to Lake Zurich where he looked for ways to reduce his holdings so he could pay every debt he owed.[263]

Meanwhile the entire banking industry in Chicago was also turned on its head. Many blamed it on John Wentworth, *The Chicago Democrat's* editor and an aspiring politician. "There can be no doubt that Mr. Wentworth was in a measure responsible for this state of public opinion. In large measure he was responsible for the hostility shown in this community to all banking enterprises and Credit, the basis of modern business transactions, was daily damaged by his philippics. But he was not alone."[264]

Back in Lake Zurich, Seth found the repose he needed. He went back to growing his hair long and wearing long white shirts as he contemplated the future. Slavery was still a simmering issue, and life at home was presenting its own challenges. Initially, he reacted to the hypocrisy and injustice with anger, but he quickly realized that anger and hate no longer served him. There was a time to be full of dreams and new ideas and a time to face reality, find gratitude, and move

---

[263] Abstract of Land Title, Lake County Recorder of Deeds, #29025, book 228, Page 870. Describes the later cases from Seth's children attempting to reclaim land by suing their parents and the estate of their mother for losing land during the trials.
[264] Goodspeed, W.A., Healy, D.D. *History of Cook County, Illinois*. Goodspeed Historical Association. 1909. Page 154.

forward.

With the help of his friends, Seth now understood how his enemies had used his own passion to conspire against him. He reflected on how his critique of the Congregational Church and its members had impacted his livelihood. The irony was not lost on him that like his Uncle before him, he was jailed for challenging established norms. Even though he was still convinced the Congregational Church was wrong, he conceded that it was more powerful than one man alone. He felt like the world had pulled the curtain back tighter over its corruption and hypocrisy. The hypocrisy still existed, but no one else dared to acknowledge it publicly. He felt blessed to find sanctuary in his beloved community around Lake Zurich. He realized how fragile his successes had been, and how they were nearly erased by the ordeals of the last year.

For a time Seth happily stepped away from the hustle and bustle of Chicago. In the daytime, he walked to his Stable of Humanity and mingled with the community. In the evenings he enjoyed standing on the banks of Lake Zurich and watching the sun set over the lake. He resolved to emerge from this time by holding tight to a passage from Hebrews 13:3, "continue to remember those in prison as if you were together with them and those who are mistreated as if you yourself were suffering." He had faith he would be called to another mission where his deep compassion would be needed. For now, he was glad to be with his family.

One Sunday evening, Frances came to his side, embraced him, and let him know that dinner was ready and the family was waiting for him. He wasn't sure who he was, or where his future would take him, but he felt the warmth of being home. The world thought Seth had lost everything when he lost a good deal of money, his credibility in business, and a number of acquaintances, but he knew he had so much left. As the weeks passed, he felt more strongly that his failures were helping to point him in a new direction. Seth embraced his family, thankful for the meals before them, and the peace at his home.

Announcement of Frederick Douglass coming to Lake County 1859
The Porcupine newspaper, Waukegan, Illinois, 1859,
microfiche collection located at the Waukegan Public Library

Chapter 12

Rebuilding the Dream; 1854-1860

Back home in Lake Zurich, Seth recommitted himself to being a wise and faithful servant to the world. His Union Store was running successfully on its own merits as if the Bank of Chicago travesties had never occurred. The Stable of Humanity, the Fourier-like community center and hall, were used frequently by local groups to meet and exchange ideas. His friends still wanted his help for those in need and to safely transport the formerly enslaved to safety. His family was thriving and grateful to still have his mother, Fanny, who helped with the four children. That joy was not long lived. In late Spring 1854, Fanny became ill and died swiftly at the age of 65. In his grief, Seth realized how much his mother's values had shaped his own. Seth dedicated his future to his mother, continuing to seek where he could best serve.

That autumn, the Kansas-Nebraska Act was passed. Replacing the Missouri Compromise of 1820, the Kansas-Nebraska Act allowed settlers to determine whether or not slavery would exist in new territories. Its passage caused a great deal of conflict across the country. [265] Many young Americans rushed to the newly opened territories in an

---

[265] Garrison, Z. Kansas-Nebraska Act. *Civil War on the Western Border: The Missouri-Kansas Conflict, 1854-1865*. The Kansas City Public Library.

effort to claim them for their respective causes. This led to confrontations between those who wanted to continue slavery and those against it at the borders of these new states. This conflict over the status of slavery in the Western frontier continued until the start of the Civil War in 1861.

After their mother passed, Seth's sister Ruth and her husband Isaac Mayo decided to move westward with their four young children. In late spring they embarked from Lake Zurich and headed to Iowa, carrying their abolitionist spirit with them. Ruth's family stayed and farmed for many years in Iowa but remained in touch with the family in Illinois. After the Civil War, Seth's niece Nellie headed West following Ruth's children Charles and Helen to Kansas, where land was plenty and opportunities were rich for young settlers.[266] Seth's own family was growing. He proudly announced in the Rockford paper under the headline *More Than One Baby:* "Seth Paine of the Lake Zurich Banker notices an event of Europe, but a similar one, the Empress of France has got a baby, and my wife has got another."[267]

When the Burbank family came through town in 1856, their oldest son Edwin described Seth as, "an extraordinarily queer looking person driving alone in a light wagon. He seemed above medium height and sat

---

[266] Federal census records, 1860, 1880, and cemetery records for Fayette County, Iowa.
[267] *Rockford Republican.* April 16, 1856. Rockford. Page 1.

very straight in the seat. The rim of a soft black hat shaded a pair of uncommonly keen eyes. His reddish brown hair fell over his shoulders in straggling locks and a flowing beard nearly covered his face. I remember my Mother's expression of horror, though he gave us a smiling salutation as we passed. Aunt Ann told us it was Seth Paine, a well-known character of fine intellect, but unbalanced mind, his specialty for the moment being Spiritualism."[268] They settled nearby in the town of Wauconda, just up the road from Lake Zurich. The Burbank family may have thought he was strange at first, but John Burbank eventually accepted a job with Seth at the Union Store, his wife Almira oversaw the boarding house at the Stable of Humanity, and their daughter taught music in the music hall. The two families eventually became close friends, particularly Almira and Frances.

Dipping his toes back into politics at the urging of his friends, Seth became part of the movement to form the Republican Party in response to the Kansas-Nebraska Act. The Republican Party would replace the Whig party created during the Jackson administration.[269] The Whigs supported the abolition of slavery but were divided on how they should

---

[268] Winter, E. W. *Memories of Edwin W. Winter*, self published for private family collection. 1922. Courtesy of the Ela Township Historical Society collection. June 2016. Page 16.

[269] Whig Party - Definition, Beliefs & Leaders - HISTORY, Formed by supporters of Andrew Jackson in 1834, the party was abandoned in 1854 and replaced by the Republican party.

act upon that support. The Republicans—made up of strong abolitionists—felt that the Federal Government needed to intervene and abolish slavery altogether in the United States. The Democrats of the day defended the rights of each state to decide for themselves, at a minimum many felt that the states had the right to keep or abolish slavery.

Politically, Seth was active but he was more reserved than he had been prior. Despite his reticence to be in the spotlight again so soon, Seth was determined to revive his newspaper in 1856. Initially, he renamed it the *Lake Zurich Banker* and included articles and insights with a little more humor, tongue-in-cheek political commentary, and satire. The paper's masthead read, "The Voice of the People is the Voice of God."

Having gained public notoriety during his trial, Seth's activities and especially his publications, were often the subject of national scrutiny. Every couple of months a national newspaper reprinted an article from the *Lake Zurich Banker* under titles like, "the Lake Zurich queer chicken" or similar descriptions.[270] The *Daily Free Democrat* said that the paper was, "the most purely original and unique paper we have seen. Its editor does not hesitate to speak as he thinks."[271] Seth was not

---

[270] *Squatter Sovereign*. August 19, 1856. Atchison, Kansas. Page 3.
[271] *Daily Free Democrat*. May 7, 1856. Page 2.

bothered by the mockery. He believed publishing the paper was an effective way to spread messages about slavery, oppression, and what he saw as the truth. He would even reprint things other people would say about him in his own paper. "Seth Paine, notorious throughout the west as the crazy banker of Chicago, has commenced the publication of a newspaper. It is the boldest, honestest, truest, craziest paper ever published."[272] In addition to his commentary, Seth wrote about speakers and events hosted at the Stable of Humanity such as J. B. Merwin—a prominent speaker and advocate for temperance, who had worked alongside Abraham Lincoln on the issue of temperance throughout Illinois from 1854-1855.[273]

As a progressive, Seth was keen to criticize those who resisted progress. In August of 1856, he wrote that, "Daniel brought new Truth to light—for him the Lions's Den, Jesus took a long stride ahead, for him - the cross of calvary, Garrison says slavery is wrong—he is haltered in the streets of Boston, the Railroad is invented and wise men call it 'Gray's Iron Road' and send the inventor to the mad house for insanity."[274] Sorting through the ironies of the times, he remarked that the bankers in Chicago were criticized by the public for being sensible, while at the same time everyone is paying 5% a month to have accounts

---

[272] *Seth Paines Banker.* August 19, 1856. Page 2. From the *Elkhorn (Wisconsin) Independant.*
[273] J.B. Merwin spoke on April 30, 1856 at the Stable of Humanity.
[274] *The Lake Zurich Banker.* August 19, 1856. Edition XXI, Page 1.

with them. "I established the best system of banking which people ever had and the old fogeys jumped upon my bank and shut me up in jail."[275] He wrote about how technological advances like the cotton gin, would save men from manual labor, its own form of slavery, while the men who resisted it complained and made money off the backs of those laborers. He also openly criticized the irony of the fact that the preamble of the Constitution of the United States, stated that all men are created equal, then went on to intentionally exclude Native Americans, Scotsmen, the enslaved, and women from this equality. Seth concluded, "now the battle of principle has to be fought among ourselves, and to God it might be done without bloodshed!"[276]

With Seth's support, the town of Barrington soon became the first town northwest of Chicago to offer rail service to and from Chicago, opening the floodgates for more people to commute to the city. In 1857, Seth ventured back into Chicago to work with his friend Philetus Woodworth Gates, the owner of Gates Iron Works. Gates Iron Works produced steel plows for farming and manufactured Chicago's first steam sawmill. The men had met when they were involved in the Engineer/Mechanics Institute where they bonded over their support of both labor and progressive mechanisms for farms and where Seth had

---

[275] *The Lake Zurich Banker*. August 19, 1856. Edition XXI, Page 1.
[276] *The Lake Zurich Banker*. August 19, 1856. Edition XXI, Page 1.

used Gates steam sawmill in Lake Zurich years earlier.[277] From Gates Iron Works, Seth published the *Chicago Daily Ledger*, a small evening journal where he was the editor. Its tagline was "A Very Large Paper for the Country". Only a few issues ever made it to publication, however because it was not well received. In 1857, Gates Iron Works was heavily invested in the railroad industry and deeply impacted by the banking panic.[278]

The panic began in March with the Supreme Court's decision in the Dred Scott case. Dred Scott was an enslaved person who with support from abolitionists and other supporters sued his enslaver for his freedom. Over the course of ten years, the case made its way through the lower courts with every trial reversing the prior's decision until it reached the Supreme Court in 1856. The Supreme Court ultimately ruled that Scott had no right to sue in federal court because he wasn't an American Citizen. The decision also declared the Missouri Compromise of 1820 as unconstitutional.[279] The verdict made many abolitionists

---

[277] Andreas, Alfred Theodore, *History of Cook County, Illinois, From the Earliest Period to the Present Time,* Chicago, 1884, In three Volumes. Page 423.
[278] Calomiris, C.W., Schweikart, L. *The Panic of 1857: Origins, Transmission, and Containment.* Journal of Economic History. 1991. 51 (4): 807–834.
[279] Dred Scott was an enslaved person who sued his enslaver for his freedom in 1846 on the premise that he and his family had been moved to a number of free territories during their enslavement and should have been freed. The Supreme Court ruled that Scott was not an American citizen, and therefore had no right to sue in federal court. The decision overruled the Missouri Compromise and some felt a catalyst for the impending Civil War.

wary of westward expansion, causing them to withdraw financial backing from the railroad industry.

******

Seth was happy to be in Chicago during the week and Lake Zurich on the weekends, where he spent time helping his children fish and teaching them about farming. By this time, Seth had again shaved off his beard and trimmed his ragged locks. In his spare time, he turned back to writing letters to editors and working behind the scenes on progressive issues. With unwavering passion, Seth worked to keep his commentary on slavery in the forefront of local interests.

Having read about the continued conflict resulting from the Kansas-Nebraska Act, Seth reached out to Senator Stephen Douglas on December 14th 1857 from the offices of the *Chicago Daily Ledger*. Seth complimented Douglas on his support of the Kansas-Nebraska Act, and appealed to him to continue his support of the abolition movement. The issue of slavery was boiling in 1857, with many politicians agreeing it was time to finally resolve the issue. Douglas felt the states should make this decision, while other politicians argued that the decision should be made by the federal government.[280]

---

[280] *Stephen Douglas letters*. University of Chicago. Box 10, Folder 13. Dated December 14, 1857. Correspondence between Stephen A. Douglas and Seth Paine. Whether Douglas responded or not is unknown.

The progressive abolitionists were breaking into three factions; those who believed that the only way to make progress was through voting, those who believed violent action was needed (such as John Brown), and those who felt non-violent actions were warranted, such as protesting and hosting public presentations and voting.[281] Seth was a believer in influencing the way people voted through outspoken and prolific advocacy and commentary. Frederick Douglass's paper *The North Star* published one noted Letter to the Editor in September 1858. In the letter, Seth invited Frederick Douglass to come to Waukegan as an advocate for the 'true' Republican Party. On February 2nd 1859, Frederick Douglass came to Waukegan to speak on "The Races of Man" though it is unclear if he came because of Seth's invitation or for another reason.[282] Several hundred local residents attended the event at Dickinson Hall. At the time, Douglass had been spending considerable time with John Brown, though he did not think violent action was the way to abolish slavery. Douglass was admired for his eloquence and considered a brilliant speaker and an inspiring leader of the abolition movement.

In May 1859, Frances contracted a brief illness and died, shocking

---

[281] John Brown Biography | American Battlefield Trust, John Brown was a controversial character with strong ties to Lake County.
[282] Halsey, J. J. *A History of Lake County, Illinois.* Chicago, Illinois: Roy S. Bates, 1912. Page 140. Article from the *Waukegan Democrat,* announcement, published 1-22-1859.

the family.[283] Seth prepared for the funeral in a state of numbness, as he wrangled his five children for the service held at the cemetery in Barrington next to Seth's mother's gravesite. As he listened to his wife's eulogy, he reflected on how strong she was, and how patient she had been with him. The support and kindness he had been shown by his wife and his mother had been never-ending. He looked at his kids wriggling around him and prayed for guidance. Holding back tears, he worked hard to contain his overbearing sorrow and to act as gracefully as he remembered his family behaving when his grandfather had passed so many years prior. He glanced around at the crowd of mourners and witnessed just how many lives Frances had touched in their community. He felt as if he were seeing the community for the first time, humbled by the outpouring of sympathy. Frances had worked in her own way, bringing friendship and comfort to new settlers and old friends alike.

A tiny woman approached him, "Mr. Paine," she said, "I don't know if you remember me, my name is Almira Burbank; I run the boarding house in the Stable, my late-husband ran the Union Store and my daughter is the music teacher. Frances was such a blessing to myself and my family since we arrived in the area and she was such a comfort to me when my husband passed last winter. Please, let me know if there is anything I can do to help you in this difficult time." Seth's children

---

[283] Frances's cause of death is unknown as death records were not required at that time in the United States.

circled around her and hugged her amiably.

After Frances' memorial, Seth was overwhelmed by the practical matter of caring for five children on his own while continuing his other endeavors. Almira extended her friendship to Seth because of her strong relationship with Frances. She and her children already knew the Paine children well. Almira appreciated Seth's respect for women and knew of his great compassion for the world. One year after his wife's death, Seth and Almira married on May 7, 1860.

From her first impression of Seth on the wagon in 1854, Almira's opinion of him had softened considerably. He was quirky, but his allegiance to his family and passion to make a difference in the world were fundamental and earnest to him. Almira's son Edwin described him as, "kindness itself to all about him. An affectionate father, generous beyond his means, but still conceived in his appointed mission to regenerate mankind or, as he expressed it, to 'work for Man, not for Men,' and in the vastness of the foggy field of activity he was inclined to overlook his own family responsibilities."[284] With Almira running the household, Seth was able to renew his focus on business and the world. The two families merged together in his large home on Lake Zurich's shores.

---

[284] Winters, E. W. *Memories of Edwin W. Winters*. Self published for private family collection. 1922. Courtesy of the Ela Township Historical Society collection.

When Frances passed, Seth completely lost his passion for writing. His heart was more interested in action and less in writing and speaking. Bigger world issues called his attention. The Union Store still functioned as a cooperative where members could buy in for a trading privilege and receive a discount. For several decades, the system worked well. The profits with this model were not like those Seth had generated in his Chicago businesses, but Seth maintained faith that he did not need a large fortune to continue living comfortably in his little town. The school—fully funded by Seth—operated out of the Stable of Humanity providing children an excellent education under the tutelage of the well-admired main instructor, Gordon Dresser. Community members hosted meetings in the hall and embraced the community gathering place. As the 1860 election neared, tensions throughout the country mounted on the issue of abolition and slavery and debates flared up frequently around the region and throughout the nation.

On April 2, 1860, Abraham Lincoln took the new railroad from Chicago to Waukegan to speak to supporters in the county.[285] His speech in Waukegan began and ended quickly when a large warehouse nearby started on fire and sounded an alarm that drew the attendees away, including Mr. Lincoln himself. Lincoln was a pro-abolition candidate for the Republican party, and his support was guaranteed by

---

[285] Halsey, J. J. *A History of Lake County, Illinois*. Chicago, Illinois: Roy S. Bates, 1912. Page 142.

the largely abolition supporting Lake County voters even if they did not get to hear him speak that day.

A few other tragedies disrupted the election season. On September 8th, in the early hours of the morning the *Lady Elgin* steamship was returning to Milwaukee carrying nearly 400 Irishmen from a local militia unit who had attended a Stephen Douglas rally in Chicago earlier that day. Accounts describe a storm that arose on the lake causing the steamship to collide with a lumber boat. In the melee of the storm, some survivors found their way to the banks of Lake Michigan, south of today's Highland Park, but most were never recovered.[286,287] Press speculation about the cause of the accident abounded, including suspicions that the ship was hit intentionally to reduce the number of Democratic votes at the upcoming elections. Because of the accident Senator Stephen Douglas came through Waukegan on October 13th to address an audience on the shores of Lake Michigan. The *Gazette,* a Republican paper, covered the event and reasoned that, "though 'duty bound' to disparage him and his audience, it is a part of history that the 'Little Giant' was an eloquent and attractive speaker."[288]

---

[286] The *Lady Elgin* was owned by an avid abolitionist and neighbor of Seth Paine, Gordon Hubbard, who had been running his ship from Chicago to Ontario for years.
[287] Lady Elgin Disaster, The Lady Elgin tragedy was considered to have a significant impact on the election of 1860.
[288] Halsey, J. J. *A History of Lake County, Illinois.* Chicago, Illinois: Roy S. Bates, 1912. Page 143.

Abraham Lincoln's election in the fall of 1860 brought hope that emancipation of the enslaved and the eradication of slavery might finally be realized. This great hope was followed by the rapid secession of seven states in the winter of 1860-61 who called themselves the Confederate States.[289,290] As each state seceded, unease grew throughout the country leading up to Lincoln's inauguration on March 4, 1861. The sitting President, James Buchanan, both forbade the states from seceding and Federal troops from forcing them to stay, encouraging the tension.

The cold settled in January 1861 in Illinois. Snow and a few warmer days broke the monotony of the gray chill.[291] Seth and Almira spent that first winter together as a new family. Seth felt a renewed responsibility as the patriarch to guide spirited discussions—keeping them lively, morally charged, and full of family warmth. With young adults in his household, Seth worked carefully to ensure that family dinner discussions revolved around the hope of Lincoln's election.

---

[289] The first seven states to secede following the election of Abraham Lincoln included: Texas, Mississippi, Georgia, Louisiana, Alabama, Florida and South Carolina.
[290] Confederate comes from the latin word, "*confoederatus*" meaning leagued together.
[291] Andsager, K. (Midwestern Regional Climate Center, Champaign, Illinois); Ross, T. (National Climatic Data Center, Asheville, North Carolina); Kruk, M.C. and Michael L. *Climate Database Modernization Program: Key Climate Observations Recorded Since the Founding of America, 1700's – 1800's*. Spinar Midwestern Regional Climate Center, Champaign, Illinois. Page 5.

Washington Jail, ca. 1862, photo from St. Lawrence University Law Library, Pryce Lewis photo from Box 2, Folder 10.

Chapter 13

A Higher Calling; 1861

The Civil War began on April 14th 1861 when Fort Sumter, a strategic location, in South Carolina fell to secessionists. President Lincoln sent out a call to arms to North Carolina, and North Carolina responded by seceding from the Union on May 20th 1861. Lincoln then called for 75,000 men from the rest of the country to defend the Union. Young men responded in droves to enlist, leaving many families with little time to process the thought of their children going to war. Seth's eldest son, Charles, wanted to enlist right away, but missed the first call. Three months later, when Lincoln issued a second call for men on August 1st 1861, it was clear that the war would last some time. Between 1861 and 1865, more than 2,000 young men joined the war effort from Lake County alone.[292]

A call to arms meant more than just putting out a notice in the newspapers. War wagons would pass through towns as the boys were working in the fields. Often compared to the Roman call for gladiators, someone rang a bell, its clanging resonating throughout rural America, calling young men to carry them off to register and fight the war.[293]

---

[292] Schumm-Burgess, N. *The Barns of Lake County.* Donning Company Publishers. The Land Conservancy of Lake County. 2004. Page 26.
[293] Bill Pierce, interview by author, Village of Lake Zurich, Summer 1996.

Young recruits had a few minutes to say goodbye to their parents and loved ones before hopping on board the wagon.

In Lake Zurich, the war wagon recruited Charles Paine and Byron Cadwell—who notably hung his scythe in the tree in front of the Stable of Humanity as they left.[294] His mother went to remove it but his father stopped her and said, "he will remove it himself when he comes home." When the tree was cut down in the early 1900s, the scythe remained.[295]

At the age of 20, Charles Paine proudly joined the ranks of the 12th Illinois Infantry in Company K. The regiment was known as the '1st Scotch Regiment' because of its leader, Colonel John McArthur.[296,297] Charles was initially assigned the rank of Corporal with the task of filling out reports because of his formal education. Enlistment and training for the 12th Illinois Infantry took place in Cairo, Illinois until September 1861. Sixteen-year-old Seth Jr., was inspired by his brother and wanted to do his part as well. On October 17th 1861, he enlisted in Ela Township, Lake County as a Bugler in the 9th Illinois Infantry, posing as an 18-year-old. Though they understood, the family worried about them both, and were relieved when the 9th Infantry met up with

---

[294] Illinois Civil War Muster and Descriptive Rolls Database. Illinois Civil War Muster and Descriptive Roles.
[295] Bill Pierce, interview by author, Village of Lake Zurich, Summer 1996.
[296] The Scottish regiment included several of Seth's friends.
[297] McArthur was affiliated with Excelsior Iron Works in Chicago and was a friend of Seth Paine.

the 12th in Paducah, Kentucky in September 1861—reuniting the brothers.

As his eldest sons headed to war, Seth considered how he could support the cause. At the age of 45 with no prior military experience, he was not a good candidate to be a soldier. Instead he reached out to his old friend Allan Pinkerton to see if his skills could support the Union cause elsewhere.[298]

******

That fall, Allan Pinkerton was in Washington D.C. serving in a unique capacity for President Lincoln. Pinkerton's security work protecting railroad shipments and connection with George B. McClellan had earned him a position supporting intelligence gathering for the Union. McClellan and Pinkerton had met through their mutual work on the railroads, when McClellan was with the Illinois Central Railroad in 1857.[299] In the early winter of 1860-61, one of Pinkerton's security associates operating between Baltimore and Philadelphia intercepted information about a plot to assassinate the President-elect on the way to

---

[298] Pinkerton, A. *The Spy of the Rebellion.* G.W. Carleton & Co., New York. 1883.
[299] Library of Congress McClellan Papers, Timeline and biography. George Brinton McClellan graduated from the United States Military Academy in 1842 and helped construct roads and bridges as part of his military service. McClellan had served as a career military officer, West Point alumnus and trainer, and had been in the Mexican War of 1847. After the Illinois Central Railroad, McClellan moved east to Ohio as part of the Ohio & Mississippi Railroad.

his inauguration.[300] Pinkerton brought the information to Lincoln's security team and was immediately hired to create an alternate transportation plan to keep Lincoln safe. After his inauguration, President Lincoln invited Pinkerton to Washington D.C. to work full-time with his security team.

Pinkerton established an office in Washington D.C. at 181 Pennsylvania Avenue near the foot of Capitol Hill. When Seth reached out to him, Pinkerton was actively looking for good men to fill positions ranging from local security in Washington D.C. to supporting the Union Intelligence Service. Knowing Seth's passion and skills firsthand, Pinkerton connected with local friends to find a position appropriate for Seth. There were a number of opportunities to assist the formerly enslaved in finding work in the region or in other Northern states. The detective agency also needed a good writer to put together reports on the ongoing war efforts, and there were congressmen to lobby to advance the plans to abolish slavery. None of these seemed to be quite the right fit for Seth's skills until Pinkerton heard about what was happening at the Washington Jail.

At the time, Pinkerton's friends were determining how to begin emancipation of enslaved people at the federal level. The District of

---

[300] Pinkerton National Detective Agency | History & Facts | Britannica. *History of the Pinkerton Detective Agency*. Seth served as one of Pinkerton's agents in Washington D.C. during the Civil War.

Columbia had strict 'Black Codes' allowing local constables and magistrates to arrest and detain men, women, and children they suspected could be freedom seekers until they could prove themselves otherwise. They would send them to the Washington Jail while they awaited proof of their status. Throughout 1861, local officers aggressively upheld these codes in the streets, markets, and homes in D.C. as the war progressed. When Union forces made their way through Southern states, formerly enslaved people flocked to D.C. They assumed they would be granted their freedom when they arrived after being liberated by the Union army, but they instead found a place in the Washington Jail. At its peak, the jail housed nearly 3,300 formerly enslaved.

On August 6th 1861 Congress passed the Federal Confiscation Act to protect the formerly enslaved from being arrested in D.C. under the Black Codes. "As the Senate met in extraordinary session from July 4 to August 6, 1861, one of the wartime measures it considered was the Confiscation Act, designed to allow the federal government to seize property, including slave property, being used to support the Confederate rebellion. The Senate passed the final bill on August 5th 1861, by a vote 24 to 11, and it was signed into law by President Lincoln the next day. Although this bill had symbolic importance, it had little effect on the rebellion or wartime negotiations." Unfortunately, the local constables, who were not necessarily Lincoln supporters, ignored the act and continued to jail black people coming into D.C. In September 1861, *Frank Leslie's Illustrated Newspaper* published a series on the deplorable prison conditions at the Washington Jail. Pinkerton sent word to Seth that he had the perfect job for him, and he started packing up his things for the journey.

The journey to Washington D.C. in September 1861 was vastly different from the trek Seth had made to Illinois from Vermont twenty-five years earlier. The railroads made travel faster and smoother particularly with the expansion of the Baltimore and Ohio Railroad.[301] Pinkerton guaranteed Seth's safety himself, assigning one of his detectives to keep Seth company on the many jaunts between rail lines. Leaving Illinois behind was no problem for Seth—he was anxious to serve his country, God, and humanity. This Seth was an older and wiser man than the one who left Vermont years earlier. As he traveled, Seth read the stories from *Frank Leslie's Illustrated Newspaper* and wondered, "how could it be that the same government that was elected on the basis of abolition could still be harboring freedom seekers as fugitives within the boundaries of the capital of the Union?" Seth was moved by the stories and hoped he would be able to help.

As soon as Seth arrived in Washington D.C., Pinkerton went to work

---

[301] The Martin F. O'Rourke Memorial Railroad Library at Bowie Tower, Maryland.

to get him access to the Washington Jail. He appealed directly to the jail's warden on October 17th 1861, with a request to send a private, prescreened reporter to formally document the conditions, talk to the prisoners, and have unrestricted conversations.[302] Because of the Leslie articles and the recent poor publicity, Pinkerton's appeal was accepted.

Seth wasted no time jumping into the task at hand. Walking into the Washington Jail, the sights, smells, and sounds reminded Seth of his own jail time. The conditions were not for the faint of heart.[303] The more he witnessed, the more he realized that these circumstances were far worse than those he had experienced in Illinois. Food, if there was any, was unrecognizable as edible, no privacy was afforded to any male or female, as they were jammed into cells in large groups where one could barely sit down. Children were mixed in the cells, and the smell implied that there was no sanitation standard being maintained. He was acutely conscious that his own experience did not compare to these atrocious conditions. The task at hand appealed to his compassion and like a bloodhound he resolved to complete it.

While preparing his report, Seth appealed to Ward Hill Lamon—chief U. S. Marshall, close friend of Lincoln, and overseer of the Washington Jail—to take care of the basic needs of the prisoners.

---

[302] National Archives Administration, Library of Congress, Pinkerton Agency Records, Box 44, Reel 1, #16574, Reports and Letters.
[303] The Washington Jail was on G street in Washington D.C. in 1861.

Butting heads with the large and boisterous Lamon, a known southern sympathizer, did not make his job any easier, but Seth enjoyed antagonizing and pestering Lamon with his demands. Through his own unique and determined style, Seth demanded the jail management provide cleaner conditions, heal the wounds of the sick, improve the food that barely sustained the prisoners, separate men and women, and move prisoners meeting certain criteria to other jails with better conditions. Seth worked for two weeks within the prison walls to improve conditions and presented a complete report on the conditions of the jail to Pinkerton on October 30th 1861.[304] Pinkerton passed the report on to his connections and sympathetic congressmen promptly to address the matter.

In the meantime, the press was also working to encourage emancipation. William Lloyd Garrison criticized Lincoln for not taking a stronger stance and sympathizing with the South. Suggesting he intended to restore the Union to its original state rather than to re-establish the country without slavery.[305]

Henry Wilson, a Senator from Massachusetts, presented Seth's report to the Senate on December 4th 1861, underscoring that, "slavery was morally wrong, all free people had a right to equal treatment before

---

[304] National Archives Records Administration, Library of Congress, Pinkerton Agency, Library of Congress, Box 44-45, Reel 1, Page 597.
[305] *Liberator.* September 6, 1861. Page 1.

the law, and the government should stand for freedom and equality, not slavery and oppression."[306] Senator John Hale seconded that position stating Congress had a duty "to look into the administration of justice in this District, and to see to it that those who have been ground to the earth heretofore may not be ground still more under your auspices." Other congressmen joined the call for better accountability from Lamon. Compared to the resistance Seth had found for prison reform in Illinois, his work with Pinkerton restored Seth's faith in humanity and his ability to affect real change.[307] His biographer recalled, "Seth Paine had hated man-stealing for a life-time and he followed like a sleuth-hound the sinuosity of management of the storehouse for slaves in Washington and at the end saw Liberty triumph, and the great work of National Emancipation begin in the District of Columbia."[308] With abolitionists collaborating together in D.C. Seth and others worked to garner additional support for the cause throughout the winter of 1861-1862.

Around April 8th 1862, Seth received word from Almira that both of his sons had survived the Battle of Shiloh in Tennessee, the bloodiest battle in the Civil War to date. However, Charles had shattered his leg

---

[306] Masure, Kate, Washington's Black Codes - The New York Times, NY Times Blogs, 12-7-2011.
[307] *Chicago Daily Tribune.* July 7, 1872. Page 5.
[308] *Chicago Daily Tribune,* July 7, 1872. Page 5.

and was heading home.³⁰⁹ Seth Jr. would continue on with the soldiers of the 9th Infantry. Seth and Almira exchanged letters discussing whether Seth should return to Lake Zurich or stay in D.C. Almira reassured him that Charles was in good hands, and Seth decided to remain in Washington D.C. to continue his work. The push to eradicate slavery in the District of Columbia was nearing success, and it felt premature to leave now. One year after the war began, President Lincoln signed the Compensated Emancipation Act on April 16th 1862 to formally emancipate the formerly enslaved in Washington D.C. and allow enslavers to be compensated for releasing them.³¹⁰

Seth sent word of this success back home to his family via telegram. They celebrated the victory with the hope that the war would end soon. Seth was grateful for his time in D.C. His progressive companions, like-minded collaboration, and potential for impact excited and humbled him. With this first effort accomplished, Seth looked for other ways to help Pinkerton. He quickly found his next task. Meanwhile, Seth's son Charles managed the family home in Lake Zurich as he recovered from his battle wound. His step-sister Permilia assisted with kindness and compassion, and she became his wife in 1862.³¹¹

---

[309] *Chicago Daily Tribune.* July 7, 1872. Page 26.
[310] The Civil War: The Senate's Story. Washington D.C. was the first place in the country to implement emancipation on April 16, 1862.
[311] Charles married Permilia in 1862.

Photo of *Pinkerton men in Cumberland Landing, Virginia, May 14, 1862*. James F. Gibson. Seth Paine is on the right, Allan Pinkerton is in the background. National Archives Records Administration, photo by James F. Gibson, #522914.jpg

Chapter 14

From Jail to the Battlefields; 1862

Lincoln tasked McClellan's army in January 1862 to protect the region south of Washington D.C. in an effort to advance the Union toward the Confederate capital of Richmond. The mission was called the Peninsula Campaign. From March to May 1862, the Union army creeped its way through Virginia.[312] Critics, including William Lloyd Garrison, claimed McClellan "deliberately slowed his military efforts in order to create the basis for stalemate and truce."[313] The pace of the advance was assumed to be orchestrated by Lincoln and McClellan, but the reality was that poor intelligence and difficult terrain was impeding their progress.

By May of 1862, McClellan's forces were struggling to protect Yorktown Virginia. Yorktown held importance for the Union forces, because of its historical significance from the end of the Revolutionary

---

[312] Davis, Major George B, U.S. Army, Perry Leslie J. Civilian Expert, Kirkley, Joseph W. Civilian Expert Capt. Calving D. Cowles, 23rd U. S. Infantry, *The Official Military Atlas of the Civil War,* The Fairfax Press, New York, 1983 reprint edition of the: *Atlas to Accompany the Official Records of the Union and Confederate Armies.* Published under the Direction of the Hons. Redfield, Proctor, Stephen B. Elkins and Daniel S. Lamont, Secretaries of War, by Maj. George B. Davis, U. S. Army et al. Washington: Government Printing Office, 1891-1895. The Peninsular Campaign ran from March 17-September 2, 1862.
[313] Mayer, H. *All on Fire, William Lloyd Garrison and the Abolition of Slavery.* St. Martin's Griffon, New York. 1998. Page 534.

War when American forces had coerced a surrender from the British there in 1781. While nearly 80 years had passed since the end of the Revolutionary War, the stories of Yorktown history were imprinted in the families of early Yankees. The secession works in Yorktown were an important way for the Confederate forces to protect Richmond from advances by sea between the York and the James Rivers. For nearly a month, the Battle of Yorktown had raged with little advancement on either side, even though history later revealed that the Union forces outnumbered the Confederates threefold. The Union's goal was to secure the peninsula between the rivers, as General George Washington had successfully done in 1771. McClellan brought troops in by land and backed them with river support from the ironclad *USS Monitor*, which had successfully suppressed the Confederate frigate *CSS Virginia* in March. Establishing a base at Fort Monroe on the lower tip of the peninsula, McClellan's hope to secure the southern capital of Richmond was hindered by General Johnston of the Confederate forces. McClellan frequently feared he was outnumbered and his miscalculations led to Confederate soldiers slipping through defenses and moving before the Union army could react.[314] McClellan appealed to Lincoln for reinforcement from Pinkerton and his team to help improve his intelligence reports.

---

[314] The Peninsula Campaign was focused on the area between the James and York Rivers.

In mid-May 1862, Lincoln assigned Pinkerton to work directly on the front lines of the Civil War with McClellan who had been recently promoted to General-in-Chief of the Army of the Potomac.[315] The Pinkerton team headed out from Washington D.C. to meet McClellan on the battlelines of the Peninsula Campaign. The assignment involved gathering and reporting intelligence to the General under the newly formed Union Intelligence Service.[316] Pinkerton saw the value in expanding his work beyond the Northern lines and hired his first formerly enslaved agent John Scobell, as well as one of his first female agents Kate Warne, to assist with gathering intelligence on the Confederate army. Pinkerton's operatives began by moving throughout the Southern states to infiltrate Southern strongholds and report back on key army details and confederate movements. While men like Scobell operated on the front lines, Pinkerton invited Seth along to write field reports, counter-espionage reports, and letters on Pinkerton's behalf.[317] Out of fear of interception by counter intelligence agents, Pinkerton signed his letters E.J. Allen.[318]

---

[315] Library of Congress. *Timeline of the Civil War*. 1862. The promotion came after the retirement of General Winfield Scott in the fall of 1861. McClellan had been leading the Army of Virginia as the Supreme Commander since January 1862.
[316] This was the start to what would eventually become the Secret Service.
[317] St. Lawrence University Law Library. Pryce Lewis photo from Box 2, Folder 10. *Pinkerton Men, with William Pinkerton (brother of Allan) and John Babcock*. Pryce Lewis describes Seth, "as one of the 'very reliable' Pinkerton men, though not one who made daring exploits. He wrote excellent reports."
[318] Pinkerton, A. *The Spy of the Rebellion*. G.W. Carleton & Co., New York. 1883.

Seth was not interested in the glory of war. He had never approved of violence or aggression. He preferred to resolve conflicts with reason. He had never owned weapons, but he was motivated to support the Union in his own way. Field reporting was not an easy task. As he reported operatives' findings, drafted daily reports, and helped the men in McClellan's army, he was a firsthand witness to the bloodiness of warfare. In his soul Seth felt that the Union must win the war because the evil of slavery was so unjust, but every day he spent in the field he longed for the war to end. To counter what he witnessed, he sought opportunities to pray over the injured soldiers. Seth also attempted to bring the soldiers together over meals, sharing wisdom and comfort in this time of struggle.

Pinkerton's intelligence team gathered data on the number of Confederate troops and their locations using reconnaissance balloons, information from captured prisoners, scouts in the field, and agents who were infiltrating enemy lines. One of McClellan's favorite Pinkerton men was John Babcock, a cartographer and architect from Chicago who created intricate maps using acquired intelligence. With the slow advance of McClellan's army, Babcock kept up with troop movements throughout the Spring. After a bloody battle at Williamsburg on May 5, Confederate General Johnston lost nearly 5,000 soldiers, forcing him to retreat towards Richmond and allowing the Union army to press forward towards Richmond.

The next couple of weeks saw the Union push Confederate troops further toward Richmond. After several skirmishes and aggressive actions, the Union troops were finally making slow and steady progress. There were several challenges due to the terrain—including earthworks where confederate soldiers hid and struck unexpectedly—and roadways that were blocked with felled trees. Small streams and landings, with spots where the Confederate army could hide small boats and bring additional troops ashore, were also challenging Union soldiers.

The heat and humidity of late May, as well as the advancing and retreating over this difficult landscape was impacting morale amongst the Union troops. To rally their spirits, Lincoln sent a number of motivational speakers to help inspire the men. One such speaker was J. B. Merwin, an old friend of Seth's. It had been six years since they had last seen each other when Merwin had presented on temperance at the Stable of Humanity. Merwin—a passionate speaker, frequent visitor, and advisor to Lincoln —brought news about the rest of the country and inspiring prose to encourage them in the midst of the toil of war.

At Seven Pines on May 31st, General Johnston attacked the Union army head-on and was wounded. He was quickly replaced by General Robert E. Lee. Lee proved to be a formidable opponent. He conducted aggressive offensive charges and succeeded in pushing the Union Army back to where they began. After a month of relentless attacks, including seven days of heavy fighting near Richmond (June 26–July 2nd 1862), the Union army retreated to the James River, officially ending the Peninsula campaign.

Seth witnessed the advances and retreats firsthand, lending assistance wherever he could from behind the front lines. The bloodshed and the mangled bodies made him consider leaving behind the brutality of war and heading for home many times. Buckets of bloody remains, the howling cries of wounded soldiers, and the general loss of morale among the men chilled Seth unmercifully.[319] Seth was not a commissioned officer and he could have left at any time, but his commitment to Pinkerton and the Union cause kept him there. Despite the rumors of Pinkerton's failures, Seth's loyalty to him was unwavering. As long as Pinkerton needed him, he would stay.

1862 became a pivotal year for both Pinkerton and McClellan. Intelligence was provided to the Union by the U. S. Military telegraph, with twenty-three operators manning all major headquarters. Partnering with them were classical Signal Corps operations on Navy ships and on land. One of the first telegraphic lines had been installed along the Eastern coastline leading from Delaware down to Washington D.C.

---

[319] Graphic representation and information was informed by the National Museum of Civil War Medicine in Frederick, Maryland.

creating a 300-mile direct link for communication. The telegraph utilized morse code to send messages, but provided nearly instant communication for the first time. Pinkerton's field intelligence team included Pinkerton himself, fourteen operatives, and a number of bureau agents. An additional team of ten agents remained in Washington D.C. to provide counter intelligence. Despite increasing criticism that information gathered by Pinkerton's team was inaccurate and misleading, his data was strategic and mostly correct. The best example was a report after the Seven Days Battle ended July 2nd 1862, "of Lee's 39 infantry brigades, 36 were fully identified; 6 other brigades were listed, 3 of which, had their correct names been known, probably would have raised the 36 to a complete 39. And the 211 regiments that were listed included every one of the 178 regiments Lee had."[320] The over-estimation by approximately 20% in the favor of the Confederate army often prompted an early retreat by the Union. The Confederacy had their own operatives. After the war it was discovered that General John Magruder of the Confederacy would strategically march the same men time and again across the same clearing and back into woodlands to suggest to their opponents a larger number of soldiers than he actually possessed. These factors potentially delayed what might have been an early end to the war.

---

[320] Fishel, E. C. *The Secret War for the Union, The Untold Story of Military Intelligence in the Civil War.* Houghton Mifflin Company, New York. 1996. Page 144.

Adding to speculation, a rumor circulated in late spring that Pinkerton was ill of an unknown cause serious enough to curtail his best performance.[321] Information from behind enemy lines was complicated by the arrest of several of Pinkerton's agents who had infiltrated the southern lines. The first two agents arrested were of British descent, Pryce Lewis and John Scully. They had been sent to find intelligence from Baltimore secessionists who were in Richmond. Someone in the street recognized them as Pinkerton agents and reported them. The men were interrogated. Later accounts claimed that Lewis and Scully turned in Timothy Webster, another Pinkerton agent.[322] The arrest of Webster, however, saved Lewis and Scully from execution. They were held in the southern prison called Castle Thunder in the spring of 1862. Webster was condemned to the gallows although Pinkerton and a member of McClellan's staff attempted to intercede on his behalf under laws of leniency toward rebel spies, they were unsuccessful.[323] The tragedy had an emotional impact on Pinkerton who considered his agents his family. Seth was concerned for his friend and the stresses he faced with his operatives in captivity. He watched and listened to the drama unfold from Pinkerton's field headquarters with a pain in his heart at the

---

[321] Fishel, E.C. *The Secret War for the Union, The Untold Story of MIlitary Intelligence in the Civil War.* Houghton Mifflin Company, New York. 1996. Page 147.
[322] This charge was denied by Lewis and Scully and caused them great distress.
[323] Pinkerton, A. *The Spy of the Rebellion.* G.W. Dillingham Publishers, New York. 1883. Chapter 36, starting at page 530.

helplessness and bloodshed they all shared.

Whenever he could, Seth sent word home to Almira to let her know how he was doing. He worked hard to keep spirits high among the men, and he trudged forward with them wherever they ventured. After the Peninsular Campaign, a new commander was assigned to the southern branch of the Union Army, Major-General Henry Halleck. Halleck, among other commanders, faced General Lee, who was determined to break the morale of the Union army while aggressively advancing his troops through Western Virginia to Maryland in an effort to surround Washington D.C. and weaken the northern railroads.

With Halleck covering the peninsula, McClellan and Pinkerton retreated to defend D.C. Pinkerton was a trusted confidant of McClellan and despite the criticism and speculation about his abilities, Pinkerton was requested to accompany the Union army on their next assignment to defend Northern Virginia and Western Maryland. Army intelligence in these campaigns coordinated between information gathered, mapped the size and location of the enemy, and supported leadership to determine their next move. After skirmishes, battles or other contact with the enemy, army intelligence reported on what they saw, documented maneuvers that worked well, and strategized to avoid making the same mistakes prior to next encounter. All the intelligence gathered and the strategies utilized were passed on to incoming general field commanders to translate, interpret, and utilize as well.

Confederate armies were circling Washington D. C. and McClellan successfully defended Southern Mountain and Crampton's Gap in Maryland by reclaiming the area from the Confederates on September 14th 1862.[324] His army however failed to protect Harper's Ferry on September 15th, losing nearly 12,000 soldiers to the Confederacy as prisoners. In an effort to recoup the loss of Harper's Ferry, McClellan's troops raced to defend the next major town north, Antietam.[325] Antietam was located along the northern railroad line where Union soldiers—struggling with low morale—faced determined Confederate troops.

McClellan took up camp at the home of the Pry family due east of Antietam bridge along an oxbow in Antietam creek. The home stood up on the ridge above the bridge and adjacent fields and afforded a view of what would become the battlefield at Antietam on September 17th. Through providence or good intelligence, a "copy of Lee's special Orders Number 191 fell into Union hands."[326] The secret orders

---

[324] Maranzani, B. Why do some Civil War battles have two names? - HISTORY. Crampton's Gap was also called Burkettsville. Union army's tended to name battle sites after waterways or natural features and Confederate army's named them after towns or other man-made structures.

[325] The Battle of Crampton's Gap | American Battlefield Trust. The small battle was a win prior to the loss of Harper's Ferry which inspired McClellan's army to continue on to Antietam, also called Sharpsburg.

[326] Woodworth, S. E.,Winkle, K.J. *Atlas of the Civil War.* Page 138.

outlined plans to split the Confederate army and allow for some vulnerability at Antietam. What followed was a full day of fighting, with each side moving against each other resulting in devastation. From their headquarters at the Pry home above the battlefield, the team of commanders and Pinkerton's men watched the terror unfold along Antietam creek. When the day was done, the roadways ran red with blood from troops on both sides.

At the time, Anteietam was considered a win for the Union.[327] With 23,000 soldiers dead, wounded or unaccounted for, it was penned the bloodiest battle in the Civil War's history.[328] Union Soldier George Allen described the local field hospital, "comrades with wounds of all conceivable shapes were brought in and placed side by side as thick as they could lay, and the bloody work of amputation commenced."[329]

When Lincoln visited the remnants of the battlefield between October 1st–4th, recovery efforts were ongoing. Seth was part of the team that met with Lincoln during that visit. Meeting Lincoln was a

---

[327] Battle of Antietam Begins - HISTORY. Antietam was a turning point in the Civil War.
[328] National Park Service U.S. Department of the Interior. *Antietam National Battlefield*. History reports the results at Antietam were considered a stalemate, rather than a victory for either side in Civil War history.
[329] National Park Service U.S. Department of the Interior. *Antietam National Battlefield*. The antietam field hospital was where Clara Barton was christened the Angel of the Battlefield by the local surgeon, Charles Dunn, after she brought lanterns and food to the site following the battle.

thrilling, but bittersweet moment for Seth. What impressed Seth the most was Lincoln's humanity and kindness towards the people he met. The meeting was somber on the ridge overlooking the battlefield. Witnesses described it as a, "landscape turned red."[330] Even after two weeks, the fields still held the remains of soldiers from both sides who were killed in the battle. The town itself was also impacted. "For the people of Sharpsburg, the battle and presence of thousands of soldiers caused sickness and death from disease, and great property damage."[331] It may have been considered a win for the Union at the time, but for the men involved there was no victory.

The battle of Antietam proved to be the downfall of General McClellan. Lincoln reported, "I said I would remove him if he let Lee's army get away from him, and I must do so."[332] McClellan was quickly replaced with General Ambrose Burnside. News media proclaimed that, "George McClellan, the innovator who gave the nation its first intelligence bureau, lost his command partly because of an intelligence failure."[333] McClellan, Pinkerton, and their teams retreated to

---

[330] Meacham, J. *Smithsonian Civil War, Inside the National Collection.* Smithsonian Books. Washington, D.C. Page 172.
[331] National Park Service U.S. Department of the Interior. *Antietam National Battlefield.* Summary of local impacts.
[332] Meacham, J. *Smithsonian Civil War, Inside the National Collection.* Smithsonian Books. Washington, D.C. Page 172.
[333] Fishel, Edwin C. *The Secret War for the Union, The Untold Story of MIlitary Intelligence in the Civil War.* Houghton Mifflin Company, New York. 1996. Page 255.

Washington D.C. with a dark cloud of misinformation following them. The battle at Antietam was however an early turning point in the war and served as a catalyst for emancipation. President Lincoln declared on September 22nd that "on the first day of January . . . all persons held as slaves within any State, or designated part of a State, the people whereof shall then be in rebellion against the United States shall be then, thenceforward, and forever free."[334]

Pinkerton's detectives who were with him through Antietam left the battlefields and returned to Washington D.C. John Babcock, the architect and cartographer, resigned from Pinkerton's service and took over leadership of the Union Intelligence Service under General Burnside. Pinkerton spent the remainder of the war investigating insurance claims, working on civil crimes, and solving fraud related to the New Orleans cotton trade and the railroads. For a while, Seth remained with Pinkerton in Washington D.C. wrapping up reports and reaching out to operatives still in the field or who were captured by the Confederacy, including Pryce Lewis, who was still behind Confederate lines in the Castle Thunder Prison in Richmond.[335] Seth felt this was his way of still contributing something to the war effort. He needed time to

---

[334] National Archives Records Administration. Quote by President Abraham Lincoln in the Emancipation Proclamation. September 22, 1863.
[335] St. Lawrence University Law Library Pryce Lewis Collection. Letter from Pryce Lewis collection, Box 2, Folder 1. Dated December 12, 1862.

process the horrors he had witnessed firsthand at Antietam.

Pryce Lewis was eventually released by the Confederacy because of his British citizenship. He went back to work for Pinkerton during the war as a bailiff and special detective at the Washington D. C. Prisons. After the war, he moved to Chicago where he formed his own detective agency. Because he never became a U.S. citizen, he had difficulty later in life and was not eligible for a pension. Lewis and Seth remained friends and reconnected during his time in Chicago.[336]

After wrapping up his final report, with little else left to keep him in D.C. Seth decided it was time to return to Lake Zurich. Christmas of 1862 was almost here, and he needed his family. He boarded the train from Washington, D.C., bid farewell to his friends, and headed home.

---

[336] Information from the Pryce Lewis Collection at St. Lawrence University Law Library, donated to the University by the St. Lawrence County Historical Association from Harriet Schoen of Massena.

William Pinkerton, Seth Paine, John Babcock and unknown agents during the Civil War, 1862, photo from St. Lawrence University Law Library, Pryce Lewis photo from Box 2, Folder 10

Chapter 15

Back to A New Reality; 1863-1865

When Seth first laid eyes on the little town he founded after the long journey home, his heart filled with sadness and relief. He was happy to be home, but troubled by the horrors he had witnessed on the battlefield. Returning to his simple life seemed like a dream far removed from the Union-Confederate conflict in the east. Seth and his son Charles, who was still incapacited by his leg injury, compared experiences. Almira attempted to cheer everyone up with warm meals, good companionship, and keeping the house comfortable. Sitting around the dinner table was bittersweet that winter. For a long time after returning from Pinkerton's service, he struggled to realign his moral compass. He felt trapped by his mental anguish. As the cold Chicago weather settled in, the business of the town coaxed Seth back into focus. By the time spring arrived, his family's love and support softened the rough edges of the walls he had built to protect himself during the war, and in the end they came tumbling down.

Seth's return to Lake Zurich was met with the reality of conventional life during wartime. The war had impacted economic prospects for residents in the Northern states in a variety of different ways. Families worried about their loved ones and they gathered every day at noon at the Stable of Humanity where Mr. Dresser, the Headmaster of the Lake Zurich academy, would read the latest news of the war.[337] Women formed war relief societies to help the war effort, providing bandages and clothing to send to the front lines. Baseball teams were formed to raise money and provide entertainment for the locals in deference to Lincoln, who favored the game.[338]

The strength of the northern economy was its railroads and industry. With his entire family out of work, Seth picked up employment again with Gates Iron Works on Canal Street and Adams Street and rented a home on Halsted Street nearby in a neighborhood called Chicago's West Side. Seth's connections with Gates and Pinkerton garnered his stepson, Edwin, a job with American Express as an assistant clerk for the railroads before he enlisted in 1864.[339] For Seth, the work at Gates did not last long. He returned to Lake Zurich in late 1863 to serve as the Lake Zurich Postmaster.[340] Nearly 20 years after he had last filled the role, he worked once again in the community center he built.

Returning home, Seth found that the steady reality of the post office, Union store, and the Stable of Humanity brought order to his days and

---

[337] Winters, E.W. *Memories of Edwin W. Winters*. Self-published for private family collection. 1922. Courtesy of the Ela Township Historical Society collection. Page 28.
[338] American Civil War for Kids. *American Civil War, Civilian Life in the North*.
[339] Winters, E.W. *Memories of Edwin W. Winters*. Self published for private family collection. 1922. Courtesy of the Ela Township Historical Society collection.
[340] *U.S. Register of Civil, military and Naval Service 1863-1959*. Page 342.

his mind. As the war continued, Seth and others established the Lake Zurich Home Guards composed of men and boys too young to enlist who would be ready to protect the homefront if needed. The Home Guards drilled every Saturday on the prairie or in the Stable of Humanity, they had uniforms and appeared like real soldiers."[341]

The peace in Lake Zurich seemed like an oasis as the Civil War continued to unsettle most of the country, but it was not without its challenges. Smallpox broke out amongst the lodgers at the Stable of Humanity in the summer of 1863, effectively depopulating the site. It was believed to have been brought in by a soldier whose family lived in the Stable. Lewis Brockway recalled, "every room in the building was soon vacated. The entire family, except the soldier's wife, had smallpox, and one child died. Mr Whipple, who taught at the public school and lived across from the old Paine house, erected a large shelf outside of one of the windows and placed groceries and provisions on this shelf and the wife took them in. When the children died he placed a casket on the shelf, and the woman, with the aid of the doctor, placed the body in the casket and put it out on the shelf again."[342]

---

[341] Brockway, L. O. *History of Lake Zurich*. Transcription of the address to the Lake Zurich Community Women's Club by Brockway on September 25, 1930. The presentation was copied and edited by Ray Syverson of the Ela Township Historical Society. Page 10.

[342] Brockway, L. O. *History of Lake Zurich*. Transcription of an address to Lake Zurich Community Women's Club by Brockway September 25, 1930. The presentation was copied and edited by Ray Syverson of the Ela Township Historical Society. Page 10.

The Civil War continued and the sons of community members who were off in the war fighting were often missing or mourned. Finally, in April of 1865 General Lee surrendered at Appomattox, effectively ending the main conflicts of the war, though battles in Texas and states would take more time to resolve. When President Lincoln was assassinated on April 14th 1865, the community of Lake Zurich mourned alongside the rest of the country. Seth felt the loss deeply and mourned him as if he were a beloved family member. Having met Lincoln on the battlefield at Antietam, Seth could not understand why anyone would want to kill such an honorable man.

That summer, Seth Jr. finally returned home. However, the celebration was short-lived for the Paines when Seth's eldest son Charles died in September 1865 at the age of 24, from the injuries he sustained in the war. Seth buried Charles next to his mother Frances, and grandmother Fanny, in Evergreen Cemetery in Barrington. Two months after his death Charles' wife Permilia, gave birth to Seth's first granddaughter Minnie. Seth was struck by how even after tragedy, new life begins again.

Like many others at the end of the Civil War, Seth became overwhelmed with financial strain. Barely recovering from the last smallpox outbreak at the Stable, Seth woke up one cold night in 1866 to the sound of fire alarm bells in the village. He threw on shoes and a coat, and ran out to help, but he knew before he made it to town that the fire was serious. He could feel the heat of the fire from blocks away. When he stopped, he saw the Stable of Humanity was engulfed in flames. Among the crowd of onlookers drawn from their beds, he could only watch as the fire blazed and within an hour, only a small pile of rubble simmering in the snow remained. After nearly two decades of service to the community, the Stable of Humanity had been turned to ash.

As Seth and his neighbors examined the debris the following morning, he felt only a weariness in his soul. "What now?" He thought to himself. He kicked the rubble, seeing the remains of his entire life's work in the ashes covering his boots. He was thankful that no one had been hurt, as he listened to the comforting words of his neighbors and friends. "You can always rebuild," someone suggested, but he knew his vision for a Fourier Utopia was over. The poignancy of the loss shook Seth. After all he had experienced in the war and the recent loss of Charles, he could not imagine starting over in what had been the perfect location for his family so many years prior. He dropped his head, lowered his eyes, and walked home defeated.

The fire was the final sign that the time had come for Seth to leave his beautiful little town. Seth had outgrown Lake Zurich and his original vision. New leadership and a fresh generation of residents were rebuilding after the war had taken their sons and fathers. They had big plans for the sprawling countryside, shifting their focus to farming the land on a larger scale now that they could ship their produce to Chicago using the railroads. The rapid expansion of railroads had brought small spurs to Lake Zurich and new ideas about harvesting ice from the lake, expanding roadways, and commerce throughout the region. Most communities were reinventing themselves as they rebuilt after the war, but a restlessness had gripped Seth since the war ended. Political sentiments had shifted again and the reconstruction of post-war America was very different from what had existed prior to the war. This was enough to convince Seth to move his family to the city of Chicago permanently in early 1866. "Surely," he thought, "I will be of some value in Chicago, or I'll die trying."

On his last morning in Lake Zurich, he stood at the edge of the lake facing the rising sun. His family and their belongings were loaded on the wagons ready to move to the city. Seth thought about all the memories he had made in this place and who he was. At fifty, he had already lost many loved ones, witnessed the atrocities of war, and nearly lost his fortune. He wondered where and how he would recover and protect his family. His wife, Almira, found him on the shoreline. As she put her arms around him to comfort him, she was impressed by his dedication, unshaken faith and endless determination. She knew that they would recover. Seth was like no man she had ever known before, and his resilience and fortitude inspired her every day. He looked down at her and smiled, "Let's go Almira. Chicago awaits."

Photo from Chicago History Museum Public Domain photographs. The Woman's Home in Chicago, Erected 1868, 1869 on W. Jackson corner Halsted. Chicago, Residences, Exteriors, 1888, Wooden sidewalks still standing in 1888, There were gas street lamps. Document #G1994.0247. 39-5-163.

Chapter 16

Chicago's West Side; 1866-1871

Between 1850 and 1865 Chicago's population blossomed with the completion of the Illinois-Michigan Canal (1848) and the expansion of the railroads.[343] Chicago became an important gateway to the west and a hub for exchange of goods and opportunities in the midst of post-Civil War reconstruction in 1866. Chicago was divided into wards and the West Side included all lands to the west of the South branch of the Chicago River, with the north and south boundaries approximately defined by the railroad feeding into the city. From Chicago's early days this western side of the city had evolved from open prairie to working class tenements and industrial buildings in only 30 years.

After all he had endured, Seth had lost his taste for commercial business. Seth felt that the city could use more social efforts, particularly on the West side, and he could not shake his desire to help. Seth had $9,000 in his pocket and an unrelenting will to do good. Once again he looked to his well worn Bible for guidance. The Book of James reminded him that, "religion that God our Father accepts as pure and faultless is this: to visit orphans and widows in their distress, and to

---

[343] Dreyfus, B. W. *The City Transformed, Railroads and Their Influence on the Growth of Chicago in the 1850s.* Copyright 1995.

keep oneself from being polluted by the world" James, 1:27. As the son of a widow himself, he remembered how lucky his family had been to have the support of others during that challenging time. Seth was determined to move forward with a plan to help Chicago's West side.

Chicago had a large population of immigrants from around the world by 1866. Famines, factory closings, and world events had led to an influx of immigrant populations to the United States seeking sanctuary and work. Chicago's rapid growth and ample opportunities attracted many to work on the railroads, canals, and ancillary industries. The immigration process was rife with tragedy, leaving many women seeking work to support their families during a time when many jobs were unavailable to women. Women were perceived as unhireable in most industries, even if they possessed valuable skills. As an added risk, homeless widows and single women were particularly vulnerable to exploitation. These women needed a way to find training, work, counseling, and safe housing. Seth compassionately moved forward to find the funds, leverage his social connections, and drum up support to help these women.

Seth envisioned establishing a home for these women that would be a sanctuary for them. He knew personally that sometimes all a person needed to get their feet under them was a place to call home. He pictured this home being the catalyst for change and advancement, the difference between desperation and success for generations of women. Seth set out to raise additional funds, using his own money as a starting-point. The vision in his mind soon became a reality with the help of other Chicago progressives. Seth did not envision simply a boarding house for women but a real home from where they would find what they needed to succeed. The women would be entirely supported, with training opportunities, sanctuary, encouragement, and clothing, if they needed it.

Seth's team of supporters included his good friend P. W. Gates, Reverend Robert Collyer of the Unitarian Church, and Reverend William Henry Ryder, who led St. Paul's Universalist Church of Chicago.[344,345] Reverend Collyer agreed to provide Seth with counsel and guidance and offered the support of the church's women's aid society to help find tenants. Seth knew Reverend Ryder from his Underground Railroad days. When Seth reached out to him about this project, Reverend Ryder was running an industrial school for black children in Chicago which he founded just after the war. Also joining the formation team were Seth's wife Almira and step-daughter Permilia who provided their own experience as widowed women. Together his team refined Seth's vision for the West side and what would be called,

---

[344] Reverend Robert Collyer was a former Methodist minister who had formed the 1st and 2nd Unitarian Churches in Chicago. He was an abolitionist and supporter of women's suffrage.
[345] *Chicago Daily Tribune.* July 7, 1872.

the Woman's Home of Chicago.

The team found a vacant lot adjacent to an existing home near the corner of Halsted and Jackson Streets. Here, Seth modeled the design for the home after the Stable of Humanity in Lake Zurich. A reporter described Seth's process in 1871 saying, "Mr. Paine first put in his own little property, then obtained a load of stone from one, a load of lumber from another, glass from a third, and so on, until all that he required was gradually accumulated, and the accommodations from time to time enlarged as means permitted."[346] The two buildings took nearly two years to finance and build.

When construction was completed between 1867–1868, the property featured two buildings, a sizable play yard, and a garden surrounded by a grapevine covered pergola. The first building was a three-story rehabilitated boarding house featuring balconies on the front facade and a dormer and basement that was half a city block in depth. The second and newer building—also made of wood—was four stories tall with a brick facade, large basement, and a front entry secured by a wooden double door. News of the Women's Home of Chicago spread across the country quickly. One article out of Pittsburgh commented on their shock that a young woman who was not yet twenty was hired to paint

---

[346] *Chicago Evening Mail.* Thursday January 18, 1871.

the interior?[347]

The Women's Home of Chicago gave the women the option of paying rent on a sliding scale depending on their income level, a revolutionary idea at the time. The press criticized Seth for establishing a charity for women unable to provide for themselves.[348] Seth had learned his lesson about the media, and ignored them. To Seth's delight, with the local churches' help, women soon filled the rooms to capacity—with 140 women living in the home by 1870. Residents originated from countries as far away as Egypt and from states as close as Wisconsin.[349] Most of the women worked in the garment industry, as secretaries, bookkeepers, telegraph operators, or as laundresses. In exchange for their rent, they had access to meals and a telegraph. A few children resided in the home including Seth's granddaughter Minnie. The entire Paine family and a few old friends also found residence in the buildings.

One tenant remarked that Seth, "not only gave all he possessed of this world's good, but what is far more valuable, his heart, his health, his increasing labors, to the industry and worth of the working women of Chicago to be self-supporting, not a charitable asylum where their

---

[347] *Pittsburgh Daily Post*. August 21, 1869. Page 3.
[348] Halsey, John J. *A History of Lake County, Illinois,* Chicago, Illinois: Roy S. Bates, 1912, page 273.
[349] 1870 Federal Census records.

self-respect would be wounded by a painful sense of obligation."[350] In the Women's Home of Chicago, Seth had finally found his mission for humanity.

As sustaining financing fell into place and more women came through the doors, Seth knew that he was exactly where he needed to be. Social reform for women was an issue dear to Seth after the Women's Suffrage movement began in earnest with Elizabeth Cady Stanton's conference in 1848 at Seneca Falls, New York and he was pleased to see it in action.[351] Seth understood that progress in the women's movement, like the abolitionist and temperance movements would be slow, but he felt it would ultimately succeed. Social reform and women's advocacy was advancing around the world and Seth was ready to stand at the forefront here in America. Instead of promoting his women's program using the media, Seth worked quietly with local sponsors to grow the effort organically. This method proved to be effective for him. Not only did the Women's Home of Chicago save hundreds of women from living on the streets, but the home ultimately supported and encouraged them to achieve their own independence and advance their careers.

An investigative reporter described the home in detail in 1871,

---

[350] *Chicago Daily Tribune*. July 1, 1870. Page 3, column 4.
[351] Hansan, J.E. *National Expansion and Reform 1815 – 1880 in: Colonial and Post-Revolutionary Era, Eras in Social Welfare History.*

several years after its construction, "the sleeping-rooms are not small by any means. Each room contains two wardrobes, closets, and two beds. There are ten bathrooms in the building. I took a warm bath and I felt it, indeed, to be a great luxury. As we passed through the library, reception room, parlor, kitchen, and wash-house, I thought how delightful it would be, how conducive to intellectual, aesthetic, and spiritual culture it would be if an engine could be introduced to do all the heating."[352] Seth had found an engineer to design a water heating system for the entire property, with a boiler in the basement to provide hot water to all the bathrooms like a 'tea-kettle'. Almira Paine functioned as the hostess on the reporters' tour, hoping to help the world see that the Woman's Home of Chicago was not just a hovel for poor women, but a truly reformatory home for those in need. The reporter remarked that both Almira and Permilia were kind and gracious hosts to the reporters and the tenants of the home alike.

One of the traditions that Seth introduced in the Women's Home of Chicago was his treasured family dinner. Every Sunday evening all would gather for lively conversation, Bible reading, and communal discussions around a series of tables in the dining room, like Seth had done with his own family for over 55 years.

One evening after dinner, Seth sat on the porch of the Women's

---

[352] *Chicago Evening Mail.* January 18, 1871.

Home reflecting on his life. Seth considered this home the most beautiful he had ever created for himself. He felt a chill pass over him that reminded him of the cold prison floor of Bridewell. He recalled how his body had been weakened and his mind strengthened by that experience. In many ways, his life had felt like an unending struggle and weariness often overtook him physically and spiritually. He could see how each and every event that had shaped his life had brought him to this moment. He was tired, but peaceful. He coughed, unaware that bacteria was beginning to take over his lungs. It would not be until 1882 when the bacillus, *Mycobacterium tuberculosis,* or tuberculosis would be officially identified by Dr. Robert Koch.[353] Though not yet diagnosed, Seth had a sense that he was approaching the end of his life.

---

[353] History | World TB Day | TB | CDC. Centers for Disease Control, it is estimated that 1 in 7 people died from tuberculosis prior to the discovery of the bacillus.

Chicago Fire community flyer. 1871. Public domain records.

Chapter 17

Consumed; 1871-1872

On October 8th 1871, the landscape of the city of Chicago was forever changed by a fire that started in a barn on DeKoven Street. Later dubbed The Great Chicago Fire, the flames spread quickly through the city to the north and the east. After 24 hours much of the city was reduced to ashes, with 17,500 buildings gone and an estimated 300 people dead.[354] The homes of nearly 300,000 people were lost.[355] Charity poured in from around the world to support the city and help rebuild after the fire.

The fire spared the Women's Home of Chicago and much of the west side, but only by a few blocks as if a wind from the southwest blew just past to protect it. Seth and the residents at the Woman's Home of Chicago, watched the city burn from across the river helplessly. As people poured across the remaining bridges at Lake and Adams Streets, the Women's Home of Chicago opened its doors to help.

Reverend Collyer was at the front lines of assistance and relief efforts in the city. He said, "I think that in these weeks the good women of our city have already won the crown, and the angels have sung their

---

[354] National Geographic. The Chicago Fire of 1871 and the 'Great Rebuilding'.
[355] Encyclopedia of Chicago. Fire of 1871. A large part of the devastation was that the business district was in ruins.

praises. They have done such work as men never could have done; they have been as steadfast and calm through all the terrible scenes as great captains who know the whole fate of an army lies in their hands. They not only worked to save their own children, sisters, brothers, mothers, fathers but any who happened to come in their way."[356] Rebuilding began right away and many of the displaced found temporary homes in the city. Those willing to work were transported to suburban farms to work as farm hands. While industrial buildings were rebuilt, orphan trains brought hundreds of children to the suburbs for adoption. The Great Chicago Fire unified the city in a way that Seth had never seen and the event filled him with bittersweet admiration of the collective power of people. The newspapers concluded that the city would survive. "In three days after the fire there was no one selfish enough to complain of his individual losses, nor any one weak enough to doubt the reconstruction and on a grander scale, of this great marvel of the world."[357]

A few weeks after the fire in early November 1871, Seth sat under the pergola as the autumn cold enveloped the city. He always enjoyed the change of season, watching the leaves drop from the trees, and the garden colors change. The heaviness in his lungs was persistent now.

---

[356] Sheahan, J.W., Upton, G.P. *History of the Great Conflagration.* Union Publishing Co. Chicago, Illinois. 1871. Page 313.
[357] Sheahan, J.W., Upton, G.P. *History of the Great Conflagration.* Union Publishing Co. Chicago, Illinois. 1871. Page 329.

Reflecting on how his life had not gone as he expected, he realized that this is the very essence of life; it is beautiful and ugly, and scary and real, all at the same time. "The best we can do is be ourselves in the end," he said to the trees. Seth had always wanted to be an authentic source of light and hope to the world. Much of his disappointment in people was around the facade, the artificiality, that so many created for themselves. He never expected how pervasive it would be, even after years of witnessing it in action. However he found that when the facade was peeled back, so many people were not who they professed to be. Seth's upbringing had taught him to be the same as the person he presented to the world. 'To talk the talk and walk the walk' was the example set by his father and grandfather before him. He chuckled aloud as he thought about the trials in his life and felt a sharp pain in his chest as he struggled to catch his breath. He went back inside and wearily collapsed into his favorite chair. Almira passed him and called the doctor at once.

Doctors confirmed that he had consumption, sometimes called the wasting disease. Prior to the discovery of the bacteria, tuberculosis was simply called consumption because it began with cold symptoms and spread to other organs effectively consuming a person. Almira and Permilia gathered around trying to convince themselves and Seth that he could fight this infection. Seth allowed them to fuss, but he knew his time was drawing near. Some people struggled for years with consumption but for Seth the struggle would only last about eight months. Those who witnessed Seth's decline, could only watch helplessly as he struggled to breathe. He would spend hours in his favorite chair in the front parlor watching the comings and goings of his family and the women at the home. His family worked to keep him as comfortable as possible, with visitors and old friends stopping by regularly, but Seth could see the discomfort on their faces as they spoke to him, reflecting his own decline back at him.

He spent his last few days in his favorite chair. Trapped by the prison of his heavy lungs, Seth lost himself deep in thought. He hoped he had made his family proud in his lifetime. He knew his story would go unwritten since his righteousness had upset too many people in his day. He felt a sense of humor that he had been anointed to help people like himself, whose stories would also never be told. He thought about the freedom seekers he had assisted, the prisoners in Washington D.C., the men who had died on the battlefield, and the women in this home. He looked forward to seeing his family again; his grandfather, grandmother, father, mother, his first wife Frances, and his son Charles who had preceded him in death. His faith had taught him that heaven would be the sweetest home of all. He was not afraid. In front of his chair on the wall was a framed needlepoint that said, "God Bless our

Home" and those were the last words he spoke to his wife.[358] Seth died on Friday June 7th 1872, at the age of 56.

Until the end of his life, Seth's family believed that he would recover. The family had spent all of their money in establishing the Woman's Home of Chicago, and they never discussed where to bury him or how to handle his affairs if he passed. Almira sought the counsel of Reverend Collyer and other friends to determine how to address Seth's funeral and on-going care of the home. The complicated journey to bury Seth in Barrington with his first wife, son, and mother would be too much to ask others to help fund.[359] John Bryan, who owned Graceland Cemetery in Chicago, had known Seth for years and wanted him to be laid to rest in the city where he had had such an impact. Bryan donated a space for him to be buried there.

Seth's funeral was held on June 9th. He was laid in an open casket in the front parlor of the Woman's Home of Chicago. The news reported that hundreds of mourners came to pay their respects and there were few dry eyes in the house.[360] The eulogies presented at Seth's funeral reflected an array of supporters from different denominations. William

---

[358] *Chicago Daily Tribune*. Funeral Obsequies: Services Over the Remains of Seth Paine, the Founder of the Woman's Home. June 10, 1872.
[359] His second wife's mother Elizabeth Goodhue is also buried with the Paines in Evergreen Cemetery in Barrington.
[360] *Chicago Daily Tribune*. Funeral Obsequies: Services Over the Remains of Seth Paine, the Founder of the Woman's Home. June 10, 1872.

Henry Ryder, the preacher at St. Paul's Universalist Church in Chicago, said, "he had a generous heart, was a high-minded, self-sacrificing man. Who was earnest, eloquent, and impressive and his charity knew no bounds. He asked God to bless the home, and permit no harm to come to it."[361] Reverend Collyer followed with his own tribute, "Mr. Paine, he had come to know as one of the noblest men the grain of his soul ever met. His thoughts did not seem to have a practical tendency but were surging and boiling in his heart. He listened with ever-growing reverence and love and on one occasion it seemed to him that he was listening to one of the prophets of God."[362] In the minds of his friends and family, Seth had been a remarkable man who had lived a remarkable life.

It took around forty-five minutes to traverse the eight miles through the city from the Woman's Home of Chicago to Graceland Cemetery in the Lakeview neighborhood. The horse-drawn caisson led the parade through the streets where Seth had spent so much of his life. He was buried in good company amongst family and friends who preceded him in death and those that would eventually be interred there.[363]

---

[361] *Chicago Daily Tribune.* Funeral Obsequies: Services Over the Remains of Seth Paine, the Founder of the Woman's Home. June 10, 1872.
[362] *Chicago Daily Tribune.* Funeral Obsequies: Services Over the Remains of Seth Paine, the Founder of the Woman's Home. June 10, 1872.
[363] Some of Seth's other friends buried at Graceland include: Charles Volney-Dyer, James Collins, and Allan Pinkerton. His sister Jane Paine and her family are also laid to rest there.

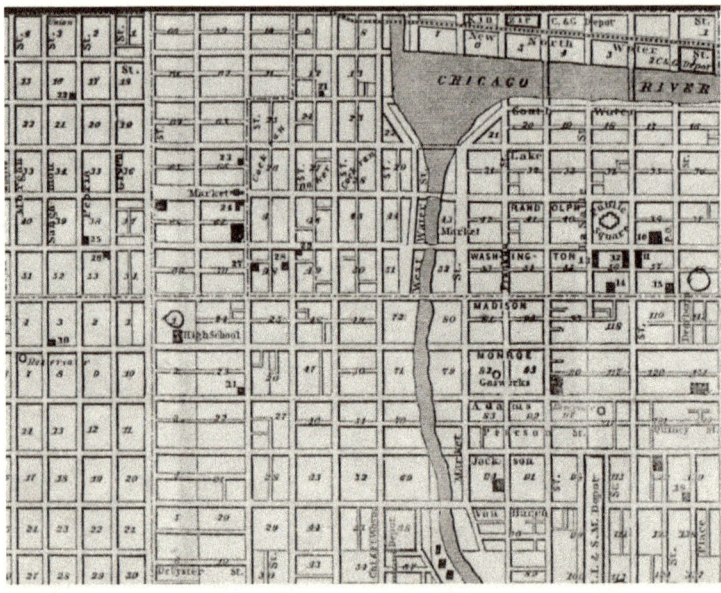

Blanchard's Map of Chicago 1857. Chicago's west side included everything west of the Chicago River. Public domain records.

Epilogue

The Seeds Sown

Joseph Medill, editor of the *Chicago Daily Tribune,* wrote a biography of Seth's life a month after his death. "When the other day, a brief mention was made in these columns that his earthly career had ended, the brevity of our news mention had in mind the reservation that his share in the reminiscences of our early days was too remarkable in its class to be thus lightly chronicled." He went on to say, "Thirty-eight years, the name of Seth Paine had a familiar sound in Chicago. The entire period which comprises progress of a ragged settlement to a thriving city. In 1834, he came as a young Vermonter, who in struggling westward, found himself stripped so thoroughly, that when kindly old Peter Cohen, the French merchant on Water Street, picked him up it looked like a Samaritan act."[364] Cohen's first act was followed with a lifetime of Seth's actions to do the same for others, but outside of Lake Zurich his legacy remained mostly a quiet one.

As a charismatic, optimistic, and eager young adult Seth was frequently frustrated with a society that attempted—yet never succeeded —to squelch his quest to find meaning and purpose in his life. Unlike his family before him who built cemeteries and constructed

---

[364] *Chicago Daily Tribune.* July 7, 1872.

railroads, the fruits of Seth's labor were not realized in his lifetime. In all of his activities, he was passionate and determined. He left a lasting imprint on the Chicago area, including establishing the village of Lake Zurich with its own cemetery. As a humanitarian, a Christian, and a loyal family man, Seth had gathered and nurtured like-minded families in his community. Despite his quirks, Seth was an important individual in Lake Zurich's history and legacy. Today there is an elementary school bearing his name and even a local folk song written about his antics.[365] Lake Zurich historians took pride in his involvement in the Underground Railroad, service to the community, and stories about the Stable of Humanity. In 1874, he was acknowledged by the *Chicago Daily Tribune* for putting Lake Zurich on the map as a popular retreat for folks from Chicago who liked to hunt and fish.[366] Seth's legacy rippled across the community again in the 1920s when Lake Zurich rose again in popularity. Its lake and bucolic picnic groves drew traffic along the first paved road out of the city of Chicago.[367]

Chicago historians barely mention Seth's name, most likely because of his controversial years and criticism of several peers who later became high ranking community members and state legislators. Although he stepped on a few toes in his lifetime, his primary

---

[365] Dan and Jenny Kortmann, folk singers in Lake Zurich, 2016.
[366] *Chicago Daily Tribune*. October 9, 1874.
[367] Modern day Rand Road was paved in 1928 and was the first paved road out of Chicago.

relationships were long standing with men like Allan Pinkerton, P.W. Gates, Henry Blodgett, James Collins, and others. Seth's relationships with these men were not based on what he could gain from their acquaintance but rather on the similar values they held—dedicating their lives to benefit others. Even when his idealism brought him to his knees, he was always true to his desire to serve others. Seth sought neither fame nor notoriety for himself. He acted based on what he believed was right.

His children and stepchildren took his lessons to heart. His son Seth Jr. eventually shed his earlier criticisms of his father and followed in his footsteps traveling the transcontinental railroad west to Audubon, Iowa. When he arrived, he started his own newspaper as a seed investor, an endeavor that challenged him greatly. Seth Jr. poured his energy into the young community, investing in its future, and drawing in new residents with his paper.[368] He was eventually compelled to move his own growing family out of Audubon, to the small town of Leroy, after his managing editor nearly destroyed his investment. In Leroy, Seth was a member of the Independent Order of the Odd-fellows, The Grand Army of the Republic, and the Knights of Pythias, which operated under the oath "to speak the truth and to render benefits to each other" in the

---

[368] Andrews, H. F. *History of Audubon County, Iowa, Its People, Industries and Institutions*. B. F. Bowen & Company, Inc. Indianapolis, Indiana. Page 180.

interest of the cause of universal peace.³⁶⁹ Seth Jr. involved himself in the mission of The Knights of Pythias just like his father had with the League of Universal Brotherhood.

Later, Seth Jr.'s son Timothy started his own newspaper in Audubon, Iowa called the *Liberator,* which he published with a hand-press. He was generously supported by professionals in the community. Timothy's paper is remembered as "one of the bright spots in the history of Audubon"and thrived until his untimely death in 1888.³⁷⁰

Seth's stepson Edwin Winters described Seth as generous beyond his means. With the help of his step-brother, Charles, Edwin received business training at Dyrengurth's School of Trade in Waukegan, Illinois.³⁷¹ Seth later used his connections to get Edwin a job with American Express which led him to a continued relationship with the railroad industry throughout his career. Family lore reports that he drove the first spike in the transcontinental railroad. From humble beginnings, Edwin continued to work hard, becoming President of the Northern Pacific Railroad in 1896. He eventually self-published his memoirs for his family in 1922.

---

[369] History — The Knights of Pythias, the current slogan of the organization is "We Help People."
[370] Andrews, H. F. *History of Audubon County, Iowa, Its People, Industries and Institutions.* B. F. Bowen & Company, Inc. Indianapolis, Indiana. Page 181.
[371] Winter, Edwin W. *Memories of Edwin W. Winter.* Self-published for private family collection.1922. Courtesy of the Ela Township Historical Society collection.

The Women's Home of Chicago was still active into the early 1890s. A news article in 1885 reported a local group of church women rescuing a young woman from a house of ill repute and delivering her to the safety of the home.[372] In 1892, a fire reportedly broke out in the basement of the Women's Home of Chicago. It is unclear how much damage it caused.[373] However by 1895, the two structures were separated and another prominent Chicago resident, John Farwell, purchased one of them.[374] History can only guess the impact Seth's work had on the lives of the women who lived in the Women's Home.

In 1889, Jane Addams opened the Hull House two blocks south of the Woman's Home of Chicago. Hull House was the first social settlement house in the United States. The social settlement house was designed to attract educated, native-born middle and upper middle class women to settle in poor urban neighborhoods and share their knowledge of basic skills such as arts and literature with their neighbors.[375] It is hard to imagine that the Women's Home of Chicago did not have an impact on Jane Addams and the plans for the Hull House.[376]

---

[372] A Good Work *Inter Ocean*. Monday, January 20, 1885. Page 4.
[373] *The Times*. Philadelphia, Pennsylvania. December 6, 1892. Page 2.
[374] 1895 Sanborn Fire Insurance Map
[375] Jane Addams | National Women's History Museum. Hull House was located just south of the Woman's Home of Chicago along Halted Avenue.
[376] Jane Addams and Seth Paine only had a few degrees of separation between them: Ellen Starr Gates, Jane's partner and investor in the Hull House, was the daughter of Caleb Gates who had helped form the Southside Congregational Church with P. W.

Throughout Seth's life, he used his unfaltering passion to help the underserved, to give them value when the world treated them as worthless. Seth was part of a bigger plan. He left an imprint on the history of Chicago, on women's rights, on immigrants, on civil rights, on the banking industry, on Spirituality, and on the history of the early Republican party.[377] Despite being relegated to nothing more than a quirky part of Chicago's history, in the end Seth accomplished much more than his critics could have predicted. In his own eccentric humble way Seth had lived up to the meaning of his name, *the Anointed One*.

Gates, Seth's longtime friend and supporter of the Women's Home.

[377] The early Republican party had a value system more closely aligned with today's Democratic party.

Author's Note

In a strange twist of fate, Seth's death and burial records were mysteriously lost. Chicago researcher, Adam Selzer, (Mysterious Chicago) uncovered that Seth was initially buried at Graceland Cemetery in Chicago in section E-7, Lot 407. According to the sales book, no one actually owned the plot until 1880, when Nathanial Rice purchased it.[378] Rice sold it to the James C. King Home for Old Men a couple of years later. Records show that a couple of months before Rice purchased the plot, Seth was moved to Lot 272 in the same section. Carrie and Walter Brown were also buried there, but there was no owner of record. In 1890, someone bought that section, and all three graves were moved to section R.[379] Seth remained in an unmarked grave in Section R for 150 years. In 2022, a proper headstone was donated to mark his grave.

~Nancy Schumm 2022

---

[378] Nathaniel Rice was a pallbearer for Seth, a Universalist, and supporter of Women's Suffrage.
[379] Mysterious Chicago, Adam Seltzer, researcher and author of a book on the history of Graceland (to be published Autumn 2022).

Timeline of Seth Paine's Life

1816, April 21	Seth Paine is born to Elijah & Fanny Paine in Tunbridge, Vermont.
1826	Seth's father Elijah dies in Vermont and the family moves to Northfield with Uncle Charles.
1833	Seth's mother, Fanny Paine, marries Abel Keyes in Washington County, Vermont.
1834	Seth leaves Vermont and heads west to Chicago.
1834	Seth starts working with Peter Cohen, a French Merchant on Water St. in Chicago.
Summer 1836	Seth first arrives in Cedar Lake, lays claim to land, and puts up the first buildings.
August 1836	Seth marries Frances Whitlock Jones in Cook County, Illinois.
1836	Seth enters into a partnership with Theron Norton, under the name of Paine and Norton.
1837	Seth's sister Jane arrives in Chicago.
1839	Seth's mother and Abel Keyes arrive in Illinois.
1839	Seth is listed as a Merchant in Chicago working with Taylor, Breese & Co. (Co. is Theron Norton).
1841, February 9	Seth secured land claims through the Cook County land office, in partnership with Daniel A. Baldwin.

1841	Seth and Frances officially move to Cedar Lake.
1841	Seth builds a communal store, and invites friends and colleagues from Chicago to visit Cedar Lake.
1843	Seth builds the first steam saw mill in Cedar Lake along Flint Creek and later a grist mill.
1843 Aug. 18	Seth is appointed U.S. Postmaster for Zurich, his newly renamed utopian town.
1846 September	Seth organizes a chapter of the Washington Temperance society in Lake County, Illinois.
1846	Seth works with Owen Lovejoy, Ichabod Codding, and James H. Collins on anti-slavery events and attends Allan Pinkerton's gatherings in Kane County. He joins the Liberty party in Lake County.
1847, March 24	Seth publicly renounces his allegiance to the Liberty Party after disillusionment with the politics.
1849, March 13	Seth sells nearly 250 acres of land around Lake Zurich to a group called the League of Universal Brotherhood.
1852	Seth joins the Spiritualist movement.
1852	Seth Paine & Co. the Bank of Chicago and publish a paper called the *Christian Banker*.
1853, Jan. 5	Seth and his colleagues from the Bank of Chicago are indicted for illegal banking and arrested.

1853, March 5	The "Spiritualist Trials" begin.
1853 April	Seth posts bail to leave Bridewell jail.
1853 May/June	Seth voluntarily checks himself into an asylum.
1853 July	Seth's banking trials begin.
1854 April	Seth's mother Fanny dies and is buried in Barrington, Illinois.
1857, Feb. 21	*The Chicago Daily Ledger*, an evening journal published by Barnes, Stewart & Paine, is edited by Seth and printed at P. W. Gates.
1858	Seth writes a letter to Frederick Douglass inviting him to Lake County to speak. Douglass comes to speak in Waukegan in January 1859.
1859, May	Seth's wife Frances Paine dies, leaving behind Seth and their five children.
1860, May 7	Seth marries Almira Burbank Winter, a friend of his late wife's who was also widowed in 1859.
1860, Nov.	Abraham Lincoln is elected as 16th president of the United States.
1861, April 12	The Civil War begins
1861, Aug. 1	Charles Paine, Seth's eldest son, joins the war effort.

1861, Oct. 17	Seth Paine Jr. lies about his age to join the army as a bugler.
1861	Seth's old friend Allan Pinkerton gets permission to bring someone into the slave prison in Washington D.C. to draft a report on the conditions, he taps Seth to do this work for him.
1862 April	Seth's son Charles is wounded at the Battle of Shiloh and sent home with a shattered leg.
1862 Spring	Allan Pinkerton's National Intelligence Service is assigned to work closely with General George B. McClellan and the Army of the Potomac. Pinkerton brings Seth along to write reports for the team during the Peninsula campaign.
1862, Sept. 17	Seth is with the army at Antietam working at the Army Command Post on the Pry Farm.
1862 Nov./Dec.	General McClellan is replaced by General Burnside, Seth and Pinkerton's men return with McClellan to Washington D.C.
1862	Seth returns to Chicago, and works with Gates Iron Works.
1863	Seth is once again appointed U.S. Postmaster in Lake Zurich.
1865	Smallpox strikes the Stable of Humanity in Lake Zurich twice, reducing its population significantly.

1865, April	General Lee surrenders at Appomattox, effectively ending the Civil War.
1865 September	Seth's son Charles Paine dies from the wound he suffered during the war, leaving behind his pregnant wife (Philmelia Winter - his step-sister).
1865	The Stable of Humanity burns down in Lake Zurich, and Seth decides to move his family to Chicago.
1867	Seth and some old friends establish a home to help women on the West side on Jackson Street called the Woman's Home of Chicago.
1871 October	The Great Chicago Fire ravages the city. The Woman's Home of Chicago is spared.
1872, June 10	Seth dies of consumption in Chicago and is buried at Graceland Cemetery in an unmarked grave.
2019	Cemetery archivist, Adam Seltzer, finds Seth's remains at Graceland Cemetery.
2022	150 years after he is buried, Seth receives a marker on his grave.

Paine Family Tree

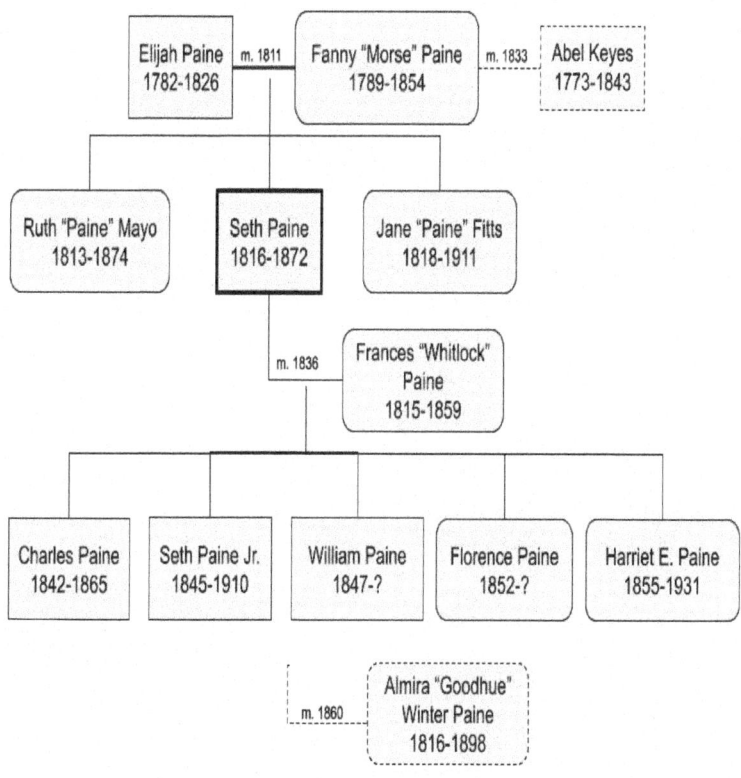

Bibliography

BOOKS

Andreas, Alfred Theodore, *History of Cook County, Illinois, From the Earliest Period to the Present Time,* Chicago, 1884, In three Volumes.

Andrews, H. F. *History of Audubon County, Iowa, Its People, Industries and Institutions,* B. F. Bowen & Company, Inc. Indianapolis, Indiana, page 180.

Arnosky Sherburne, Michelle, *Abolitions and the Underground Railroad in Vermont,* The History Press, Charleston, SC, 2013, page 20.

Baldwin, Elmer, *History of Lasalle County, Illinois,* Chicago, Rand McNally and Co. Printers. 1877.

Blanchard, Rufus, *Discovery and Conquests of the North-West, With the History of Chicago,* Volume 1, O.L. Baskin and Company Historical Publishers Lakeside Building, 1882, Volume 2 1900.

Blanchard, Rufus, *History of Dupage County,* O. L. Baskin and Company Historical Publishers, Lakeside Building, Chicago, Illinois, 1882

Blodgett, Henry W. *Autobiography of Henry W. Blodgett,* Waukegan: 1906

Chamberlin, Everett, *Chicago and its Suburbs,* T. A. Hungerford & Co., 1874

City Publishing Company. *Portrait and Biographical Album of Lake County, Illinois.* Chicago: Lake City Publishing Company, 1891.

Clark, George W., The Liberty Minstrel, LEAVITT & ALDEN, Boston: SAXTON & MILES, N.Y., MYRON FINCH, N.Y., JACKSON & CHAPLIN, N.Y, 1844.
https://www.gutenberg.org/files/22089/22089-h/22089-h.htm

Coffin, Levi, **Reminiscences of Levi Coffin, the Reputed President of the Underground Railroad:** *Being a Brief History of the Labors of a Lifetime in Behalf of the Slave, with the Stories of Numerous Fugitives, who Gained Their Freedom Through His Instrumentality, and Many Other Incidents,* R. Clarke & Company, 1880.

Cook, Frederick Francis, *Bygone Days in Chicago,* A. C. McClurg &Co., Chicago, 1910

Davis, Major George B, U.S. Army, Perry Leslie J. Civilian Expert, Kirkley, Joseph W. Civilian Expert Capt. Calving D. Cowles, 23rd U. S. Infantry, *The Official Military Atlas of the Civil War,* The Fairfax Press, New York, 1983 reprint edition of the: *Atlas to Accompany the Official Records of the Union and Confederate Armies,* Published under the Direction of the Hons. Redfield, Proctor, Stephen B. Elkins and Daniel S. Lamont, Secretaries of War, by Maj. George B. Davis, U. S. Army et all. Washington: Government Printing Office, 1891-1895.

Dorsey, James, *The **Underground Railroad**: Northeastern Illinois and Southeastern Wisconsin.* Sons of Thunder Ministry, Waukegan, Illinois, 2000.

Dretske, Diana, *What's in a name?: The Origin of Place Names in Lake County, Illinois,* Lake County Discovery Museum, January 1, 1998.

Dreyfus, Benjamin, The City Transformed, Railroads and Their Influence on the Growth of Chicago in the 1850s, Copyright 1995, Benjamin W Dreyfus

Fishel, Edwin C. *The Secret War for the union, The Untold Story of MIlitary Intelligence in the Civil War,* Houghton Mifflin Company, New York, 1996

Foner, Eric, Gateway to Freedom, W.W. Norton and Company, New York, 2015

Goodspeed Historical Association. *History of Cook County, Illinois.* Chicago: Goodspeed Historical Association, 1909.

Haines, Elijah M. *Past and Present of Lake County,* Illinois, Chicago: Le Baron, 1877

Hall, S.R. LL D., *The Geography and History of Vermont,* Montpelier, Freeman Steam Printing House and Bindery, 1875.

Halsey, John J. *A History of Lake County, Illinois,* Chicago, Illinois: Roy S. Bates, 1912

Hardinge, Emma, *Modern American Spiritualism, A Twenty Year Record.* New York, by the author, 1880

Hatcher, Harlan, Erich A. Walter, *A Pictorial History of the Great Lakes,* Crown Publishers, New York, 1963

Hazen, Henry Allen, *The Climate of Chicago*, Weather Bureau, 1893, Chicago Illinois.

Hemenway, Abby Maria, *The Vermont Historical Gazetteer, Volume II,* Published by Miss A.M. Hemenway, Burlington, Vermont, 1871

Hill, Libby, *The Chicago River,* Lake Claremont Press, Chicago, 2000

Historical Encyclopedia of Illinois, Cook County Editions, Vol. 2.

Hull, Moses, **Two Volumes in One; Or, The Question of the Spiritualism of the Bible Settled:** *Together with a Series of Startling Contrasts Between Creedal Christianity and the Facts and Philosophy of Modern Spiritualism,* M. Hull & Company, Buffalo New York, 1901.

Hyde, James Nevins, *Fergus Historical Stories. Early Medical Chicago,* Fergus Printing Company, Chicago, 1879.

Kinzie, Juliette M., *Wau-Bun, Early Day in the Northwest,* New York: Derby and Jackson, Cincinnati: H. W. Derby & Co. 1856

Lake County Genealogical Society. *1838-1888 Report of the Semi-Centennial Anniversary of the Fremont Congregational Church, Ivanhoe, Illinois, Monday, February 20, 1888.* Libertyville, IL: Lake County (IL) Genealogical Society, 2004.

Lawson, Edward S. *A History of Warren Township.* Gurnee, Illinois: Warren-Newport Public Library, 1974.

Lines, Arnett T. *History of Cook County and its Environs*, Barrington, 1937.

Lyman, Frank H. *The City of Kenosha and Kenosha County Wisconsin: A record of Settlement, Organization, Progress and Achievement.* Vol 1. Chicago: S.J Clarke, 1916.

Madsen, John, *Where the Sky Began; Land of the Tallgrass Prairie,* 1982.

Mansfield, J. B., *History of the Great Lakes, Volume I,* Chicago: J. H. Beers & Co., 1899

Mason, Edward G. of the Chicago Historical Society, *Early Chicago and Illinois*, Fergus Printing Company, Chicago, 1890

Mayer, Henry, *All on Fire, William Lloyd Garrison and the Abolition of Slavery,* St. Martin's Griffon, New York, 1998

Millburn Congregational Church. *The First Hundred Years Plus Forty: The Story of the MIllburn Congregational Church, 1840-1980, Millburn, IL:* Millburn Congregational CHurch, 1980.

Paige, Lucius R, *History of Cambridge, Massachusetts, 1630-1877,* H. O. Houghton and Co., Boston 1877.

Partridge, Charles A. *History of Lake County, Illinois.* Chicago: Munsell, 1902.

Palmer, Russell, *A Factual Study of Allan Pinkerton and Larch Farm,* 1968

Pierce, Bessie Louise, *A History of Chicago, Volume II: From Town to City 1848-1872,* University of Chicago Press, 2007

Pinkerton, Allan, *The Spiritualists and the Detective,* G.W. Carleton & Company, New York, 1896

Pinkerton, Allan, *The Spy of the Rebellion,* G.W. Carleton & Co., New York, 1883,

Price, Steven, *By Gaslight,* Farrar, Status and Girou, October 2016.

Sandefur, Timothy, *Frederick Douglass, Self-Made Man,* Cato Institute, 2018, Washington D. C.,
https://www.cato.org/sites/cato.org/files/sponsor-ebook-page/frederick-douglass-self-made-man.pdf.

Sheahan, Jas. W., Upton, Geo. P. *History of the Great Conflagration,* Union Publishing Co. Chicago, Illinois, 1871.

Siebert, Wilbur Henry, *The Underground Railroad from Slavery to Freedom,* The MacMillan Company London, New York 1898,

Slotkin, Richard, *The Long Road to Antietam,* LIveright Publishing Corporation, W.W. Norton & Company, New York, 2012

Smithsonian Institute, *Smithsonian Civil War, Inside the National Collection,* forward by John Meacham

Stern, Philip Van Doren, *Secret Missions of the Civil War*, Garrett County Digital, 2012

Swan, Oscar, J.B. Merwin, State of Humanity 1856

Thompson, Zadock, *History of Vermont, Natural, Civil and Statistical,* (also called *Thompson's Vermont) in Three Parts*, Published for the author by Chauncey Goodrich, Burlington, Vermont, 1842.

Westerman, Al, *Public Domain Land Sales in Lake County, Illinois,* Zion, Illinois 2006

Western Historical Company, *History of Jefferson County, Wisconsin, Containing a History of Jefferson County*, pg 347. Western Historical Company, Chicago, 1879.

Western Historical Company, *The History of Fayette County, Iowa,* Western Historical Company, Chicago, 1878

Wilson and St. Clair, *Biographical Sketches of the Leading Men of Chicago*, Wilson and St. Clair Publishers, Chicago, Illinois, 1868.

World Publishing Company, *The Holy Bible,* Revised Standard Edition, The Letter of James, Chapter 1, verses 19-20

Turner, Glennette Tilley. *The Underground Railroad in Illinois:* Glen Ellyn, IL Newman Educational Publishing, 2001.

INTERVIEWS

Bill Pierce, Bills Boats and Bait, Lake Zurich, Illinois, July 1996

Euclid Farnham, President of the Tunbridge Historical Society, January 29, 2017 interview.

Adam Seltzer, Mysterious Chicago, 2020

MANUSCRIPTS AND UNPUBLISHED SOURCES

Abraham Lincoln Presidential Library, Springfield, Illinois. Coffing, Ichabod, biographical Sketches, Box 3, Memorandum envelope, page 7.

Barrington Area Public Library, Barrington, Illinois Public Library archives, https://www.balibrary.org/files/atlas_corr.pdf

Chicago History Museum, Chicago, Illinois. Chicago City Directories.

Chicago Historical Society, Print Department, *Chicago Photographers 1847-1900, As Listed in the City Directories,* North Avenue at Clark Street, 1858.

> The Woman's Home of Chicago, Erected 1868 and 1869, W. Jackson St. Corner of Halsted, Chicago Historical Society,

> James W. Hedenberg Chicago, 39-5-163 Chicago-Residences-Exteriors 1888 Wooden Sidewalks Still, Standing in 1888, Gas Street Lamps G-1994-0247, Samuel Bridgeman

Kenosha Civil War Museum, Kenosha, Wisconsin; Studies on Underground Railroad, various documents.

Cook Memorial Library Libertyville, Illinois;

> *Ivanhoe Congregational Church Records.* Self published by the church, June 15, 1973.

> Sharf, Albert F., *Indian Trails and Villages in Lake County, Illinois*

Detroit Public Library; Burton Historical Collection.

Dumbarton House, Washington D.C.; January 2020 Newsletter, www.dumbartonhouse.org

Ela Historical Society Museum, Lake Zurich, Illinois

> Winters, Edwin W., *Memories of Edwin W. Winters*, self published for private family collection, 1922, courtesy of the Ela Township Historical Society collection, June 2016

> Abstract of Title #29025, book 228, page 870

Ela Area Public Library, Lake Zurich, Illinois; Local History Files

Graceland Cemetery, Chicago, Illinois; Archives

Illinois History Society Conference 2001; Kelsey, C.L., *Bureau County Republican, June* 16, 1864, OWEN
LOVEJOY'S TRANSFORMATION FROM THE LIBERTY PARTY TO THE FREE SOIL PARTY, By the Rev. William F. Moore, Illinois State Historical Society Symposium, December 1, 2001.

Illinois State Archives, Springfield, Illinois; ourtland, T. Millow Jr., *Southern Illinoisan*, Carbondale, Illinois, June 18, 1972.

Illinois State Library; Letter from James Collins to Owen Lovejoy, March 17, 1847

Lake County Clerk, Waukegan, Illinois; Probate records, Plat book and deed recordings.

Lake County Discovery Museum Archives, Wauconda, Illinois; 1840 Census records

Library of Congress, Archives, Washington, D.C.

    Manuscript Division Collection Request, Frederick Douglass Papers, 1854-1864.
    Pinkerton papers, Allen or E. J. MF #16574, Box 44 Reel 1, Reports and letters
    Pinkerton Agency Records Admin Box 24, Filed reports to army 1853-1990
    Pinkerton Agency Records Admin files Box 20-68, 1857-1999
    Library of Congress, *Timeline of the Civil War,* 1862
    George B. McClellan Papers

Millburn Historical Society, Millburn, Illinois. Millburn Congregational Church Records

Museum of Civil War Medicine, Frederick, Maryland

Newberry Library, Chicago, Illinois

    Chicago City Directories, 1839
    Encyclopedia of Chicago, Banking, Commercial,
    www.encylcopedia.chicagohistory.org/pages/108.html
    Newspapers on microfiche
    Chicago City maps
    Sanborn Company Fire Insurance Maps, 1896, 1905

PRIVATE COLLECTIONS

>RJ Quinn Training Academy and Chicago Fire Department, *History of the Chicago Fire Department*, revised 6/10/2004
>Snetsinger, Helen Mills, *A Prairie Farmer and His Family,* Memoirs of Helen Mills Snetsinger, ca. 1962.

St. Lawrence University Law Library, New York

>Letter from Pryce Lewis collection, Box 2, Folder 1. Dated Dec. 12, 1862

>Pryce Lewis photo from Box 2, Folder 10, Pinkerton Men, Seth Paine with William Pinkerton (brother of Alan) and John Babcock.

University of Chicago, Guide to Stephen A. Douglas Papers 1764-1908, Box 10 Folder 13, Correspondence 1857, December 14. *From Seth Paine.* University of Chicago Library, Hyde Park, Illinois.

Waukegan History Museum, Waukegan, Illinois

>Blodgett, Henry W. Autobiography of Henry W. Blodgett, Waukegan 1906

Historical Encyclopedia of Illinois, and History of Lake County, Edited by Charles A. Partridge, Chicago: Munsell Publishing Company, Publishers, 1902

Waukegan Public Library, Waukegan, Illinois, Newspaper archives on microfiche.

MAPS

From the Library of Congress archives, *Canal Guide, for the Tourist and Traveler*, LOC #G3800 1826.W5

Chicago Sanborn Fire Insurance Map 1895

Map of Chicago, Rufus Blanchard, 1857

Map of Lake County, Hixon, W.W & Co, Rockford 1845

Map of Lake County, Illinois. St. Louis: L. Gast & Brothers, 1861

Map of Lake County, Illinois. Chicago: Frost & MCLennan 1873

Illustrated Atlas of Lake County, Illinois. Chicago: H.R. Page & Co., 1885

McAlpine, WM. J. C.E., *Map of Various Channels for Conveying the Trade of the Northwest to the Atlantic Seaboard,* New York, 1853, State Engineer of New York and Surveyor.

Sharf, Albert F. *Indian Trails and Villages in Lake County, Illinois,* (ca, 1908), 1-2. Cartographer, Indian villages (numbered), minor camps, chipping stations, principal Indian trails lettered and numbered, portage, springs, heights and signal stations, Indian mounds, mound builders trail, published 1900. (Copy can be found at the Cook Memorial Library in Libertyville, Illinois).

Washington District of Columbia 1865

Williams, William and S. Stiles, *The Travelers Pocket Map of New York from the best authorities,* (Utica, N. Y. Williams, 1826) Map: https://loc.gov/item/83694242.

NEWSPAPERS

Baltimore Sun, Baltimore, Maryland

Chicago Daily Tribune

Chicago Democrat, Chicago, Illinois

Chicago Evening Mail

Chicago Press

Chicago Tribune

The Christian Banker, Chicago, Illinois

The Daily Intelligencer, Wheeling, West Virginia

Daily Register Gazette, Rockford, Illinois

Daily Illinois State Register, Springfield, Illinois

Democratic Press, Chicago, Illinois

Elkhorn (Wisconsin) *Independant.*

Frank Leslie's Illustrated Weekly, National

Hornellsville (New York) Tribune

Illinois State Register, Springfield, Illinois

Inter Ocean, Chicago Illinois

Janesville Daily Gazette, Janesville, Wisconsin

Journal, Pittsburg, California

Kenosha (WI) Times

Lake County Citizen, (Waukegan, Illinois)

Lake County Independent, Libertyville, Illinois

Lake Zurich Banker

The Liberator

Pittsburgh Daily Post

The Porcupine, Waukegan, Illinois

The Rockford Forum, Rockford, Illinois

Rockford Republican, Illinois

Rock River Democrat

The Times, Philadelphia, Pennsylvania,

Waukegan News Sun, Waukegan, Illinois

Waukegan Gazette/Waukegan Weekly Gazette, (Waukegan, Illinois)

The *Weekly Wisconsin,* Milwaukee Wisconsin

Western Citizen, Chicago, Illinois

Vermont Historical Magazine

280

PUBLISHED ARTICLES

Antietam National Battlefield, National Park Service U.S. Department of the Interior, battlefield publication.

Benzkofer, Stephan, *The Original Private Eye,* Chicago Tribune

Calomiris, Charles W.; Schweikart, Larry (1991). "The Panic of 1857: Origins, Transmission, and Containment". Journal of Economic History.

Centers for Disease Control, it is estimated that 1 in 7 people died from TB prior to the discovery of the bacillus. History | World TB Day | TB | CDC.

CLIMATE DATABASE MODERNIZATION PROGRAM: PRE-20TH CENTURY TASK – KEY CLIMATE OBSERVATIONS RECORDED SINCE THE FOUNDING OF AMERICA, 1700'S – 1800'S Karen Andsager Midwestern Regional Climate Center, Champaign, Illinois Tom Ross National Climatic Data Center, Asheville, North Carolina Michael C. Kruk and Michael L. Spinar Midwestern Regional Climate Center, Champaign, Illinois.

Common Sense, quoting an article of the *Evening Post* from the 1850's. Volume 1-2, 1874.

Daily Register Gazette, Rockford, Illinois, page 17, Friday, December 7, 1928. *Chicago's Early Banks.*

"Sugar Grove's Historic Role in the Kane County Anti-Slavery Association and Underground Railroad," Sugar Grove Historical Society, accessed December 22, 2021, Sugar Grove's Historic Role in the Kane County Anti-Slavery Association and Underground Railroad.

Garrison, Zach, "Kansas-Nebraska Act" *Civil War on the Western Border: The Missouri-Kansas Conflict, 1854-1865.* The Kansas City Public Library. Kansas-Nebraska Act | Civil War on the Western Border: The Missouri-Kansas Conflict, 1854-1865

Haines, Michael R., *The urban mortality transition in the united states, 1800-1940 [*],* The urban mortality transition in the united states, 1800-1940 [*] | Cairn.info

Howarth, Richard J. *Through a glass darkly: patients of the Illinois State Hospital for the Insane at Jacksonville, USA (1854–80)* University College London Shirley A. Aleguas Genealogist, Waverly, IL Corresponding author: Richard J Howarth,

Department of Earth Sciences, University College London, Gower Street, London WC1E 6BT, UK. patients of the Illinois State Hospital for the Insane at Jacksonville, USA (1854-80) Richard J Howa

The Martin F. O'Rourke Memorial Railroad Library at Bowie Tower, Maryland

Masure, Kate, 12-7-2011, NY Times blogs, *Washington's Black Code,* Washington's Black Codes - The New York Times

National Expansion and Reform 1815 – 1880 in: Colonial and Post-Revolutionary Era, Eras in Social Welfare History, The United States Expands: 1815 – 1880, By John E. Hansan, Ph.D.
https://socialwelfare.library.vcu.edu/eras/colonial-postrev/national-expansion-and-reform-1815-1880/

National Research Council 1995. *Colleges of Agriculture at the Land Grant Universities: A Profile.* Washington, DC: The National Academies Press. Colleges of Agriculture at the Land Grant Universities: A Profile.

Semi-centennial History of the University of Illinois, Volume 1, University of Illinois, 1918. 3rd Industrial Convention, November 24, 1852.

The *Strand Magazine,* Volume 30 article by Charles Francis Bourke, 1905, G. Newnes

WEB REFERENCES

Ancestry.com

American Battlefield Trust; www.battlefields.org, *The Peninsula Campaign*

Antietam; www.history.com, *Battle of Antietam*

Applegate, Debbie, informality, eastern educations, and unabashed showmanship." Beecher's 'gospel of love', set the groundwork for theological and social reform. (www.biogtraphy.com/people/henry-ward-beecher-9204662.

Beriah Green; Beriah Green - NATIONAL ABOLITION HALL OF FAME AND MUSEUM

Black Codes of Illinois
:http//www.google.com/books/edition/Black_Code_of_Illinois/NjY1twEACAAJ?hl=e

The Chicago Fire of 1871; The Chicago Fire of 1871 and the 'Great Rebuilding' | National Geographic Society

Chicago Fire of 1871: Fire of 1871

Chicago After the Great Fire: http://gildedage.lib.niu.edu/islandora/object/niu-lincoln%3A34907, Fergus' Director of workers 1839 Chicago

Chicago Post Fire: Northern Illinois University Digital Library; http://gildedage.lib.niu.edu/islandora/object/niu-lincoln%3A34907, Fergus' Director of workers 1839 Chicago

Confederate comes from the latin word, "*confoederatus*" meaning leagued together. What is a confederate? | Macmillan Dictionary Blogr

Crampton's Gap; The Battle of Crampton's Gap | American Battlefield Trust

Father Dodge; www.lakecountyhistoryblogspot.com, June 18, 2019, William B. Dodge

Dusable Museum; interview with Glinette Tilly Turner, Early Chicago: Slavery in Illinois

Elgin Conferences; Elginhistory.com/eaah-ch02.htm, quote by Caroline Gifford in a letter to her father

Encyclopedia of Chicago, Banking, Commercial, www.encylcopedia.chicagohistory.org/pages/108.html

Findagrave.com

Fox Sisters; https://www.smithsonianmag.com/history/the-fox-sisters-and-the-rap-on-spiritualism-99663697/

George Brinton McClellan; George McClellan - Biography, Civil War & Importance - HISTORY

https://www.google.com/books/edition/The_History_of_Jefferson_County_Wisconsi/4h UrAQAAMAAJ?hl=en&gbpv=1

History of the Congregational Church, www.congregationallibrary.org/researchers/congregational-christian-tradition, *The Puritan Heritage*

Illinois infantry; http://www.civilwararchive.com/Unreghst/unilinf1.htm

Jane Addams and the settlement house goal was "for educated women to share all kinds of knowledge, from basic skills to arts and literature with poorer people in the neighborhood. Jane Addams | National Women's History Museum.

The Knights of Pythias; http://www.pythias.org/index.php/the-pythian-story

The Lady Elgin Disaster; Lady Elgin Disaster.

The League of Universal Brotherhood; https://connecticuthistory.org/apostle-of-peace-elihu-burritts-quest-for-universal-brotherhood/#:~:text=In%201846%20Burritt%20sailed%20to,encouragement%20of%20friendship%20between%20nations.

Lovejoy and Missouri; http://collections.mohistory.org/exhibit/EXH:CWMO-61, *The Alton Observer article in the Missouri History Collections, May 5, 1836.*

Mount Tambora, Indonesia Volcanic eruption, (www.britannica.com article 581878)

New York State Archives Erie Canal Time Machine 1830*s* http://www.archives.nysed.gov/education/primary-source-sets-erie-canal-1830s

Quinn Chapel AME history. http://quinnchicago.org/our-history

Sandefur, Timothy, *Frederick Douglass, Self-Made Man,* Cato Institute, 2018, Washington D. C., frederick-douglass-self-made-man.pdf.

Secession; https://www.britannica.com/topic/secession

Socrates Rand, Des Plaines, IL

Taylor, Edmund D. Biography found at notesoflife.smfforfree2.com/index.php/topic,365.0. from *The National Magazine,* volume 16, April-November, 1892, "The Originator of the Greenback Currency"

Temperance: http://drwilliams.org/iDoc/index.htm?url=http://drwilliams.org/iDoc/lincolnandliquor.

php

U. S. Senate: https://www.senate.gov/artandhistory/history/common/generic/ConfiscationActs.htm

Vegetarianism; http://www.edu.pe.ca/sourishigh/Pages/Cmp6-03/Beth/Homepage/history_of_vegetarianism.htm

Weather in Chicago: https://www.newberry.org/weathering-sudden-freeze

Whigs; Whig Party - Definition, Beliefs & Leaders - HISTORY

Wilmot Proviso and the Republican Party http://www.history.com/topics/wilmot-proviso

Wilmot Proviso; From the Wilmot Proviso to the Compromise of 1850.

William Lloyd Garrison and The Liberator, *U. S. History Online Textbook,* 28a. William Lloyd Garrison and The Liberator, 2017

Yankee, 'yanks' or yankee doodle's. Yankee | National Geographic Society

VITAL RECORDS

Fayette County, Iowa cemetery records

Illinois State Marriage records

Lake County Illinois, Census 1850

Lake County Illinois, Census 1840

U. S. Agricultural census records: 1855, 1865

U. S. Federal census records: 1820, 1830, 1840, 1850, 1853, 1860, 1870, 1880, 1900, 1910

U.S. Register of Civil, military and Naval Service 1863-1959

Vermont Probate Records, Elijah Paine, November 1828

Vermont vital records 1720-1908

Index

9th Illinois Infantry, 202
12th Illinois Infantry, 202
Addams, Jane, 258, 259, 283
Allen, E.J. 215, 276
Allen, George, 223
Alton, 82, 85, 87, 88, 284
Anthony, Susan B., 103
Antietam, 222, 223, 224, 225, 232, 266, 273, 280, 282
Antioch, 68, 105
Antislavery, 55, 85, 86, 87, 88, 89, 90, 109, 120, 125, 131, 141, 156
Appomattox, 231, 266
Audubon, 256, 257, 269
Babcock, John, 216, 225, 228, 277
Baldwin, Daniel, 71, 72, 134, 262, 270
Bank of Chicago, 145, 148, 149, 151, 154, 156, 157, 158, 167, 168, 185, 264
Barrington, 190, 193, 232, 251, 265, 272, 274
Baumfree, Isabel, 103
Beaubien, Mark, 52, 53, 54
Beecher, 54, 87, 88, 282
Black Codes, 56, 57, 106, 107, 109, 204, 205, 281, 282
Black Hawk Indian War
Blodgett, 83, 84, 85, 87, 88, 108, 124, 153, 255, 270, 277

Bloodhound Law, 130
Bradley, Cyrus, 15, 53, 54, 165, 166, 169, 172
Bridewell, 161, 164, 165, 166, 171, 178, 243, 264
Brockway, Lewis, 131, 231, 232
Brown, John, 98, 99, 192
Bryan, John, 251
Burbank, Almira, 186, 187, 194, 265
Buritt, Elihu, 127, 128, 283
Burnside, Ambrose, 224, 225, 266
Burroughs, Reve. Dr., 173
Cadwell, Byron, 202
Canal Street, 42, 43, 77, 78, 232, 277, 284
Capitol Hill, 170, 204, 287
Carpenter, Philo, 52, 150
Castle Thunder, 220, 225
Cedar Lake, 10, 61, 62, 64, 65, 66, 68, 70, 72, 73, 75, 76, 77, 263
Certificate of Freedom, 107
Chicago Marine and Fire, 89, 140
Chicago River, 46, 253, 271
Chicago Spiritualist Society, 138
Childs, S.D., 133

287

Christian Banker, 141, 152, 153, 154, 155, 156, 157, 171, 172, 173, 264, 279
Civil War, 132, 204, 216, 218, 220, 222, 223, 224, 228, 230, 231, 232, 237, 265, 266, 270, 271, 273, 275, 276, 281, 283
Clarke, George Washington, 101
Clarke, Hiram, 54
Codding, Ichabod, 102, 103, 109, 264
Coffing, Churchill, 133, 134, 140, 274
Cohen, Peter, 47, 50, 51, 52, 56, 57, 58, 59, 71, 76, 78, 254, 263
Collins, James H.,110, 116, 125, 126, 133, 252, 255, 264, 276, 293
Collyer, Robert, 239, 240, 247, 251
Compensated Emancipation Act, 210
Congregationalists, 27, 28, 32, 90, 100, 105, 108, 131, 133, 158
Cook County, 13, 38, 47, 48, 50, 54, 55, 73, 75, 92, 139, 144, 148, 149, 150, 154, 155, 156, 158, 164, 167, 179, 180, 181, 191, 263,269, 271, 272
Cook, Isaac, 54, 55
Crampton's Gap, 222, 223, 282

CSS Virginia, 214
Davidson, Daniel, 15, 16, 113, 133, 171
DeKoven Street, 247
Democrat, 28, 112, 114, 157, 166, 167, 187, 188, 189, 193, 197, 259, 279, 280
Detroit,43, 45, 275
DeWolf, Calvin, 133, 134
Dickinson, D.O., 102, 105, 112, 156, 193
Dix, Dorothea Lynde, 177
Dodge, William B., 102, 105, 106, 282, 289
Douglas, Stephen, 149, 176, 192, 193, 197, 277
Douglass, Frederick, 184, 193, 265, 273, 276, 284
Dred Scott Case, 191
Dresser, Gordon, 129, 131, 195, 229
DuPage County, 38, 83, 270
Dyrengurth School of Trade, 258
Easton, John, 105
Eddy, Ira B., 137, 138, 140, 141, 143, 148, 158, 159, 160, 161, 168, 170, 173
Ela Township, 64, 66, 77, 131, 132, 187, 196, 202, 230, 232, 258, 275
Elgin, 120, 122, 125, 127, 129, 196, 197, 283, 284

Erie Canal, 42, 284
Federal Confiscation Act, 205
Fittz, Caleb, 62, 75, 160
Flint Creek, 78, 91, 151, 264
Fort Hill, 89, 112
Fort Paine, 37, 83
Fox Sisters, 137, 149, 283
Freer, L.C. Paine, 133
Fugitive Slave Act, 130, 131
Galloway, James, 64, 66
Garrison, William Lloyd, 79, 80, 83, 84, 86, 97, 98, 99, 103, 121, 122, 123, 125, 136, 137, 189, 208, 213, 273, 281, 285
Gaston, Chancey T., 152
Gates, Philetus W., 78, 79, 151, 190, 191, 230, 239, 256, 260, 265, 266
Graceland Cemetery, 251, 252, 253, 261, 262, 267, 276
Great Chicago Fire, 53, 54, 246, 247, 248, 267, 277, 282
Green, Beriah, 123, 124, 125, 282
Hale, John, 87, 208
Halleck, Henry, 221
Halsted Street, 230, 239, 275
Harper's Ferry, 222, 223
Harrison, William Henry, 99
Hawley, Cyrus, M., 151
Herrick, Mrs., 138, 139, 142, 149, 150, 157, 167, 168
Holmes, John, 151

Hull House, 259, 260
Hurd, Harvey B., 113, 134, 172, 173
Illinois Central Railroad, 203, 204
Illinois Constitution, 110, 140
Indian Creek, 37
Ivanhoe, 89, 90, 102, 104, 105, 272, 275
Jackson, 69, 103, 187, 188, 236, 239, 267, 270, 272, 275, 281
Kane County, 106, 109, 110, 121, 264, 281
Kansas-Nebraska Act, 185, 186, 187, 192, 281
Kennicott, John, 150, 152
Keyes, 35, 37, 73, 76, 100, 263
Kimberly, Ira, 54, 55, 60, 74
Kinzie, 52, 272
Knights of Pythias, 257, 258, 283
Koch, Dr. Robert, 244
Liberty Association, 106, 107
Lake Mills, 74
Lake Zurich, 64, 77, 79, 92, 105, 113, 126, 127, 128, 131, 140, 144, 151, 172, 173, 174, 177, 180, 181, 182, 185, 186, 187, 188, 190, 191, 195, 201, 202, 209, 210, 226, 229, 230, 231, 232, 233, 234, 240, 255,

289

256, 264, 266, 267, 274, 275, 276, 279
Lamon, Ward Hill, 207, 209, 213, 271
LaSalle County, 125, 132, 133, 140, 270
League of Universal Brotherhood, 126, 257, 264, 284
Lee, Robert E., 217, 219, 221, 222, 224, 231, 266
Lewis, Pryce, 2, 200, 215, 216, 220, 221, 225, 226, 228
Liberty Minstrel, 102, 103, 270
Liberty Party, 109, 110, 120, 121, 122, 123, 124, 125, 128, 131, 134, 264, 276
Libertyville, 89, 90, 100, 101, 102, 104, 105, 272, 275, 278, 279
Lincoln, Abraham, 70, 102, 104, 127, 189, 196, 197, 198, 201, 203, 204, 205, 207, 208, 210, 213, 214, 217, 223, 224, 225, 230, 232, 265, 274, 282, 284
Little Fort, 128
Lovejoy, 85, 86, 87, 88, 90, 96, 98, 99, 109, 120, 125, 126, 264, 276, 284
Lusk, Julia, 137, 138
Magruder, John, 219
Mansfield, J.B., 45, 46, 272

Maunk-Suk, 60
McArthur, John, 202, 203
McClellan, George Brinton, 5, 203, 204, 213, 214, 215, 216, 218, 220, 221, 222, 224, 266, 277, 283
McIntosh, Francis, 87
Mechanic's Grove, 89
Medill, Joseph, 255
Meeker, George W., 179, 180
Merwin, J.B., 189, 190, 217, 274
Millburn, 101, 273, 276
Missouri, 82, 86, 87, 119, 179, 185, 191, 281, 284
Mundelein, 89, 112
Naper Settlement, 37
Northern Pacific Railroad, 258
Northfield, 29, 32, 33, 34, 35, 36, 41, 263
Norton, 9, 16, 17, 88, 89, 91, 263, 271
Oneida Institute, 124, 125
Orange County, 29, 33
Parsons, Theron, 102, 105, 108
Patterson, R.W., 173
Payne, 38, 89, 105, 158
Peninsula Campaign, 213, 214, 217, 221, 266, 282
Phillips, Wendell, 103
Pinkerton, Allan, 109, 110, 111, 113, 121, 124, 126, 148, 149, 203, 204, 206-210, 212,

214-216, 218, 219, 221, 223, 225, 228, 229, 230, 252, 256, 264, 265, 266, 273, 276, 277
Plainfield, 36
Polk, James Knox, 111, 119
Pollock, Robert, 105, 108
Prairie Du Chien, 45
Presbyterian Church, 89, 100
Quinn Chapel, 101, 102, 284
Rand Road, 129, 256
Republican, 105, 106, 111, 186, 187, 193, 196, 197, 260, 276, 280, 285, 291
Rice, Nathaniel, 261
Richmond, 213, 214, 216, 217, 220, 225
Rossiter, 54, 109
Ryder, William Henry, 239, 251
Sargent, Ann, 130
Scammon, J. Y., 88, 105, 173, 179
Scobell, John, 215
Scully, John, 220, 221
Seven Days Battle, 219
Seven Pines, 212
Sharpsburg, 223, 224
Sherman, E.L., 103, 156, 157, 160, 168, 169, 171
Smith, Chester, 36, 37, 38, 41-44, 46, 57, 83
Smith, Crawford, 179
Smith, George, 139, 140

Spiritualist, 17, 133, 138, 139, 142, 144, 148, 149, `52, 168-170, 172, 173, 180, 264, 265, 273
St. Paul's Universalist, 239, 251
Stable of Humanity, 77, 107, 128, 131, 166, 182, 185, 189, 196, 202 ,217, 229-233, 239, 256, 266-267
Stanton, Elizabeth Cady, 242
Strang, John, 105
Swedeborgians, 169
Taylor, 69, 70, 71, 72, 88, 132, 140, 263, 284
T.B., 244, 280
Tracy, E.W., 179, 180
Truth, Sojourner, 102-104
Tunbridge, 23, 29, 30, 31, 34, 35, 41, 262, 274
Tyler, John, 91, 92, 99
Underground Railroad, 56, 85, 92, 102, 109, 110, 113, 118, 120, 122, 132, 133, 134, 138, 144, 148, 172, 239, 256, 270, 271, 273, 274, 275, 281
Union Intelligence Service, 204, 215, 225
Union Store, 77, 113, 115, 128, 185, 187, 194, 195, 230
University of Illinois, 150, 152, 281
USS Monitor, 214
Utopia, Ohio, 59

Utopian Socialist, 59
Vermont, 16, 22, 23, 27, 29, 32, 34-37, 41-44, 54, 55, 61, 66, 70, 71, 73, 78, 206, 255, 262, 263, 270, 271, 272, 274, 280, 285
Volney-Dyer, Charles, 109, 110, 111, 113, 133, 138, 252, 253, 292
Wacker Drive, 57
Warne, Kate, 215
Washington Jail, 200, 204-208
Washington Temperance, 98, 102, 113, 264
Waukegan, 5, 85, 86, 102, 104, 121, 127, 128, 141, 151, 153, 184, 193, 197, 258, 265, 270, 271, 276-280
Webster, Timothy, 220
Wentworth, John, 140, 147, 153, 173, 174, 181
Westminster, 30, 32
Whig, 99, 100, 112, 131, 153, 187, 188, 285
Whipple, Mr., 231
White River, 30
Whitlock, 69, 70, 72, 263
Williamsburg, 216
Wilmot Proviso, 111, 119, 124, 285
Wilson, Henry, 208, 274
Winters, Edwin, 196, 230, 258, 275, 276

Wisconsin, 61, 73, 101, 102, 139, 154, 155, 271, 272, 274, 275, 279, 280
Woman's Home of Chicago, 240, 243, 247, 251, 252, 259, 260, 267, 275
Wright, Daniel, 92, 102
Wynkoop, Tobias, 104
Yankee, 55, 119, 120, 213, 285
Yorktown, 213, 214